D0043096

"*Nazaré* brings to mind the work of Jorge Amado, Louis de Bernieres, Alejo Carpentier, Mario Vargas Llosa, and Ngũgĩ wa Thiong'o. But it's no imitation. JJ Amaworo Wilson is a topnotch novelist in his own right. I fell in love with his troubled city, its eclectic characters, with their unlikely alliances, comedic turns, bursts of magic, and with the depth and nuance of a community rising against tyranny and corruption."

    —David Anthony Durham, author of *The Risen*

"Steeped in awe and everyday mysticism, *Nazaré* captured me with its stunning opening scene and never let go. It is a story both timeless and urgent, and every passage is alight with humor, ingenuity, and surprise. A singular voice in contemporary fiction, JJ Amaworo Wilson offers readers both an energizing escape and a look at how to live with courage and clarity through absurd times."

    —Adrienne Celt, author of *End of the World House* and *Invitation to a Bonfire*

"An epic of everywhere. Of autocrats and inequality, of profiteers and their police. But also of revenge and solidarity, of rebels and the righting of wrongs, and of Kin das Ondas—Kin of the Waves—a beachcomber and street urchin turned revolutionary. A luminous novel of the margins and the lumpen and their due."

    —Raymond Craib, author of *Adventure Capitalism*

Nazaré

a novel

JJ Amaworo Wilson

ISBN: 978-1-62963-908-6 (paperback)
ISBN: 978-1-62963-920-8 (hardcover)
ISBN: 978-1-62963-919-2 (ebook)

Library of Congress Control Number: 2021936596

Cover by John Yates / www.stealworks.com
Interior layout by briandesign

10 9 8 7 6 5 4 3 2 1

PM Press
PO Box 23912
Oakland, CA 94623
www.pmpress.org

Printed in the USA

For Chris and Jenny

"La vida es sueño." ("Life is a dream.")
Pedro Calderón de la Barca

"Let justice roll down like waters."
Amos 5:24

CHAPTER 1

Balaenoptera musculus—Kin—

Shadrak—Jesa—the town descends—

holy man Fundogu—rice and

beans—Nazaré

AT 4:30 A.M. ON JUNE 30, EVERY DOG IN BALAAL BEGAN TO BARK. PAMPERED POOCHES IN the mayor's palace yelped at the chandeliers, mangy street hounds growled at a cloudless moon, and guard dogs yanked at their chains and bawled into the dark. It was a canine protest. A crescendo of "no! no! no!" because that was the moment nature was breached. The moment a sixty-ton blue whale washed onto the beach.

A boy called Kin rose from a dreamless sleep inside the shipping container he called home. He sensed a change in the atmosphere and a smell of brine and flesh more pungent than ever before. The port along the way was silent at this hour. There was no sound but the insistent wash of the waves.

He rubbed his eyes and walked the fifty yards to the beach, past other containers where other children slept, and he saw the whale. At first, he didn't know what it was. Just a dark mound on the sand, like the outline of a low hill. As he approached, the features began to clarify in the early morning light: the pectoral fin, the bifurcated tail. The whale was stranded on its belly, half in, half out of the water, parallel to the breakers. Gentle waves lapped at its flanks.

Oblivious seagulls flew overhead and a light breeze jostled the grass of the hummocks that fringed the beach. Balaal, city of tinkers and fishermen, slept as the sky turned orange with the first stirrings of the sun.

Slowly Kin circled it. He saw water and air bubbling from its blowhole and heard the rumbling of what sounded like a breath emanating from its belly.

The whale was a mottled gray. White and black spots covered its back as if a painter had flicked a loaded brush at it. The skin shone with a watery sheen.

Kin, at eleven years old, had seen whale fins in the distance and heard whales bellowing to one another in the deep. A child with music in his bones, he'd once perceived the sound at A minor and thought it was a ship's mournful foghorn until one of his sailor friends told him, "That's a blue whale, ten miles out."

Kin dared to get closer. The whale's presence was other-worldly—a colossal mass of indistinct blubber. It looked like a fallen zeppelin, and its stench permeated the beach.

He walked past the boats anchored off the shore to the village where the night-fishermen were bringing their catch to be placed on ice and gutted. The first person he saw was Shadrak, an old black fisherman with a round belly.

"Shadrak," he said, "there's a whale on the beach."

The old man smiled and nodded. He had a fishing rod in one hand and the butt of a cigarette in the other. He blew a miasma of smoke.

"And it be good mornin' to you, young shrimp. You tellin' tales?"

"No. I just saw it."

The old man coughed. "Where?"

"There." Kin pointed. "On the beach."

"How big?"

"Huge."

Shadrak took a final drag of his cigarette, a mess of rolled newspaper and foul-smelling tobacco, and dropped it at his feet.

"I go get some men. We take a look."

Kin walked on, a little inland, away from the whale, until he came to more fishermen unloading their catch, and he repeated his story. A few of them knew and trusted him. Some put down their tools immediately and began walking toward the ocean. A few old hands laughed it off. "They stink up the beach is all they good for."

By the time Kin returned to the whale, there was a crowd. Several women were carrying buckets and throwing water over its gargantuan body.

Kin saw Shadrak with a group of fishermen and asked him, "Why are they doing that?"

"Whale skin dry out in the sun, whale die."

One of the women, who was called Jesa, saw the group of fishermen and shouted, "Hey!" They looked at her. "Call Fundogu," she said. "Tell him to bring a stethoscope. We'll need your fishing boats. He's too big to push by hand."

None of the men moved.

"Hey, estúpidos!" she shouted again, pausing from throwing water on the whale's back. "We don't have much time. When the tide goes out, the whale will be stranded."

"It's stranded already," said a fisherman. "What's your plan?"

"What do you mean, what's my plan? We're going to rescue it. Put it back in the ocean."

Another fisherman moved forward, next to the first, and said, "How we gonna move it?"

Jesa said, "We're going to use your boats, tie lines around it, and then you drag it out to sea."

There was a murmur, a shaking of heads. More people appeared on the beach so now the crowd numbered a hundred. Some inspected the creature, walked around it in awe and silence.

The mayor arrived in a suit, along with six pampered dogs and a retinue of soldier-bodyguards, who were called the Tonto Macoute. The villagers shuddered at the sight of them and parted to let the mayor through. He had himself photographed next to the whale, prodded it with his cane, and went home.

A priest arrived on a bicycle, soon followed by a gang of harlots in fishnet tights and a drum troupe and trapeze artists from a travelling circus. An acrobat danced on the whale's back until Jesa shouted at her to get down because "the beast is sacred!" A hot air balloon soared above the scene and its pilots, from neighboring Bujiganga, looked down upon the whale and marveled.

Then came the widows of the fifty lost miners—los desaparecidos. Then troubadours and vagabonds from Balaal's backstreets. Kin's neighbors, the homeless kids from the stray shipping containers, emerged. And other kids who lived in the containers at the port along the way and who had addresses: third container, second row, Hawagashi Electronics, or second container, fifth row, Köstlich Foods.

There was an appearance from the Bruja of Laghouat, although no one knew it because the witch came in the form of a seagull and observed events from far above.

Down below, a bus cranked and creaked to a stop on the sand and disgorged a rabble of schoolchildren. They ran to the whale and made notes and drew pictures, eyes agog, nostrils aquiver at the smell.

The radio station took a break from its nonstop government propaganda and ran a story on the whale, complete with fake whale noises. Journalists from Balaal and two neighboring cities came and took photos and interviewed the locals.

"It's a gift," said the priest, leaning on his bicycle.

"It's an omen," said the fortune-teller.

"It's big," said the acrobat, still out of breath.

A posse of loosely affiliated dogs came nosing along the beach to catch the commotion, tails erect at this new wonder. To them everything was in two categories: Dog or Not-Dog. But this creature seemed to herald a third: Undog. Unlike Not-Dog, Undog was the very antithesis of Dog: huge, not moving, and incapable of wagging its tail.

Then came twenty-five Believers, who gathered sticks to build a fire and sat in a circle around the whale and made incantations and said the whale was a god.

A woman who had been shooing the dogs away asked, "Who found it?"

"This boy," said Shadrak, pointing at Kin.

The crowd parted to make way for Fundogu, who was a holy man and a doctor, which were the same thing in Balaal. He was large and black and in his seventies, with tribal scars down both cheeks. He wore a white gallabiya—a long embroidered robe—and no shoes. With great ceremony, Fundogu inspected the whale. He circled it, touching it with his long, ringed fingers, prodding at some parts, massaging others. The whale blew a jet of vapor and Fundogu pulled out a stethoscope from somewhere within his robe. He had no idea where to put it, so he placed it against the whale's vast back and leaned down to listen. The crowd murmured its approval of the learned man.

During the inspection everyone had retreated a few feet except Jesa, who continued to splash sea water on the whale.

"This whale," pronounced Fundogu, "is a distraction."

There was an audible gasp from the crowd and then a flurry of whispered questions. No one knew what "distraction" meant.

"It's this boy," Fundogu continued, and he pointed at Kin. "It's this boy you should be looking at. The future is his."

There were more gasps, some nervous laughter.

"But what of the whale?" asked the woman called Jesa.

"Get him back in the water or he will die."

With that, the holy man wandered off, head held high, through the human corridor that had let him enter. His large flippery feet were damp with wet sand. Before leaving the beach, he turned, looked again at the boy, and whispered to himself, "Everything begins and ends in the sea."

Jesa called to the fishermen, "You heard him. Get your boats ready."

Shadrak stepped forward and said, "No can do use our boats."

"Why not?" said Jesa.

"Our boats not big enough. We take this whale into water, he pull us under before we cut the line. He drag us down, boat and man 'n' all. No can do it."

Jesa dropped her bucket into the sand. Some of the other women who had begun throwing water at the whale also stopped. Jesa crossed her arms. She was in her mid-thirties, already a widow, her husband claimed by the sea. She had no progeny and wore a black scarf around her head in memory of her drowned beloved and to hide a vivid streak of white hair. It had turned white the moment she had heard her husband was dead, and the Spanish-speaking kids had taken to calling her zorrillo—skunk.

"This is a sacred animal," she said. "Older than me and you. It was sent here by God. Put your boats to work, you weaklings, and cut the lines when the whale's in the water. We'll send divers down to do it."

The fishermen were unmoved.

"Too risky," said Shadrak.

Jesa squinted her eyes at him. "Then I'll do it."

"You no got no boat, remember?"

Jesa approached Shadrak as if to slap him. She had lost the boat at the same time she had lost her husband, both taken by the sea. Shadrak didn't flinch.

"Miss Jesa, I would like help you," he said. "But my boat is my livin'. No boat, no fish."

Jesa looked around at the other fishermen. A wiry Somali. West Indians stripped to the waist. Pacific Islanders with tribal tattoos. Lean, weather-beaten Japanese. Not one looked her in the face. The whale breathed again and its massive eye opened to take in the sky and the flitting birds.

"Which of you will lend me a boat?"

The men looked at their feet. No one lends a boat to a water widow.

"Then we'll bring every man and woman in Balaal and push the creature back into the sea."

With that, the women with buckets wheeled away to gather reinforcements. Others followed them.

It was at this moment, with the crowd streaming away, that Kin alone heard the whale singing. He heard three notes in a minor key, a threnody of such sadness that the whale's mottled, dark skin seemed to tremble with the song. It sounded to Kin as though the notes conjured all the beast had seen: the glistening shoals of fish; kaleidoscopic reefs with their jagged edges; seaweed wavering like witches' hair in the tides; sunken galleons lost and canted on the seabed; the underside of trawlers and skiffs he could have upturned like toys; sunlight bursting through the water like the beams of torches.

The song ended as abruptly as it had started.

For the crowd was back, and many others with them. Volunteers, streaming down the beach, the pushers and pullers of stranded whales. Jesa ordered them in five languages to take their positions. They were going to roll the beast back into the ocean.

As he joined them, Kin could see the tide receding. Where the whale had been half-under at first light, it was now barely in the shallows.

Two hundred people were amassed now at the whale's side: bakers and road workers, farmhands, schoolteachers, knife sharpeners, cat catchers. They gathered their strength, sucking in the sea air, placed their hands on the colossal wall of gray-black flesh, and heaved with a cry that faded into groans and gasps. The whale didn't move.

Forty of them brought out shovels and wheelbarrows and dug a vast trench toward the sea to reduce the drag of the sand, to ease the whale's passage to the water. They rasped instructions to one another, mimed and gestured, wheeled away and dumped their loads of sand, even as the new ditch began filling instantaneously with water. The people took their places again and, with a shout, pushed with all their might to roll the great beast into the channel in the sand. The whale didn't move.

Three fishermen—islanders squat and sun-browned—appeared reluctantly and tied ropes to the whale's flukes and flippers. In groups of thirty, the people gripped the ropes and readied themselves like contestants in a tug of war. The remaining fishermen joined in, put their shoulders to the whale's back. At the water's edge one of the drummers from the circus troupe started up a beat on his djembes. The man, who'd been born with four arms and now whacked out a rhythm on four drums, went faster and faster till the sweat flew off him in his frenzy, and as the pounding came to a crescendo and the sun climbed higher, the people of Balaal heaved and shoved and pulled as they'd never heaved and shoved and pulled in their lives. They gritted their teeth and strained every sinew and summoned from nowhere the strength of the ancestors. The whale didn't move.

The people looked at one another. They were spent. Bruised and cut where the rope had worn a groove into their skin.

Shadrak picked up his straw hat, which he'd temporarily laid on the sand, and said, "He no gwon move."

The fishermen untied their ropes from the whale and people began to walk away.

A woman approached Jesa and said, "We did our best. All this pushing and shoving is going to kill it anyway. There's only one chance now."

"What?" said Jesa.

"The magicians are here."

A raggedy cluster of shamans arrived, most of them naked or wearing nothing but loin cloths and necklaces made of seashells. They were preceded by the smells of pipe smoke and ganja weed. They were alchemists, windtalkers, adepts, thaumaturgists, Voodoo priests.

They lit a fire under a cauldron and mixed metals and threw in bindweed and dandelion and the spines of long-dead starfish. Some whispered incantations in languages not heard for a thousand years. One blew mapacho smoke into the pot and sang to the whale in a voice so pure the stones in his pocket began to dance. And when all their spells were said and done and all their gods summoned, still the whale didn't move.

By late afternoon, the shamans had melted away into the distant rocks or returned to the hills, and the crowd was thinning out. Jesa had gone home, leaving just a few women to throw water onto the whale's back, careful to avoid its blowhole, and to warn the children to stay away from the thrashing flukes. Then even the women and children went home.

As the sun went down, Kin sat alone beside the creature in the sand. Steam came off its skin and its eye rolled above the grooves of its ventral pleats. Kin listened. There was no song, but he thought he detected a low moan.

He looked beyond the creature at the island of the abandoned lighthouse with its cluster of vegetation and the cracked, useless phallus of the building itself. Kin wondered if the whale had skirted the island on its journey to the sands of Balaal.

With the last of the women gone, he kept the creature company until he heard its breathing change. He stood up and stepped back. All around, seagulls flitted and yawped and watched this child in rags staring at the mass of blubbery flesh.

Kin hurled himself at it. He put his shoulder to the whale and pushed, running in place, kicking up sand till his feet sank. "Move, damn you!" A crab darted from a hole, looked quizzically, then skedaddled.

The stench was now tremendous, a mélange of rotted fish, garbage, and salt. It was as if the whale were inside out, discharging the fetor of its guts. Kin ignored the smell. He pulled at the creature's flipper. He yanked at the whale's fluke, which lay immobile, a massive dead flap.

He exhorted the creature in all the languages he knew. He hollered and sang and begged and howled. He clambered on top and looked into its eye and pointed at the sea.

At last, he climbed down, bathed in his own sweat and tears. His legs were trembling. He sat down again beside the whale on a bundle of kelp and sea grass. A voice startled him.

"I brought you something to eat."

It was Jesa, that widow known to be crazy with grief, that woman who had beseeched the fishermen to tow the beast out to sea, and failed. She was behind Kin, holding a plate of food.

"I'm not hungry," he said.

"You're lying."

"I'm not hungry."

"Maldito, don't you get it? If you want to push the whale back into the sea, you need more strength."

She gave him the plate. Fish, rice, and beans. He said nothing and ate with his hands.

She had been there for ten minutes, letting the food grow cold, watching this boy. Now she watched him cramming the food into his mouth. He hadn't eaten all day. Maybe not all week.

Skinny as an eel. Stubborn as a roosterfish. Maybe nine or ten years old, she figured. Another street urchin tossed up by the waves. Seen him running errands for those yellowbellied fishermen. Why was he here? Wasn't he the one who first saw the whale?

He finished the food and gave the plate back without a word.

"You're welcome!" she said, and walked away, empty plate and unused fork in her hand.

The sun was going under. Kin whispered and stroked the whale's flanks and thought about life and death. Dead fish washed up every day on the shore, large and small, sometimes fly-ridden, sometimes already shredded to bones. Death was everywhere. But this beast had been so alive. A giant traversing oceans, now reduced to shallow breaths, an expanse of fat and skin.

His thoughts were interrupted by a distant roar. The sound continued but he didn't see the wave rising, a freak, a massive veil of brine and salt, that drew over the shore like a dark, annihilating curtain.

They called it Nazaré. You heard it before you saw it. It broke the laws of nature. A wave was supposed to make a wide perfect curl like butter from a knife and then collapse on itself and dissipate onto the shore, disappear like a memory. Nazaré rose tight, like a great rearing horse, higher and higher, overwhelming the other elements.

At the last moment, Kin saw the rising tower of water. It wasn't the tide coming in. It was something sent by the spirits of the ocean, or that's what the people of Balaal would have said had they seen it. He knew it would sweep over the land and drag everything in its path back out to sea, and so he ran toward higher ground beyond the grassy patches that bordered the beach, in the direction of the hill where the shamans observed the horizon. He sprinted, not looking back, hearing the roar chasing him until it became a great fizzing sigh, stopping short of the houses perched precariously on the coast, the outer edge of its splash spitting droplets which scattered like rain.

He turned. The wave covered the whale, pulled it into the water. In one jolt like a gust of wind, the whale was borne into the ocean. It made a sound, like a lone cello, a thrum at the core of the universe. It sank and rose and waved its tail and plunged into the deep. It rode further and further out to sea, past the island with the abandoned lighthouse, until it was a mound just as Kin had first seen it. And then with a final wave of its tail flukes, it dove out of sight. At that moment, every dog in Balaal wagged its tail, collapsed onto its forelegs, and fell asleep.

Around Kin there was nothing but the sound of the receding wave and the pinprick glints of stars in the evening sky. Across the way, harbor lights glowed dimly.

CHAPTER 2

Balaal—Black Magic—Ochiades—the

trial—Lambu—Abacaxi the turtle—

high window

For centuries, fishermen had hauled their catch along the stone walkways of Balaal. Weathered marine men, faces creased and scarred by sun and wind. In later years, there were ships carrying huge metal containers packed with the world's junk: washing machines, guns, tractors, car parts. And sometimes rarer cargo: a harem of perfumed demoiselles or a travelling zoo with animals shuffling off the ship two by two, and once a boat with six boxes of dinosaur bones, each of which had to be assembled and mounted on plastic plinths. Some of the containers wound up scattered along the coast, homes for the homeless.

The ships came from everywhere. They were manned by crews of Africans who spoke in grunts and clicks or pirates tattooed with sea routes and maps of foreign lands.

The boats came in all shapes, gliding or slaloming or jumping waves. There were Japanese fishing skiffs and Indonesian jukungs, Bermudan sloops and Zambian pontoons. The crews would show up starved or red-eyed and bloody from skirmishes. Some had goods; others were looking for refuge. The sailors would stagger onto land, their oil coats steaming, and tell tall tales of wild mutinies and whales as big as islands.

For Balaal was a sea town, a city shaped and battered by water. Its coastline was craggy, a mix of sandy beach and rugged rock, and worn by the tides. Its docks were built of wood and stone and faced down a daily lashing from the sea.

The people of Balaal worshipped old spirits and seahorses and bits of tree bark and stones. There was nothing they weren't afraid of. The night itself caused terrors and led to the burning of lanterns twenty-four hours a day. Guards kept vigil, armed with bows and arrows and rickety muskets with lead balls for bullets. They prayed to the sea to keep them safe and they prayed to the gods to keep them safe from the sea. And if that didn't work, they prayed to trinkets and talismans. Some prayed to car parts and tractors. Some prayed to blades of grass.

The elders said there was a prophecy: when Balaal became too evil and corrupt, a giant wave would straddle the horizon and wash away the city, its buildings and roads, its people and animals, drown the whole tale of avarice and bloodlust that was Balaal's history, wash away the sins of the people.

Another tale claimed a sea beast would get them, come lurching like a god from the deep, finned and horned and gilled, with teeth the size of houses and a temper that would lay waste to every living thing in that place.

For now, neither prophecy had come true. The beast and the wave had arrived on the same day and laid waste to nothing. The wave hadn't touched the houses on the shore, had barely disturbed the promontory. It had fallen short of the covered fish market and Shamans' Hill inland, hadn't touched the twin bronze cannons aimed at invisible invaders from across the sea. Instead, it had done its job: swept the whale back into the ocean and receded, barely seen by the inhabitants of Balaal, besides a small boy, a few drunk fishermen, and a coterie of seagulls.

✳

Jesa emerged again from her ramshackle house. This time she had a hunk of bread for the boy. No butter or cheese. Not even a fried sardine. If the boy had no manners, he could expect nothing in return. But she couldn't leave him hungry, because the ghost of her husband would have been scandalized, and, besides, she knew the boy was homeless.

For a moment she didn't notice that the whale wasn't there. The beach appeared to her as it always did: an endless vista of low dunes fringed on one side by foliage, on the other by the waves rolling in to the shore.

Then she remembered.

"What the hell?" she said to herself.

The whale that had attracted acrobats and politicians and schoolchildren and shamans was indisputably, completely, and utterly gone.

In its place was the boy. He was sitting cross-legged on the sand, looking out to sea. The sun was a sliver of yellow light dipping under the ocean. She approached him. He turned his head. He recognized her. The one who'd brought him food. The one they said was crazy.

She looked at him, and then at the ocean, and then at him again.

"Where did the whale go?"

She immediately understood the absurdity of her question and laughed. She handed him the piece of bread. He took it wordlessly.

Jesa asked, "What's your name?"

"Kin."

"Where do you live?"

"In one of the shipping containers."

A squadron of seagulls flew toward the city. He bit into the bread.

"Tonight you can sleep at my house," she said. "It's your reward for rescuing the whale."

"I didn't rescue it," said Kin. He finished chewing the piece of bread and turned to face her. "A wave dragged it out to sea."

"A wave?" she said.

"Yes."

"Are you a shaman?"

There was a pause.

"Ah," she continued, "but you wouldn't know yet, would you? You're too young. But I know this: the whole town tried to move the whale. And then you pushed it back into the sea. Some will say you're a magician."

The boy took another bite of the bread and gazed out to sea again. She wondered if he was watching for the whale. But he was as staggered as Jesa. He sat there listening to his own breath and to the gathering whistle of the ocean breeze. His heart pounded. What had he just seen?

"Do you know where I live?" she asked.

"Yes," he said. "That house over there. The green house."

"The green house. I have a pillow. A mat. You can sleep there tonight. I have clean water outside. You can wash in the morning."

"They call you zorillo. And a witch. They say you're a witch."

"What do you care? You're a shaman."

"I'm not."

"You are the future. Fundogu said so. I'll leave the door open."

She laughed and walked away. He said nothing. Nor did he look at her. Stunned as he was by the whale's disappearance, he was also puzzled by this woman. He had interacted with adults all his life, doing odd jobs, finding a way to survive on the backstreets and beaches of Balaal, but he had never known kindness. What did this skunk-witch want with him?

When the last of the sunlight dropped under the ocean, he got up and walked to Jesa's house. He turned back twice to look at the sea roiling in the dark. The whale was truly gone. He knocked on the door.

"It's open," she called.

He went in.

＊

The following morning, two members of the Tonto Macoute barged into Jesa's shack and arrested the boy on a charge of Black Magic. The arrest itself was as mysterious as the disappearing whale. No one seemed to know who had issued the warrant. And in any case, Black Magic was completely legal. Half the city's doctors practiced it. And Kin was eleven years old. According to the Constitution of Balaal, he could not be charged with anything that didn't involve petty thieving or random violence. But no one had read the Constitution for a hundred years because it had been written by a monk in a dead language on a scroll of disintegrating pigskin and hidden in a vault with no key.

Rumors went around that the mayor was behind the arrest. Some said it was a cabal of fishermen who'd been planning to use the whale for oil and were furious at its disappearance. Others believed it was because of what Fundogu had said: the future belonged to the boy. If the present belonged to the mayor and his cronies, the future had always belonged to the priests. They, and not some homeless waif, were the guardians of the afterlife.

All Kin cared about was the fact his wrists were hurting as the two members of the not-so-secret police led him away. He could hear Jesa screaming at the men but couldn't make out her words. One of the policemen was clattering against the pots and pans hanging from the ceiling of Jesa's kitchen and the other kept swearing as he bumped into the walls.

Control your fear, the boy said to himself. Even in the chaos of noise and pain, he was already planning his escape. He would break free, but not now. These bruisers were twice his size. But there was always a way out. He knew it from his days and nights slipping in and out of shadows, reading the streets.

"Hey!" shouted the one who had hold of Kin's wrists. The man turned to Jesa just as he was leaving her house. "He's a witch! He'll be on trial tomorrow at 10:30. At the courthouse. Save your complaints for tomorrow."

And they locked him in a cell for a day and a night.

※

The courthouse wasn't a courthouse. It was a warehouse. In fact, it wasn't a warehouse either. It was a former warehouse. It sat on the edge of Balaal, half-rotted with saltwater. Mold staggered up the walls, and the rafters were occupied by a gang of anarchist bats who swooped and dangled and made alien chirping noises. In one corner was a conundrum of disused fishing nets and orange buoys the size of soccer balls. In another was the wreck of a skiff, some kind of talisman for the town, although no one could remember what had happened to the skiff or why its remnants were kept there.

A large hole in the roof let in the sun, which made a spotlight on the stone floor and on Kin, who was now standing in that spot. The sunlight from above cast him in chiaroscuro like an Old Testament martyr.

At 10:00 a.m., the door creaked open and the jury staggered in: twelve men and women from Balaal. Four of them were already drunk. A fifth was catatonic and walking in his sleep. Then the public came in, swigging on soda bottles or moonshine. With the sun blinding him and the people in shadow, Kin saw little but heard the clump of fishermen's rubber boots above the hubbub and smelled pipe smoke and tobacco. He calculated the distance between himself and the door. Looked at a high window above the wreck of the skiff and pondered the angles. He would run if he had to, scale walls, climb roofs.

At exactly 10:30, the judge, a man named Ochiades, was led in by his helper. Ochiades was 145 years old. His hands had six fingers and his feet had six toes. He hobbled in, wearing a dark blue military jacket with epaulettes that dwarfed his tiny shoulders. The jacket itself seemed to belong to another man, for it was three sizes too big for the judge, whose body had withered to a dry twig. He looked like a vulture. He was completely bald and pale, with a long, sharp nose, and that jacket, frayed and slick with the filth of decades, looked like nothing but the dark plumage of a bird of prey. Kin glanced at the old man and shivered at the sight. So this was who they'd sent to judge him.

Everybody stood up. Ochiades squinted around the room and ordered everyone to sit down again with a wave of his hand.

He perched on a rickety chair and peered around, looking for the boy who was on trial. There was a hum from a group of onlookers seated at the back on makeshift benches of wooden planks. They hadn't seen the judge for some years, ever since he'd presided over the case of The Kidnapped Cockatoo more than a decade ago. In fact, many assumed the judge had either retired or died, since most disputes in Balaal were resolved the old-fashioned way (mass brawl until the winning side won).

"This is the boy?" asked the judge of no one in particular. Despite his tiny frame, Ochiades's voice could still boom.

Kin looked up.

"Blessings be on your head, young one. You stand accused of Black Magic because you pushed a whale into the water. What do you say?"

Kin looked around. He had lived on the streets for years. He had faced down wild dogs and wolves. Slept on ledges and roofs.

"I didn't do it," he said.

"Then how do you explain it?" said Ochiades. He waved away a fly. "You were the last person seen in the company of the whale. You were seen pushing it. And the next morning it was gone. Tell me: Does this sound like a human act? An act of nature? How old are you, boy?"

"Eleven, sir."

"Eleven. And you expect me to believe you can push a whale into the water."

"I didn't do it. A wave came and took the whale out to sea."

At that, the crowd let out a peal of laughter.

"Boy!" Ochiades almost shouted. "A wave came and removed a whale. That's what you're saying?" With a skeletal, six-fingered hand, he swung at the fly that had resumed buzzing in his face. He missed.

"Yes, sir."

"But no one else saw it."

"I don't know, sir. I can't say what other people saw."

Ochiades calmly appraised the boy's face. He was a handsome child, brown-skinned, with strong cheekbones and deep-set eyes. One of those mestizos from everywhere and nowhere, his parents probably black, white, yellow, brown, a salmagundi of Balaalian chaos.

The old man intoned, "You are a sorcerer. You are a practitioner of the dark arts. You are a Black Magician. *Will someone get this fly off my face!?*"

Ochiades's assistant, a tall, thin man called Lambu, dressed in a dark suit, swished a few times with a piece of paper. The fly ascended. The old man went on.

"Have you any witnesses?"

"Witnesses to what, sir?"

"The wave, boy! The alleged, imaginary wave. The wave you invented to cover up for your Black Magic."

Jesa, seated at the back of the room, stood up and said, "I'm a witness."

She was in her finest black dress, indeed her only black dress. Unlike every other piece of clothing she possessed, it didn't stink of fish, and it was pressed so the creases looked like blades.

"Who are you?"

"Jesa."

"Jesa what?"

"Just Jesa."

"Well, Just Jesa. Speak." The fly was back. Ochiades flapped at it.

"I saw this boy that very evening. He was pushing at the whale but it didn't move. He must have been there for an hour. After a while I took pity on him and gave him food."

"What food?"

"Fish."

The gallery roared with laughter. Fish was all they ate, these poor guileless coast-dwellers. Breakfast, lunch, and dinner. Cod, sprat, and bass.

Ochiades grunted, hushed the crowd with a wave of his hand, and said, "Go on."

Jesa went on. "The boy ate it and then he continued pushing at the whale. You see, if he was a sorcerer, why would he spend so much time pushing when he could cast his spell immediately?"

Jesa wore kohl around her eyes. It was her one acquiescence to vanity, to the things of the earth. In some light she was beautiful, but she was also cursed. No man would marry a widow who'd lost her husband to the sea.

"Cast his spell?" said Ochiades. "Ah, so you admit he had spells to cast! You're saying he was a sorcerer."

"No. He had *no* spell to cast. He's a simple child," said Jesa.

Before the judge could reply, the fly launched a full-frontal attack. It lurched and buzzed and lodged in his ear. The judge craned his neck and shook his head. He shook and shook so rapidly and the fly remained so determinedly that the old man became dizzy and promptly fell to the floor with a rattling of bones. The crowd gasped and got to their feet. Chaos ensued while the fly escaped to the rafters, giggling like a fly. Lambu, Ochiades's assistant, called for help, and the old man was carried away by a retinue of four policemen and taken to his cart, which in turn took him home. Kin eyed the door and the high window, counted the police.

With barely a pause, an ancient turtle named Abacaxi was led in on a leash to serve as the replacement judge. It didn't matter that the turtle was deaf as a jackhammer and had no notion of the law; it was an elder. In Balaal, those who lived beyond sixty were revered. The turtle was two hundred and twelve.

As he pulled the turtle into place, the judge's assistant announced solemnly, "I am Lambu. I'll be assisting Abacaxi. Do go on, Just Jesa."

Jesa said, "I know the boy. So do many of the fishermen here. They employ him to help with their catch and do odd jobs. He's trustworthy."

The turtle said nothing, because it was a turtle. Lambu spoke up.

"Wait a moment. You yourself, Just Jesa, are a witch. Am I right?"

"Wrong," said Jesa.

"How can a witch be trusted in a court of law?"

The turtle nodded its head and chewed on a dandelion.

"I just told you, I'm not a witch."

"Says who?"

"It's not me who's on trial. It's this innocent boy."

"And what does he have to say for himself?" asked Lambu.

"Why don't you ask him?" said Jesa.

"Boy, what do you have to say for yourself?"

"I'm innocent," said Kin.

He knew now was his moment. The Tonto Macoute had returned, but they were scattered and distracted by the departure of Ochiades, yawning and scratching and fiddling for cigarettes. Kin ran out of the light, straight at the wall. At the last moment he leaped onto the wreck of the skiff and bounded off it on one leg, gripped the window ledge above, and swung through the gap where the glass should have been. Lambu's jaw dropped. The crowd inhaled. The turtle carried on chewing its dandelion.

The boy landed outside the warehouse on two feet. Blazing sun. Sand and stones under his shoes. Now he ran.

Inside the building, the four policemen headed for the door but found it blocked by a cabal of fishermen. Twenty of them crowded around, blowing pipe smoke and stinking of lobster. One took off his boot and dangled it like a club. Another reached into his mackintosh and pulled out a vicious looking hook. Another opened a rucksack and took out a metal anchor. Then Shadrak appeared, old and paunchy but with a look in his eye. He tossed away a cigarette, crushed it under his boot, and from nowhere produced a knife the size of a machete.

"This here for guttin' fish," he said. "But I been known to gut other things."

The policemen backed away, but the fishermen caught and disarmed them while the crowd scattered in all directions, some ogling the scene, others heading home before all hell broke loose. Finally, the fishermen chased the police to the road that led to the city and called after them, "Tell the mayor to mind his own business!"

Meanwhile, Kin ran past the priest Fundogu, who was levitating outside, cross-legged and six feet in the air, to the sanctuary of Shaman's Hill, which overlooked the village. The wave hadn't touched him there and neither would the Tonto Macoute.

Inside the warehouse, only the turtle remained. It peered around the empty room, then padded into the spotlight where the sun homed in through the hole in the roof. Then it wandered outside to take in the air and to hear the lashing of the waves against the shore, where it had been born all those years ago. The trial was over, but the boy's troubles had just begun.

CHAPTER 3

True history of The Skunk—

skedaddler—the fisherman's

apprentice—flotsam—baptism by

water

Jesa's tiny shack was made of wood reclaimed from the wreck of a Spanish galleon. It contained two chairs and a table, but these were barely visible among the coils of fishing line, old nets, barrels, ancient tins of crusted paint, hanging buoys and lanterns, pots and pans. Covering the walls and half the floor was the detritus of the sea—all the things washed up on the shore that she and her husband had rescued. The main room was the kitchen, and off it was a small anteroom that housed a bed, a rickety wardrobe, and a small wooden chest which contained the private possessions of the dead husband. The bathroom was outside, behind the house. It was little bigger than a telephone box, with a rudimentary toilet and just enough room for a crouching adult to bathe by upturning a bucket of water.

She lived her life to the rhythms and the sounds of the sea, her days punctuated by the swell of waves, the calling of fishermen, the squawks of seagulls, and the horns of far-off ships. Time was measured by the rising and setting of the sun, and food was fish and whatever else her wages and her inheritance could bring.

By day, she mended nets and clothes and cleaned boats and houses. At night, she slept.

She wore black every day, in memory of her husband, whose boat was dashed on the rocks in the prime of his life. No one knew why a great sailor, which he was, would have crashed into known rocks off the coast of Balaal. Some said he'd been murdered. Others said he'd fallen asleep or had gotten so drunk he couldn't steer. But no one said these things to her face.

When his boat was discovered, the townsfolk expected her to die of grief. Only Shadrak had had the courage to knock on her door. No one answered. He left her fresh fish, and later brought bread or vegetables. She had talked little even before her husband's death, and now she began a period of silence that was to last a year and a day. They sent a priest to ask her about a service for her husband. She closed the door in his face. A tax collector came knocking but got no answer. Shadrak paid her bill.

One day she looked in the mirror and saw a streak of white hair that had not been there before, and she took to wearing a black scarf.

Eventually, a year and a day later, she left the house. She sought work, because even a hermit needs to eat, and she knew she couldn't rely on Shadrak forever. At first, she found fossils on the rocky parts of the beach and in the hills and sold them at the Sunday market. When the fossils ran out, she went to the fishermen and asked for odd jobs. Shadrak again took pity on her and paid her to mend a net. Then she cleaned his house. Then the houses of other single fishermen. One gave her a stove and she cooked sardines on the street and sold them in packets made of old newspaper.

She carried with her an air of mourning. The black clothes, the head-scarf, the eyes rimmed with kohl. It was the children of the barrio who went from calling her zorrillo—the skunk—to la bruja—the witch.

Like everyone else in the neighborhood, she smelled of fish and gasoline. Her hands were perpetually stained and salt clawed its way into the pores of her skin, drying her out and wrinkling her before her time. Yet she was still striking. Her eyes were black as melanite, and something in her demeanor made people afraid, even fishermen who had seen fifty-foot waves rear up like stallions and said they feared nothing.

She found more work cooking for an elderly widower, and as he got sick, she began to tend to him, washing him and cleaning his messes to the sound of the local radio, which was never turned off. When he died after a year, he left everything to her, not that there was much: a creaky old house and some savings in a tin can. She sold the house. The money brought her no pleasure, but it meant she could pay her bills.

One day she knocked on Shadrak's door, a door even more battered than her own. Red-eyed and with a cigarette dangling, he answered it. She held out a fistful of notes.

"What's this?"

"You paid my bills. I'm paying you back."

"What?"

"Take the money. I know it was you, and I thank you."

He took it wordlessly.

✳

Now Jesa set about the task of educating the boy. Every time she fed him, she made him say thank you. She saw how hungry he was, a hunger born of a lifetime of scrap-scrounging. At first, he would put bread in his pockets for later, hoard it like a bird, till she finally persuaded him he didn't need to. He ate fast and fluidly. He wasn't gluttonous, but he ate with a focus she'd only seen in animals—the vultures that swooped the back roads of Slepvak or the mangy dogs outside the butcher's shop on Salamurhaaja Street.

He learned to use a toilet and a stove and to read and write. He learned to say thank you.

"Thank you, bruja," he said.

"You're welcome, shaman."

Whatever damage the streets had done to him was invisible. He'd lived off his wits and barely survived, but the boy's brown skin was clear, his limbs were strong, and he could think straight. He worked without distraction. When she gave him a task—emptying buckets, clearing fallen leaves from a gutter—he did it well.

Aged nine, he'd been a tiny motherless, fatherless wastrel. A mop of shiny black hair and big brown eyes were all that stopped him being thrown onto a trash heap, but the other street kids had worshipped him because he was fearless. He ran everywhere. Or jumped. Over fences, under bridges, up trees, down ravines. The boy had been unstoppable. He scaled walls like a spider, jumped roofs like a cat. And all the while he learned to understand the shapes of shadows and to smell danger from a thousand yards. He knew every child in every shipping container, and they all knew him.

Aged ten, he began to flirt with derring-do. He broke into warehouses. He picked the pockets of the dead in morgues. He stowed away on boats. He ate live insects. He hung upside down from trees. He impersonated crickets. He blew kisses. He threw stones. He picked locks. He goaded donkeys. He laughed with glee. He howled like a howler monkey. He was a born skedaddler, a flash of limbs and white teeth. The other kids looked on, gawping.

Aged eleven, he changed. The whale made him contemplative, as miracles must. He began to ponder the mystery of the sea. And why Fundogu had called him The Future.

Now Jesa watched him work with the fishermen. They liked his silence because they, for the most part, were silent. Out on the water only a fool talked to lure a fish and, with the fishermen, Kin never opened his mouth unless he had to. He copied their every move: the way they boarded a boat, the bend of the back to haul a net, the way they held a squirming fish. He was at one with them, and some days when Jesa looked at the fishermen from afar, she couldn't tell which was Kin because he blended in and moved just like them.

The fishermen were lean and angular like El Greco saints. They barely smiled or scowled, because they were stoics. They understood that everyone eventually returned to the sea. Balaal's graveyards were full—and in the year of the Tenth Plague they had overflowed—so the dead were now cremated and their ashes thrown into the ocean. There they became atoms. They commingled with everything else that had ever been. And it was the fishermen, as much as Jesa, who became Kin's family. They lifted his burden of solitude.

Kin cleaned boats, swabbed them daily, shined name plates with a rag and sealing wax. The fishermen gave him coins for his labors and let him compete with the cats for discarded fish parts.

At day's end he scoured the market for scraps. He was relentless in his pursuit of food. Nothing was too lowly or wretched enough to be thrown away. He would bag fish heads and guts, boil them down to get at the brine. He would hassle the butcher for pig testicles and rabbit tails, chicken jowls and cow eyes. On fallow days, he'd collect nettles and dandelion, bring them to Jesa. She took everything, and with what she took she always made something. And they always had enough to eat.

The money she'd inherited was no fortune, but Jesa had no extravagances. She wore the same black clothes day after day. Her only jewelry was what her husband had bought her or what Kin found on the beach: metal hoop earrings, a coral bracelet, a necklace encrusted with a fake ruby. Her only pleasure was the radio, listening for the rare moments when the government propaganda and the incessant jingles and ads might stop and they would play a song to raise her spirits.

Sometimes Kin would listen with her. Thus, the two lost souls under the same roof, the mother and son that weren't, coexisted.

✳

The years passed like owls in the night—flashes of light in the long darkness. And as they passed, the salt of the ocean stuck in Kin's hair and made dry white lines in his clothes. Jesa washed them by hand, until one day she looked at him. He was her height, and his voice had started to deepen like a man's. She threw the pile of clothes at him.

"You're too old for me to wash your clothes, and I'm too young to do this forever. From now on, you wash your own."

"Thank you, bruja."

"Just thank you is fine, shaman."

Now that he was doing more work for the fishermen, he needed clothes for each season. Shadrak lent him a coat, and one of the Japanese fishermen gave him some oversized pants. Hand-me-downs from his big brothers. Kin turned up the cuffs and cinched a belt tight around his waist and Jesa thought he looked like a clown, but she waved him out of the door without a word.

His nights, like hers, were punctuated by foghorns and the rhythmic lapping of the waves. He would wake to gray light and the bickering of the first seagulls and walk the shallows of the beach. Every morning he stared out at the island of the abandoned lighthouse, squinting at it through the mist, or watched for the mass of a whale banked on the sand but knew it wouldn't come again and was grateful he'd seen it and felt its skin.

The morning walks were a scavenger hunt. He shared the beach with a few ragged dogs and the returning night-fishermen and so any findings were his to keep. Along the coast was the port that took in big ships and every now and then they jettisoned their cargo or lost a crate. Everything would wash up on the beach and Kin would collect it: dolls with retractable eyes, whisky bottles, the skeleton of a two-headed dolphin, colored plastic eggs, the femur of a dinosaur.

His findings were usually warped out of shape or rusted to uselessness. The sea was a brutal caretaker. It gobbled everything in its maw and spat it out half-wrecked. But still Kin occasionally found things that he could sell. Jewels or large, perfect shells he'd take to the market and hawk to tourists. He'd flash his grin at them, set an outrageous price, and haggle.

"Come on, this is precious!" and he thrust under their noses the perfect conch/urchin/diamond/ruby. And because he was a beautiful boy and in need of a little luck, they'd grin back and buy it.

"Here, Jesa," he'd say, and hand over the money.

It was rare he kept anything for long—objects or cash—but the dinosaur femur now hung from Jesa's wall like a totem calling from another world to this.

In the winter, Jesa sent him to find wood. She taught him to light fires whose embers would glow all night to ward off the spirits, and she taught him card games to help pass the time while the wind wailed outside and made the frames of her tumbledown house creak. And she never forgot what Fundogu had said of this mysterious child who had come into her life by chance, by the whim of a stranded whale—this boy owned the future.

✳

Someone knocked on her door. Jesa opened it and saw the old man, Shadrak.

"The boy be here? I have news."

"He's not here, but you can come in," said Jesa.

Shadrak made a great show of blowing the final whorl of cigarette smoke outside, tossing the butt, and removing his shoes—great clumpy fishing boots—and leaving them by the door. His socks were black with filth and thick as a blanket. Jesa offered him a seat.

"I have news," he repeated.

"You already said that. Now tell me what."

"They be goin' baptize the boy tomorrow," said Shadrak. "They fishermen talk and talk and talk and finally say yes. Some o they Japanese no in favor. They say he livin' with a water widow, no can go out on the sea. But we got us a majority."

The ritual meant Kin's apprenticeship was over. He would be treated as an equal during fishing trips, entitled to a portion of the catch.

Jesa asked, "What time tomorrow?"

"Ain't you happy, Miss Jesa?"

"I don't know what took you so long."

"It were you, Jesa. Boy livin' with a water widow."

"I took him in. He's not my son."

"We know. That's why they agree. The stigma not on him. Tell the boy be at Socorro Point at 6:00 tomorrow mornin'. And I'm sorry: only the boy."

※

After she'd told him the news, Jesa and Kin went to Shamans' Hill overlooking the port to celebrate. They sat on the grass and watched Balaal in motion. In the other direction from the port they could make out through the haze the shape of the abandoned lighthouse half a mile from the shore, the sentinel that guarded their little lives.

"Look!" said Jesa, up on the hill.

A great black ship was edging its way out of the port. It was packed with massive shipping containers headed across the ocean. All around it were gaivota birds, battalions of them following the ship, either predators or protectors.

Kin watched and thought about the ceremony that would take place in the morning. It was along the beach where the whale had surfaced.

"You deserve it," said Jesa. "You'll be a real fisherman, ready to join a team. You can catch and sell your own fish."

"No, not yet," he said. "I'll still be an apprentice until I have my own boat."

"And you will one day," she said. She put her arm around his shoulders. "Fundogu said it. The future is yours."

✳

The following morning, Kin walked the beach as always. He had been unable to sleep, so he was there at 5:00 a.m., an hour early for his baptism. A mist covered everything, making it impossible to tell sea from sky from land. He could barely make out the Japanese fishing crew—the best of them all—bringing in their night's catch, so he went to the pier for a closer view and watched them unload.

The Japanese fishermen were muscled and ageless and they worked with a speed unmatched by the others, moving in unison, in a kind of dance, hauling nets or passing great barrels of fish from hand to hand.

"Ohayō gozaimasu!" shouted Kin.

They saw him and waved.

There were many other crews—the Spaniards, the Sudanese, the Eritreans, and the Guyanese—coexisting in shared waters, a delicate ecosystem in which no boat could bring in too big a catch. They nodded to one another and called out greetings, and made sure each had his own space in the sea.

Into this life Kin would be inducted that day. A rough life. On boats named after wives or homelands, the fishermen spent long hours contemplating and fighting the ocean, both loving and hating it and always fearing it.

Kin stood up and began walking his familiar route. He had no watch but knew by the heat of the sun that it was time to get to Socorro Point. He walked faster than normal and heard his breathing above the sound of the ocean.

When he arrived, there were a few fishermen waiting for him. Others trickled along the beach, appearing in the mist like omens, until there were twenty.

From nowhere Fundogu appeared. He was wearing a white robe and seemed much older than he had been those few years ago when he had examined the whale. Fundogu nodded to the fishermen and looked the boy up and down.

"The boy becomes a man," he said.

Kin smiled, then bowed his head. It was a time to be humble, to become a stoic like *them*. Fundogu took Kin by the arm and walked him into the water. It was ice cold and Kin shivered. Before them was the expanse of the ocean. When they were knee-deep, Fundogu said, "Learn the position of the lighthouse."

Kin looked for it in the fog, just making out the ghosted shape barely visible on its island, and wondered why Fundogu was telling him this.

"The whale," said the old man, as if in answer. "You remember the whale?"

"Yes, sir, of course," said Kin.

"It was a messenger. My days are numbered, but you have a long life ahead that will be full of trouble."

They kept walking until they were up to their waists.

"What kind of trouble?" said Kin.

"Every kind. You will do battle with monsters and you will do battle with men. And you will be a leader."

"But. . . I'll be a fisherman. Who will I lead?"

"The people. And remember, you must bury your enemies. And find out how Amador died."

"Wait, I don't know who that is, and what enemies?"

"I'm here to baptize you, boy. So I'll baptize you and we'll talk about these things another day. You have much to do and much to learn. First, I give you your new name. Kin das Ondas. Kin of the Waves."

Fundogu suddenly moved behind Kin and grabbed him under the arms. Kin could feel the rings on Fundogu's fingers digging into his skin. With surprising strength, the old priest hauled the boy backwards into the water. Kin submitted as he was supposed to and the freezing waves washed over him and turned his blood to ice. Fundogu began reciting in an ancient language some kind of paean to the ocean, begging its protection. From the shore, the fishermen looked on, arms folded, cigarettes dangling.

Fundogu pulled Kin up. The boy gasped. Salty water stung his eyes.

"Now wear this."

Fundogu pulled from his pocket a necklace of red coral and placed it around Kin's neck.

"This will protect you from evil spirits. You must wear it for the rest of your days."

"I will," said Kin, still shivering.

"Then it's done," said Fundogu, and he turned them both toward the shore. "Now dry yourself and run."

The wash of the waves annihilated most sounds.

"What did you say?" asked Kin.

"Run."

The fishermen made a huddle and applauded. They patted the boy on the back, but he looked uneasy. As a phalanx of seagulls lurched overhead, the sound of police sirens wound its way through the air. Still in the shallows of the ocean, where he walked slowly in Kin's wake, Fundogu said, "Hear that? That's your cue."

CHAPTER 4

Tonto Macoute—The Butcher—

ransack—boat in D major—the

lighthouse

BALAAL'S SECRET POLICE, THE TONTO MACOUTE, WERE USELESS AT FINDING SUCH THINGS as criminals, but they were long-established upturners. They were experts at upturning wardrobes, cupboards, chests of drawers, offices, whole houses. When they really put their backs to it, they could upturn the contents of entire mansions in minutes. They were highly experienced ransackers, possessors of advanced degrees in vandalization and berserker pillaging. They were led by a man called The Butcher, who was the mayor's brother. Between the butchery and the mayory, the citizens of Balaal were, for the most part, kept very quiet.

Three years to the day since the whale had appeared on the beach of the fishing village, the police knocked on Jesa's door. Because it was early morning, she was barely awake and had no time to answer. They barged in and began upturning.

"Where's the boy?" said The Butcher.

Jesa got out of bed and leaped to her feet. She was wrapped in a blanket.

"He's not here!" she said.

There were four of them in her house, bumping into the hanging pots and pans and tripping over the nets in the corner.

"Where is he?!" The Butcher shouted.

"I don't know!"

They began hurling things. Pans came clanging down. They smashed her dishes and swept her cups off the counter. One of them saw the dinosaur femur hanging on the wall and slapped it onto the floor. It landed with a crack. They upturned her table and left boot marks on the stove and then moved to her bedroom. One of the men looked under the bed, then kicked at the wooden chest which housed her dead husband's possessions. It skidded across the floor. Because it was neither big enough for a boy to fit inside nor easily breakable, they left it alone. The Butcher went to the back of the house and bashed at the walls of the makeshift latrine.

Then he came inside and pointed his pistol at Jesa, who was backed up against a wall.

"We know he lives here. Now where is he?"

"I don't know. He moved out."

The Butcher and his men left Jesa's house and jumped into an armored car. The Butcher began talking into a megaphone: "Fishmongers and whores, get up! This is your chief of police! We're meeting in the town square right now! Get up."

It wasn't yet 7:00 in the morning, but Balaal was already stirring, and with the police banging on doors and shouting, it didn't take long for the street to fill. Among the crowd, several of the fishermen came armed but saw immediately they were outnumbered. There was no town square, but in what constituted the center of the village, there was a bare patch of land off the beach. On this patch now sat armored cars with machine guns on turrets. Balaal's police and the military had long ago become indistinguishable, and now there were fifty of them in the street overseeing the whole community: shopkeepers, schoolteachers, housewives with cowering children under their skirts.

The Butcher stood up in his armored car and through his megaphone announced, "We wish you no harm."

The crowd snorted. The only reason the soldiers ever went anywhere was to dish out some harm.

"We're looking for the boy called Kin. We have word that he's in danger. We want to protect him."

At that, the crowd couldn't contain itself. Muffled titters. Rolled eyes. A couple of courageous washerwomen threw tomatoes, which fell short of The Butcher's armored car.

"The boy is in danger," continued The Butcher, "and as we are the police, our duty is to save him."

More laughter. A dog barked. A handful of moldy apples rent the air and landed on the hood of the armored car.

"I repeat, we are removing him for his own protection."

A flock of seagulls cackled. Someone threw a potato, which bounced off the front tire of the car.

"And we will not harm anyone."

The village elders, who remembered the Slepvak Massacre and the Night of the Sixteen Daggers, grunted and scoffed, and a wet lettuce came flying through the crowd.

"Hold your damned vegetables," hissed The Butcher, "or we'll open fire."

The people hushed and squinted nervously into the morning sunlight. Around the perimeters of the crowd the police gripped their triggers.

"We have nothing against you fishing people, but the boy comes with us."

"Why?" came a woman's voice. It was Jesa.

"For his protection. Whoever has him needs to release him *now*."

"Protection against what?"

The Butcher paused and looked at Jesa more closely. He lowered the loudspeaker so it rested by his side.

"You're the bruja," he said. "The witch who lives in the green house. We've already searched your little shack, but we can have you interrogated too. We have experts. If I were you, I'd shut up."

The sun was still ascending. A few people scuttled away to work. Others turned for home. The Butcher put down his megaphone and spoke to his men.

"Go through every house one by one. Check every attic, every cupboard, every box. If there's a loose floorboard, rip it up. If there's a chimney, climb it and find the little shit. The boy goes with us today."

The policemen lumbered into position. They carried rifles and billy clubs. Handcuffs dangled from their belts. They wore body armor under their uniforms and were so laden down they moved like oxen.

Among the dispersing crowd were the fishermen. Shadrak had his knife but kept it sheathed, and the tough Japanese walked briskly to their boat, not looking back. This was a fight they couldn't win.

In truth, several of the residents would gladly have given the boy away, for he lived with a witch and what was he to them? Just another runt, another piranha from nowhere, born in a shipping container, would probably die in one. Others remembered and admired the boy's leap through a window at his trial three years earlier and his helter-skelter escape in broad daylight. Not many people evaded the Tonto Macoute even with the help of the rough-edged fishermen. But no one except Shadrak and Fundogu had the faintest idea where Kin was, and they weren't telling.

✳

That day the police broke the mold. By custom, their atrocities and ransackings happened at night. The knock on the door. The fat beam of a flashlight. The unrecognizable silhouettes. The play of blood in the moonlight. They took pride in their history of massacres, pogroms, assassinations, and assorted slaughters, but all had been deniable. From the Night of the Sixteen Daggers to the burning of the Kandisha Citadel, the atrocities had been committed by men in masks. No one could prove it was the Tonto Macoute. Even when the loot was discovered in the mayor's office (which was in the same building as the police station), there was no proof that the police were involved. And even if there had been, the judge, Ochiades, would never have put to trial the mayor or the chief of police, a man universally known as The Butcher. After all, they were his beloved great-grandnephews. And before them, the town was ruled by his beloved grandnephews, and before them his beloved nephews.

And so that day in the fishing village in the sprawling city of Balaal was something of an anomaly because it wasn't even mid-morning when the Tonto Macoute went about kicking down doors and people. Four of those very officers felt a sweet pang of revenge, for they remembered that day three years earlier, when Ochiades had been sent home unwell (attacked by a local fly), and they themselves had been sent packing by fishermen wielding hooks and knives.

So now they thundered down the little streets of the little village that was so insignificant it had no name, moving house to house. First they knocked. Then they bashed. Then they upturned. Domestic birds went fluttering out the windows. Furniture flew.

The police for once were excellently organized. Four men to a house. One talker, one basher, one upturner, one looter. They came away with no little boy but a ton of loot: family jewelry, elaborate knives, wads of cash, TV sets, radios, ornate lampshades, leather shoes. Who knew humble fishermen had such good stuff? They loaded the booty into the armored cars and went back for more.

Shout. Bash. Upturn. Loot.

Seagulls shrieked in protest and an owl stared disdainfully from a rooftop.

The Tonto Macoute were indefatigable. Door to door. Street to street. Sacks of loot. They checked the scattered shipping containers where the homeless lived—the kids and the drunks, the lame and the addicted—and threw off the rancid blankets, upturning husks of cardboard and newspaper where the rough sleepers slept. They found a few children, but none who fit the description of the boy they were looking for.

And as The Butcher's car wound its way down the cobbled streets he observed his men roving through the village, battering and whacking away at doors, hurling cutlery and plates, pinning these dumb fishermen against walls, and he looked on approvingly and thought lovingly of his father, instigator of the Night of the Sixteen Daggers, and his grandfather, the very first Butcher, responsible for law and order (and a few unfortunate massacres) in twenty provinces of Balaal, and his uncles, outstanding police captains bemedaled and enriched by their hard work, and his brother, the mayor, the tycoon with a twirling cane, who was perhaps a bit soft for this work, who perhaps preferred not to dirty his hands, but who had a thousand men at his command and six loving dogs yapping at his feet to the sound of his fancy clock collection chiming the hours away. Family was family.

Shadrak stood at his door. Blood poured from his head. They'd shattered his lanterns and plundered his den. His plate and bowl lay smashed on the floor, and his old fishing rods were snapped in two. They'd cracked him on the head with the butt of a pistol, but despite it all, there was a glint in his eye.

"Dumb as parrotfish these Tonto Macoute," he said to himself. "They no find the boy in a million years. Boy done gone for good."

✳

An hour earlier, Kin had been walking, newly baptized, from the ocean. Fundogu was behind him when the sirens erupted, breaking open the morning's silence. Because he was a born skedaddler, Kin always had an escape route. As he began to run, he turned to Shadrak.

"I'm borrowing your boat."

"No can do use my boat. My boat my living, boy!"

Kin veered, mid-run, toward Shadrak. He stopped and spoke rapidly. "Sorry, no choice. Fundogu baptized me so I can sail now. The key's under the bucket?" He didn't wait for an answer. "I have to escape." He looked at the island of the lighthouse and Shadrak followed his eyes. "Get one of the others to send me a message when it's safe to return."

He ran and reached Shadrak's little skiff just as the sirens were winding down in front of Jesa's door. He untied the boat and jumped in. He sparked the engine and steered it into the deep. He never looked back.

✳

The island was half a mile out to sea, but in the morning mist it was hardly visible. Kin of The Waves navigated by instinct and the boat bucked and thumped over the choppy water and through the cloak of the fog. He had watched the fishermen handle their boats, imitated their every move for three years, and now found

himself steering the little skiff like it was second nature. He felt
in his wrists and forearms the spirit of the boat's owner, Shadrak,
and swore he tasted the tang of the old man's foul tobacco on his
breath.

As the police poured into the village, Shadrak said to himself,
"Switch off the engine! Switch off the goddam engine, boy! They
gwon hear you."

But they didn't because they were already hollering and
ransacking.

Kin approached the island and steered the boat around a
corner, out of sight of the mainland. There was a small, rocky beach
and a cave and a smattering of rotting wooden pylons on which
a fisherman could tie his skiff. Kin secured the boat with a clove
hitch, gathered a plastic gallon of fresh water and Shadrak's fishing
rod, and stepped on shore.

He stopped to look back at the mainland. Were they following? He saw nothing through the thick mist, and his fear dissipated.

Now he was alone on a strange island. He climbed up the
steep hill overgrown with sea fern and wrack that led to the lighthouse. The building was a crumbling wreck. Its white paint was
peeling and a pile of rubble sat at its foot next to the stone platform
that supported the structure. Scattered beside the rubble were the
remains of a deck chair, the staves of a broken barrel, and some
rusted cans. Kin ascended the platform steps that led to the lighthouse door. It was all but caved in.

He paused and looked up at the six rectangles where windows
had once been. Now they were spaces for the wind to perform. He
could just make out the gallery, with its rusted railings, and above
that the vault, which, although it was round, seemed to pierce the
sky.

The lighthouse reminded him of a recorder he'd once found
on the beach. White ivory, six tone holes, the mouthpiece an
elongated cupola. Now he heard faint notes, the wind whistling
through the windows, playing a tune as the sun burned away the
morning mist.

The door was on half a hinge, so he pushed it gingerly and went in.

＊

The abandoned lighthouse was a bestiary. Terns and cormorants had their nests in the cupola and mice skittered up and down the central stairwell. The wind and the light cymbal clash of the waves made a quiet tone poem of Kin's solitude.

He looked around the dark atrium and saw the remnants of dead animals and the evidence of the living. Tiny bones stripped clean. Droppings everywhere. At the foot of the inner stairwell he saw weather-shattered furniture—amputated chair legs and a mess of a carpet, discolored and ragged.

He placed the fishing rod and the water on the floor and slowly made his way up the stone stairs. They were narrow and crumbling, and he steadied himself on the thin metal railing attached to the wall. He heard a flapping of wings, looked up, but saw nothing except a vortex of whitewashed stone.

From the top, he looked down and the stairs appeared to him like the shell of a snail, an arabesque leading to a point of darkness at the bottom.

The lighthouse had several small anterooms, all homes to rubble and damp leaves, cockroaches and ants, and husks of insects long dead. Here and there, he saw wads of newspaper soaked to pulp. Nothing useable except a rope tied mysteriously to the railing at the lookout balcony at the top of the building. It dangled down the outside wall, reaching almost to the ground below. Perhaps, he thought, it was for pulling goods up through the high windows instead of carrying them up the narrow stairs. If that was its use, though, the bucket at the end of the rope had vanished.

His first thought, as always, was how to find food. Clearly, there was none in the lighthouse.

But the island was enchanted. Despite it being so small that Kin walked around it in twenty minutes, he found it full of riches.

He discovered an inlet full of cavorting fish and heard celestial music at its southern edge. To the west there were two palm trees which had dropped several coconuts full of milk onto the ground. He picked one up and carried it with him. Moments later, he found a shady cove half-hidden by the outer curve of the rock. How long could he survive there? And would the Tonto Macoute come for him?

He went back to the skiff and rootled under the stern sheets and found everything he needed: a small bucket, a gutting knife, matches in a plastic waterproof container, a flashlight, and a wooden board. Shadrak had been well prepared. Kin took the equipment to the inlet. He sat on a rock and cast the net. Within minutes he had a dozen fish in the bucket. At least he wouldn't starve.

CHAPTER 5

The Anteater—soldiers on a

bowrider—seagull—the cave

A FEW DAYS OF OMINOUS PEACE FOLLOWED THE RANSACKING OF THE FISHING VILLAGE. BUT one morning The Butcher appeared with four of the toughest Tonto Macoute plus The Anteater. The Anteater, otherwise known as Hormigonera, otherwise known as The Kid Sniffer, had a gift for tracking children by their smell. She was rumored to have been brought up by wolves and had the longest nose in all of Balaal, a phallic protuberance with nostrils like potholes. She was semi-feral and would be paid only in raw meat.

Like most of Balaal's population, she was of an unknown age. Her limbs were stick-thin and she had a limp from when a child had stabbed her with a knife, but she possessed a great, distended belly from all the meat she had consumed, and her face was as smooth as a peach save for two deep vertical lines between her eyebrows. She wore a washerwoman's rags and a pair of rubber chinelos, from which her fat, filthy toes protruded like slugs.

The Butcher took her straight to Jesa's house, kicked open the door and sent The Anteater to sniff the bedclothes where the boy had lain. Once she had the scent, she grunted, "Aku duwe!" and pointed her enormous nose toward the sea.

"There?" said The Butcher.

"Aku duwe! Liwat ana!" and she pointed again.

She led the way to the beach, hobbling crooked but urgent, with The Butcher and his soldiers following.

When they got there, she pointed out to sea. The Butcher saw nothing but roiling waves and mist.

"What are you saying, woman? That he's drowned?"

"Dheweke ana!"

"There's nothing there!"

"Dheweke nang pulau, sampeyan bodoh!"

The Butcher looked at his men.

"What's this peasant trying to say? Any of you?"

The men looked at one another. They knew only two languages: Smash and Grab.

She shouted it again: "Dheweke nang pulau, sampeyan bodoh!"

The wind blew the fog away, and suddenly the distant shape of the lighthouse appeared.

"Wait a minute," said The Butcher.

"Apa kowe ngerti saiki, wong bodoh?" said The Anteater.

One of his soldiers piped up, "I think she's pointing at that island, sir."

"I think you're right, genius. Let's go find a boat."

They went to the harbor and commandeered a rickety bowrider. The Butcher didn't know how to sail it, but one of his men did, and soon they were all cramped up on deck, looking out to sea. The Anteater sniffed and snuffled and ignored the boat scents of fish and gasoline.

They docked on the far side of the island and saw Shadrak's skiff moored to a rotting post. The Butcher, using all the chivalry he could muster, took hold of The Anteater's hand and helped her off the boat.

"There you are, my queen. Now go find the little shit. He needs to die today. This must be his boat."

The Anteater limped over to the skiff, shuffling on the rocky parts to avoid treacherous sand. She began nosing from the transom to the bow and caught a whiff of the boy. Skin. A trace of sweat. Then she moved inland and the soldiers followed her. They were armed to the teeth—rifles, bullet belts, kukri knives—and instinctively fell into single file.

They were hunting a terrorist like no other. The fourteen-year-old boy, a former homeless waif with the power to move sixty-ton whales and evade armies, was nothing if not deadly. The Butcher walked side by side with The Anteater because now he knew where she was going. It was right in front of her very large nose: a looming tower piercing the sky—the lighthouse.

"Dheweke nang kene," she muttered to herself, but by now The Butcher was ahead of her and unsheathing his knife. He turned to his soldiers.

"Any of you idiots know what he looks like?"

The men glanced at one another and shrugged. Like most street boys in Balaal, Kin had no papers, no ID, no photos. The boy didn't officially exist. Those who had been on the beach when the whale washed up knew the kid, but none of the soldiers had been there.

"Ach," said The Butcher. "She'll sniff him out and we'll know it's him."

✳

When The Butcher and his crew arrived, it had still been early morning and Kin was asleep, his coral necklace tight to his skin.

He'd taken to sleeping in an anteroom high up in the lighthouse. From his days on the street he'd learned that the higher he slept, the safer he was from animals and humans and the elements. The anteroom had been full of rubble and cobwebs when he'd first seen it, but he'd cleaned it out and placed a mat from Shadrak's skiff on the floor.

That morning, something in the air, something in the wind, changed with the arrival of the bowrider and its cargo, and that wind carried to the lighthouse and blew in through the recorder's tone holes that were its windows and changed the pitch of the air to something foreboding, a C minor for Caliban on that enchanted island, and it stirred Kin from his dreams.

I'm in danger.

He went to the window and looked out.

He saw The Butcher closely followed by four soldiers. Hobbling beside them was the figure of The Anteater, a witch in rags. Kin's breath began to quicken. He needed to get out of the lighthouse but it was too late. The soldiers were approaching. They were just meters from the entrance.

Control your fear, he thought. A patina of sweat gathered on his forehead. He had no time to cry or shiver. He barely had time to think. Raw panic moved him. He ran upstairs to the lookout balcony. His mind raced—a series of images like playing cards dealt at triple speed—as he tried to remember all the escapes he'd made as a homeless street kid: jumping through open windows, crawling through cat flaps, balancing on roofs, ducking under enemy flashlights. *There's always a way out. There's always a way out.*

Down below, The Butcher turned to The Anteater.

"He's in here, isn't he? Hag, I'm talking to you! The boy's in here!"

Her eyes had turned yellow.

"Dheweke ana ing mercusuar," she said and pointed at the building that soared in front of them.

The Butcher paused and looked up to get the measure of it. His soldiers pulled pistols from their holsters.

Kin waited out of sight. His stomach churned and he could barely breathe. *Control your fear.* He didn't need to see or hear the men enter the lighthouse. He would know when they were inside. The air would change. And it did.

Moments later, he clambered over the railing of the lookout balcony and gripped the rope that was hanging from it. A rope for hauling merchandise up the side of a wall. Weather-frayed twine. Bucket vanished. He prayed it would hold his weight.

He heard the clattering of doors. These soldiers never ransacked quietly. They bashed into submission even a decrepit lighthouse with nothing but cockroaches and birds' nests.

When he heard them approaching the top of the stairs, he swung on the rope over the edge. It held. He rappelled down the side of the lighthouse, feeling the frigid wind all about him, his face to the whitewashed wall. He felt sick with terror but kept going. The rope reached all the way down, almost to the ground. He moved quickly, gripping it hard, clamping it between his knees and sliding. As he got to the bottom, he jumped and landed on uneven ground and turned to run. Before he could move, he came face to face with The Anteater.

"Hormigonera!" he said, and looked into her yellow eyes. The myth turned flesh. He saw her massive nose quivering and thought *you eat children*. She grabbed at him with a paw-like hand. He evaded her and ran.

She howled to The Butcher and to the soldiers and to the sun. The boy was getting away. The Butcher ran back down the stairs, knife in his fist, and his troop followed waving their guns. When they burst out of the lighthouse, they turned and turned. No sign of the child.

"Where is he?" shouted The Butcher.

The Anteater pointed and The Butcher ran, followed by his four-strong troop.

"Why are you all following me?" he said to his men. "Spread out! And kill him on sight."

The terrain was a mixture of rocks and sand and grassy hummocks. Although the island was small, there were places for a boy to hide: nooks and holes in the ground, coves and shadows.

Minutes passed. The Butcher had quite forgotten that The Anteater could find the boy by his smell, and now she limped after the child. She was alone. She passed a cluster of trees and came to a sandy cove. The water lapped at her feet, two fat and formless claw-hooves in red flip-flops. She could smell him but she couldn't reach him. He was there, she knew it. Inside a watery cave accessible only by swimming in the shallows. He'd tried to stay in the water so she wouldn't detect him but he couldn't stay long enough and she smelled the one breath that escaped his lungs, traced it on the wind and followed it.

A lone seagull came to rest on the rocky outcrop of the cave. It cocked its head. It watched The Anteater with a schoolmasterly eye. It was an interloper in this game of cat and mouse. For no discernible reason it opened its yellow beak and let out a peal of bird nonsense, an ear-shattering caw.

Inside the cave, Kin shivered. He was soaked and trembling. He knew Shadrak's skiff was just around the corner, but there was no time to get into it. They'd see him and shoot and he'd be defenseless. Even if they didn't hit him, they'd puncture the boat and it would sink. Better to stay put.

But the island was too small. He'd walked around it in twenty minutes. Sooner or later they'd find him. He had no weapons bar the fish knife, which he realized he'd left in the lighthouse. Could he hold out until night and get away under the cover of the dark? From where he was crouched he could see outside the cave. It was still early morning. There was no way he could evade the soldiers all day. So he would have to fight. But with what? There was gasoline in the skiff. An oar. There were coconuts on the far side of the island. Coconuts against five armed men.

He couldn't fight. He had to hide. He was already in the best hiding place he could think of, but he could smell Hormigonera just as she could smell him. Sooner or later the soldiers would follow her lead. They would swim into the cave and find him. He fought off his tears. He would fight for his life.

He tried to think straight. He didn't know why they were there looking for him, but he remembered Fundogu telling the village that the future belonged to Kin. He didn't even know what that meant. And then after the baptism, Fundogu had told him to run. And so here he was, running, trapped like an animal in a cave, hiding from the monsters outside. The woman was a cannibal. He'd seen it in her face.

She stood now, unmoving, eyes yellow as sulfur, her great belly pulsing in and out with her breathing. Her legs were planted wide in the wet sand as she listened to the tide coming in and going out, the squawk of the gull on the rock.

On the other side of the island, The Butcher clambered over boulders and kicked at clumps of grass as if the boy was an insect hidden in the soil. He gripped his knife and kept moving. The child would die soon. Fundogu's prophecy would not come true. The Butcher's family would continue to own Balaal and everywhere else: the mines belching minerals, the forests and hills, the creaky fishing villages, and the great port. It was just as his father and his grandfather had told him: "Boys grow into men and men want power. Kill them before they get too strong."

The other soldiers went blundering around the island, pointing their guns. One heard a rustle in the brush and took aim at a sea turtle. Another caught a glimpse of his own shadow and thought he was under attack. Another heard a murmuration of starlings and, fearing an airborne ambush, took cover under a tree.

Kin das Ondas was trapped. He listened to the water lapping gently at the walls of the cave. He watched the horizon, hoping for succor. A boat. A fleet of fishermen. A whale. But nothing came.

He had the acrid smell of The Anteater in his nostrils. She stank of rotten meat. Was she now approaching? Was she telling The Butcher where to find him? No sooner had he thought of her than the smell disappeared. He heard an indistinct yell and then another. Someone was getting closer.

Then he heard the caw of the seagull again and realized it was talking to him. It was telling him to get out of there, to run in the other direction from the human voice, so he splashed through the waist-deep water and ran ashore. And as he ran, he felt but didn't see the beasts of the island with him. He was being followed not by soldiers or The Anteater but by a sea turtle, a coven of water rats, a shrew, a scuttle of crabs, whelks, and snails. Staying low, he dashed across rocks and sand till he was once again at the lighthouse. The door was ajar so he went inside and climbed the steps. Adrenaline and fear took him higher.

Where was the devil-woman? He ascended to the topmost floor, stopping at his adopted quarters to pick up the fish knife. He fumbled at it, dropped it, picked it up again. Sweat and seawater commingled on his skin.

Maybe if it came down to it he could fight hand to hand. He was strong for a fourteen-year-old. Muscles honed from hauling nets. He knew the terrain and the building. He could set a booby trap. He could light a fire and burn the invaders. He could summon the birds who lived there to pluck out the soldiers' eyes. Where was Jesa when he needed her? And Shadrak? And the fishermen? They must have known he was on the island and that The Butcher was after him. Why hadn't Shadrak sent word?

He crept into place and peered out of the lookout balcony. There was no sign of the soldiers or The Anteater, but he thought they would return soon.

Suddenly it came to him. Switch on the beam of the light-house. Call for help.

He went to the control room and tried to activate the great beacon. He imagined shining a light into the eyes of Shadrak and the tough Japanese fishermen, Jesa and the other women. They would see the signal and know he needed them. And they would come in a flotilla of skiffs and canoes, umiaks and shikaras. And he would be saved.

But the switches were all rusted and the knobs wouldn't turn. He tried everything twice, his hands trembling. Then a third time. He blew on the controls, rubbed them with his sleeve, invented an incantation. Nothing worked.

Could the birds save him? One had already tried, the one outside telling him to run. He whistled quietly at their nests but the birds were gone.

He sat down, out of sight. He touched the coral necklace. Fundogu had said it would protect him, but Kin didn't believe it. He fought back tears. For the first time in his life, he could see no escape.

On the other side of the island, The Butcher glanced at his men. "The little shit's in there," he said, and pointed at the cave. The soldiers followed him, wading through the water.

It was at this moment that Kin heard the distant clamor of the ocean. Six hundred feet from the shore of the abandoned island a wave began to gather. It grew. Its swell multiplied, at first imperceptibly and then with the beginnings of a roar. It was a sound Kin had heard before, and he lifted his head to stare from the lookout balcony. It was nothing like the wave that had moved the whale, but it was big.

"Nazaré," he said. "The wave."

The five soldiers splashed through the cave.

"Come out!" shouted The Butcher. "Come out, come out, wherever you are! We won't harm you."

They walked further and further into darkness, plunging knives and rifle butts into the water, until they were at the back of the cave.

"He's not here, sir," said one of the men. But by then it was too late. Nazaré, the great avenging wave, was on them.

"What's that noise?" said The Butcher.

The wave washed over the entire island. It came halfway up the lighthouse and Kin closed his eyes as he felt the impact of the tremendous swell of water batter the building.

Down on the beach, it flooded the cave, blocked off the exit. The soldiers floundered. They dropped their guns and were flung to all corners. They groped and plunged and fumbled, and gradually their life force disappeared and they became quiet as thrown puppets. The Butcher was the last to die. He raged against the wave. Death was an affront to the Matanza family name and he would have none of it in this pathetic cave searching for this Doomsday child. First he was sent tumbling to the back of the cave, where he slammed into a wall of rock. Then the water plunged him into a chaos of darkness and noise. Among that riot of blackness and cold and cymbal crash, he fought. He swam for his life, a wild self-invented doggy paddle and then a manic breaststroke. He went headlong into a wall. He ignored the pain, turned, and in the turbulent water began a ferocious front crawl. Smack, he went crashing blind into another wall. By now his breath was faltering. He bumped into one of his men, barely alive, who inadvertently blocked his way and clung to him and wouldn't let go as if to say, "I'm dead and I'm taking you with me!" With the force of sheer rage, The Butcher wrestled the soldier off him and splashed a path upward toward the roof of the cave. Surely a pocket of air would be waiting. But there was none. The top of his head clattered into the cave roof. Moments of his life flashed before him. Cat stranglings.

The frightened eyes of a freedom fighter he'd drowned in a barrel. The cleansing of a shanty town by fire and the screams from inside the burning buildings.

Finally, he sank to the sandy floor of the cave, together with his men, and turned and turned in the mad tides till his hair was seaweed and his skin went blue. Down in Hell, they say, the Matanza family has a whole block to themselves.

Up in the lighthouse, Kin sat crouched, head in hands, expecting death to come in the form of a wall of water that would knock the lighthouse off its perch. Instead, the roaring had given way to the soft rasp of receding water. The island itself seemed to breathe. The rocky outcrops poked their heads above the surface. The palm trees, now stripped of coconuts, swayed but didn't break. The lighthouse itself remained defiant on its concrete plinth.

The boat was intact. That was the first thing Kin saw when he ventured out. Shadrak's little skiff had been upended, ripped from its moorings, tempest-tossed, and sent sailing into the horizon like a boomerang, from which it had miraculously returned, unbroken, and landed in the same spot from whence it had come. He bent down to inspect it. He ran his trembling hands over the transom, bow and stern, starboard and port. He stepped into it and removed a layer of sea gunk: clumps of moss, seaweed, and silt. The few objects he'd left inside the boat—a bucket, a buoy, a spare net— were all gone, but the boat itself seemed seaworthy. He pulled the key from his pocket and switched on the engine. It clicked and then coughed into action.

"I have to get off this island," he said to himself as he jumped in, still trembling.

There was no sign of the other boat, the bowrider that had brought The Butcher and his men and The Anteater. And there was no sign of The Anteater either.

He pulled away from the abandoned island. His heart was hammering. It would be years before he set foot on that rock again and in that time he would learn that islands are prisons for madmen and killers. And he didn't know it then, but the biggest killer of them all, Augusto Matanza, aka The Butcher, had found his final resting place on the island. In a cave teeming with life, with bats and mollusks, white anemone and gooseneck barnacles, the killer was stripped down to atoms, become one with the ocean.

CHAPTER 6

Sing!—sardines—the return of

Ochiades—camel—The Popcorn

Rebellion—cacerolazo

THEY SAID THE CITY OF BALAAL WAS FOUNDED ON MUSIC. IT WAS SUNG INTO EXISTENCE BY the holy wanderers who were the namers of the universe. As they walked across the world, they would name things by singing. So the cactus was a B minor chord, and the lark was a high C. Balaal itself was a dirge, a low D that blended with the swamps and the tall grass, the thistled hills and the wastelands that stretched to the horizon. The intervals between notes were what held the world in balance.

Nightclubs sprang up that were made of little more than sound, the walls a string of random cello notes, the windows a piano arpeggio. The thrumming of a blind man's zither became the first notes of a cavernous nightclub in Sondaj. A ten-year-old girl's hammering of pencils on an upturned ice cream tub became the first beats of a recording studio where many years later a self-proclaimed president would scream into a microphone and launch a war. A washerwoman's whistling was so beautiful that it mesmerized a tycoon, who built an opera house for her there on the spot where he first heard it—a river bank in Umculi. In the south, people greeted one another with "Sing!"

In those early days, music was in the sweat of the people and in their DNA. It was in the hairs on their arms and the buds on their tongues. Music was in their inner organs—their lungs and hearts, kidneys and intestines. A string of notes could conjure the flight of a parrot. A chord progression could invoke the birth of the world or the day when six hundred workers were gunned down in the streets or the end of the first plague when Shashuuan the Prophet flew down from his mountain and announced the End of Death.

And thus when Kin das Ondas brought Shadrak's skiff to the dock, its engine sounded a low C and the birds overhead heard it and began to sing an aria so exquisite it melted the clouds.

With the gathering of the afternoon heat, the birds ceased their singing and took to their nests. Kin stumbled home so worn and weary he forgot to knock. Jesa was at her table.

"My God," she said. "Where were you?"

Kin fell into her arms. It was more a collapse than an embrace. They held each other for a few seconds and then she stood back to look at him.

"Shadrak didn't tell you?" he said.

"Shadrak?"

"I took his boat and hid out on the island."

"Sit down," said Jesa. She pulled a plate from a cupboard and heaped upon it a pile of fish from the pan and some stale bread. "Sorry. Sardines."

He took it and ate ravenously. Jesa stared at him. He looked as he'd looked that first time, on the beach when he was just a child. She'd needed to wash him in disinfectant head to toe, shave off his hair and delouse him.

"Say thank you, shaman," she said.

"Thank you, bruja."

"What island?"

"The lighthouse. I lived off the fish I caught. How long was I gone?"

"A week," she said. "No one knew where you were. We thought they'd taken you. The Tonto Macoute."

"Shadrak knew."

"He knew where you were? How?"

"I told you. I took his boat."

"Then why didn't he say anything? Ah, I'll ask him. Or kill him."

"Probably to protect you."

"They ransacked the town. They nearly destroyed the house."

Kin looked around. There were new cracks in the walls. A window was broken.

Jesa said, "Are you still in danger? The last I heard, The Butcher was looking for you."

"I don't know."

"We'll ask around. But you're home now." She put her hand against his cheek. "Why the hell didn't Shadrak say anything?"

He ate the sardines and gave his plate to Jesa for more. Soon he was fast asleep on his mat on the floor and dreaming of lighthouses and waves as big as walls.

The following morning, Kin woke early. He wanted to speak to Shadrak, tell him he'd returned the boat, and ask him why he, Shadrak, had left Kin stranded. But first, as always, he would walk the beach. Shuttered in the lighthouse on the tiny island, he'd missed wandering the expanse of sand, sidestepping crab holes, and looking for trinkets dredged up by the ocean. He tiptoed past sleeping Jesa, pushed open the door, and went out in his bare feet. On the beach he watched for the arrival of the nighttime fishermen.

And what he didn't see was the pair of Tonto Macoute officers moving across the promontory like an arrow headed toward Jesa's house. And he also missed them kicking open her door. "Witch!" said one of the men. "You're under arrest." And he missed them hauling her away, a gag in her mouth, their dragging her over the sand bank and into a spluttering car. As it coughed and kicked up black smoke, Kin turned. His sixth sense told him Shadrak could wait.

✳

The warehouse-courthouse had aged in the three years since Kin's trial. The colony of bats had become an uproar. With their constant feuding and with the ravages of three scalding summers, rubble and debris had amassed on the stone floor, the final panes of glass from the side windows had caved in, and a carpet of fungular moss had begun its steady spread.

From the hole in the roof a familiar shaft of light beamed down on Jesa. She was in the dock for harboring a fugitive. No matter that the fugitive was a child and no matter the child was guilty of nothing. The same child was now in hiding because it was clear that the Matanzas and the Tonto Macoute wouldn't rest until he and his protector, Jesa, were in the regime's hands or dead.

At exactly 10:30 a.m., Judge Ochiades was wheeled in. He was now completely blind and seemed to be made of ash. An oxygen mask covered the lower part of his face and dark glasses covered the rest. He wore his blue military uniform with huge epaulettes and six medals dangling from the shoulder, his tiny decrepit frame dwarfed by the paraphernalia of war.

Someone said "all rise" and there was a hubbub as everyone got out of their seat, scraping chairs and muttering. With a barely visible gesture of his six-fingered hand, Judge Ochiades told everyone to sit down. No one moved.

The court natterer said, "Sit down!" and everyone did.

Several moments passed as Ochiades's wheelchair pusher, one of the Tonto Macoute, maneuvered the judge into position. First, he was in the light, which disturbed him. Then he was in a draft that blew in where a window pane had been. The man thrust him back and forth, wheeling the king on a giant chess board, one move at a time. Finally, with a croak, Ochiades said, "This is fine!"

The judge removed the oxygen mask and then had a spectacular coughing fit. He harrumphed and hacked and yacked, almost bouncing in his wheelchair until suddenly, with a lurch and a clearing of his ancient throat, he stopped.

"Where am I?" he said.

"In court," said the judge's assistant, the lanky Lambu in a wool suit. "The woman in front of you, known as Just Jesa, is guilty of harboring a fugitive. That fugitive is the sorcerer-child who pushed the whale into the water some years ago."

"I remember the case well. What do you have to say for yourself, boy?"

"No," said Lambu. "The boy isn't on trial. It's the woman, Just Jesa."

"Where's the boy?"

"We don't know. He went missing."

"But isn't it the boy I have to sentence to death?"

"That's for another day, sir," said Lambu.

"Well, Just Jesa?"

There was a pause. A gang of bats in the rafters launched a commotion.

"Well what?" said Jesa.

Lambu intervened. "You will address the judge as sir."

"Well what, sir?"

"Where's the boy?" said Judge Ochiades, suddenly warming to his task.

"What boy?"

The judge coughed again and helped himself to a swig of oxygen. A bat chirruped. Ochiades swooned briefly and then began: "When I was a child I found the body of a thirteen-foot man in a cave. The cave had paintings on its walls like those Stone Age caves. I always wondered who that man was. Someone said he was a pariah. You imbeciles probably don't know what a pariah is. It's an outcast. An untouchable. A persona non grata. That's Latin. He was cast out from the tribe to die alone in the cave. But to me he was a hero. You see, he carried with him a stick. He died holding it. What kind of man dies holding a stick? Wise men and warriors hold sticks. You see, he was a judge. A man of the law. Thirteen feet tall he was."

The judge fell asleep. A bat shat a bullet-shaped pellet which just missed the back frame of the wheelchair.

Lambu spoke up, "Is Abacaxi here?"

All heads turned to look for a two-hundred-and-fifteen-year-old turtle.

"He's on vacation," said a courtroom lackey.

"Then I will assist Judge Ochiades," said Lambu. He turned to Jesa. "You are the woman known as Just Jesa. Is that right?"

"No."

"Your name is not Just Jesa?"

"No."

Someone from the gallery shouted, "It's just Jesa!"

Lambu looked perplexed. "That's what I said."

"Without Just!"

"Oh. So your name is Jesa?"

"That's correct."

"Jesa, you are hereby accused of harboring the fugitive, a boy named Kin. He's wanted by the police."

"On what grounds?" asked Jesa.

"On what grounds what? On what grounds are you accused or on what grounds is he wanted by the police?"

"Both."

"Well, he's a sorcerer. He illegally pushed a whale into the ocean. And you're accused of harboring him because he lived with you for several years."

"He was found not guilty of being a sorcerer," responded Jesa. "Which means I can't be guilty of harboring him."

Suddenly an enormous camel wandered in through the door. It moved in slow motion, as if crossing a desert, and when it opened its drool-covered mouth in a tremendous yawn, a stench of rotting vegetation emanated so powerfully that three jury members passed out. The creature circled the room, prancing all the way around the jury, the defendant in the beam of light, and the popcorn-eaters in the gallery. It stopped at sleeping Ochiades and nuzzled the top of his head. Then it wandered out again.

"You don't deny," Lambu went on, "that this boy stayed in your house?"

"Everyone knows I took him in," said Jesa.

"And you knew he was a necromancer?"

"I knew no such thing."

"Then how do you explain his moving of the whale?"

She paused. A bead of sweat trickled down her forehead. The day's heat was gathering and she was standing in the beam of light from the hole in the roof.

"I don't explain it," she said. "Why would I? I'm a simple cleaning woman. What do I know of necromancy and miracles?"

Someone in the gallery grunted. Someone else rustled their bag of popcorn. No one knew the word necromancy.

Lambu resumed, "Well, by the powers invested in me, I hereby. . ."

"What powers?" said Jesa.

"By . . . by the powers invested in me. . ."

"You have no powers. You're an illegitimate stooge of an illegitimate government."

Someone in the gallery gasped. Someone else dropped their popcorn.

Jesa went on. "The ruling powers here are unelected. They're invalid. This sleeping fool has no qualifications as a judge and neither do you. You're a tool of the dictatorship and I demand that you release me immediately."

At that moment Judge Ochiades woke up and yelled, "Fish! Banana!" Then he fell asleep again.

Lambu gasped. His thin face fluctuated between fury and incomprehension. He clenched his fists. "How dare you insult the government! By the powers invested in me. . ."

"You have no powers!" Jesa shouted.

"By the powers. . ."

"You have no powers! You're a fraud!"

Judge Ochiades stirred.

Jesa continued. "You sent this old fool to judge the boy. Now you sent him again to judge me. You tax us for nothing. Where does the money go? Our roads are cracked. Our boats are wrecked. That family of the mayor's in the big city. All it wants is gold. And what do we want? Just one thing. Leave us alone."

One of the fisherwomen in the gallery hurled a handful of popcorn at Lambu. It scattered over his suit. Soon others followed her. And then a blizzard of popcorn flew, hitting Lambu and Judge Ochiades, and with it came shouts and cries.

And thus began The Popcorn Rebellion.

Ochiades's wheelchair pusher grabbed the handles of the judge's wheelchair and made a run for the door. Suddenly the camel reappeared, sidled into place, and blocked his way. The assistant swerved, and the judge went sailing out of the chair. His black glasses and the oxygen mask hit the floor together with a brown toupee made of badger pelt, revealing a head as bald and white as a boulder.

A shout came up: "Hang the judge!" and it became a chant: "Hang the judge! Hang the judge! Hang the judge!"

Lambu, showered with popcorn, backed off, tried to creep out the door, but the fisherwomen jostled him against a wall. They assailed him with hands calloused by the scraping of a million fish scales, foul sardine-breath, and the kicking of yellow rubber boots sloppy with cod guts and octopus slime. Lambu, spectacles askew, arms flapping in feeble defense, howled like a baby.

In the courtroom, besides the wheelchair pusher, there were six police officers whose job was to keep the peace. Three of them became embroiled in a battle with a throng of the anarchist bats who'd descended from the rafters to join the brouhaha. The other three were hunkered down in the corner of the warehouse beside the wreck of the old skiff.

Some of the jury members were outraged. They'd come from the bourgeois, tree-lined streets of Balaal's suburbs. They were literate and chalky white and dressed in summer attire and had nothing to do with this sun-scarred tribe of fishermen. They stood in appalled silence as the fishermen hoisted Judge Ochiades up by his ankles. Meanwhile, someone untied Jesa's wrists and helped her to clamber atop the shaggy camel and perch between its humps. The judge was draped face down behind her, across the camel, as the beast wandered into the street at the head of an impromptu procession.

Within minutes, hundreds of the citizens of the Fishing Village with No Name were marching, banging pots and pans, chanting and singing, and eating popcorn. Half of them didn't know if it was a protest or a party. Some of the elders remembered the Slepvak Massacre, when the mayor of Balaal had ordered the deaths of fifty fishermen for refusing to pay a tithe. But most were too young or too recently arrived to know the history of the Matanza family's rule over these lands. So the people settled on the chant invented by the bruja/washerwoman: "Leave us alone!"

The noise spread to the seafront, where the fishermen's rickety houses stood. Kin, hiding in a shipping container, clambered out, squinted into the sun, and joined the procession. Above them a yellow hot air balloon floated like a distended sun, with two distant figures waving in the basket below. On the side of the balloon was written "Freedum." All heads inclined and someone said, "Ah, the Bujigangans are with us."

They marched along the promontory, past the jetty where a dozen boats were docked, past the covered fish market, past the craggy outcrops of rocks, past Shamans' Hill, past the pair of bronze cannons pointed at the ocean. They picked up revelers and protesters: the same motley legions as the whale pushers three years before: schoolchildren, priests and prostitutes, acrobats, a bull-headed blacksmith, chimney sweeps, net menders, worm catchers, crab boilers. From the roofs, there came a raucous cacerolazo as housewives and scullery boys bashed rhythmically at pans in time with the drum troupe that had joined the procession.

At one moment it appeared as if they really were going to hang the old man Ochiades, but the moment passed and instead the judge was stripped down to his underwear, stuffed into a child's buggy, and smothered in popcorn. He was wheeled to the outskirts of the fishing village and left there like a toddler, sucking on popcorn, his false teeth having been removed and placed in the pocket of his pantaloons hung on the side of the buggy. He would later be rescued and wheeled to his mansion amid the din of traffic and street hawkers' cries.

Lambu, seeing little alternative, joined the procession. Stoopshouldered in his wool suit and a head taller than everyone else, he made a strange mascot, but he found himself chanting with increased vigor even as he forgot he had been sent by the Matanza government to assist the judge. By the end, he was waving his fist and shouting, "Leave us alone!"

The fishing village had inadvertently found its Joan of Arc on a camel instead of a horse: Jesa Maria Isabella Todos los Santos (her parents couldn't remember the names of all the saints) Ochoa Hernandez, better known as Jesa, or in court Just Jesa, the sad widow who had looked after an old man and taken in a homeless boy. She had defied the Matanzas. Now, in the commotion of pots and pans and popcorn, she removed her black headscarf, and although the streak of white hair was still there, no one called her zorrillo.

CHAPTER 7

Matanza—the Jadoogah tells the

future—the mayor plans a massacre—

Kin heads for the hills

THE MAYOR'S NAME WAS PORFIRIO FULGENCIO MELGAREJO TRUJILLO MATANZA. HE LIKED small dogs. He kept six in his yard, which is to say he kept six in Balaal, because Balaal was his yard. He held dominion over the city and the hinterland. He had an army and a police force and the private group of thugs called the Tonto Macoute, although no one knew the difference between the three, and he owned dozens of businesses, and those he didn't own had to pay him anyway because he was the mayor of Balaal.

He had a collection of one hundred antique clocks, with which he fiddled every night, teasing them open with screwdrivers and brass tweezers and vice pins. It was said that he occasionally used these tools to torture his enemies—pluck out an eye, remove a fingernail or two—but no one could be sure because no one saw it and his biggest enemies weren't talking because they were all dead.

He owed his position to no election or popular mandate. It was simply the position his father and grandfather and great-grandfather had held, and anyone who challenged the family's sinecure ended up in a hole in the ground or in a cage.

Like all of his kind, Porfirio Fulgencio Melgarejo Trujillo Matanza was deeply superstitious. He employed a woman to read his tea leaves. He consulted soothsayers and tarot readers. If he saw a black cat, he had the thing strangled.

He was correctly paranoid. Although it had never been invaded, Balaal was always on the brink of catastrophe. Its borders changed with the wind. Communities broke off and proclaimed independence. Disputes erupted about rivers and hills, trees and stones. Gangs annexed strips of land or muddy creeks. There were battles with clubs and slingshots, ancient harpes and arquebuses. Protests broke out in the street, and the family name was traduced, hollered from mountain to sea.

He'd once tried to employ a mapmaker to demarcate his lands. The man gave up after a week. Balaal was constantly shifting.

Towns would disappear under mudslides, rivers suddenly dry up, and nature kept encroaching, trying to swallow the city. The forest in the south kept creeping back. Overnight, in the rainy season, huge swathes of foliage would emerge and the people would bring machetes to battle against this incursion. Elsewhere, weeds erupted through cracks in the road. Ivy climbed the walls of the edificios. Moss spread like fire. In a pueblo called Nyagburu, a bird's nest took over the whole floor of a building and then the building itself.

Everyone knew that eventually the city would return to nature, disappear under giant leaves and trees or be washed away by the wave they called Nazaré, but for now they fought the elements. For Porfirio Fulgencio Melgarejo Trujillo Matanza this wasn't good enough. How can a man control such a city?

But there was worse.

He had a Jadoogah, a man named Vinegar Shalom, whose job was to tell him the future. Shalom was from a family of Jadoogahs who had been born with their heads on backwards. This was a punishment from the gods for daring to proclaim the future. One day at a feast Mayor Matanza asked Shalom, "When should I procreate, so there's an heir to Balaal's throne?"

Shalom paused. "An heir?"

"Yes, an heir. To take over Balaal. Take over the running of my city."

Shalom looked him in the eye. A Jadoogah cannot lie even if it means he will be executed.

"You may have a son whenever you wish, but he will never rule these lands."

"What do you mean?" said the mayor.

"Your family will no longer hold dominion over Balaal."

"What are you talking about?"

"Your days are numbered. The boy in the fishing village will end your family's rule."

"What boy?"

"The boy who saved the whale."

And so it began. Dog-loving Porfirio Matanza would try to outrun the future. He had the Jadoogah executed the same day—the firing squad wasn't sure whether to shoot him in the back or in the chest as his head was on backwards—and sent his brother to kill the boy. But there was no word. A week passed, then another. Finally, he sent more troops. They found nothing but a community of sullen fishermen hauling in their nets and still repairing the damage done by the earlier ransacking.

"Where's the damned boy?!" the mayor bellowed at his servants.

"Find the little shit!" he hollered at his guards.

"Break the child's bones!" he screamed at his shoe polisher.

"Rip the runt's lungs out!" he shrieked at his umbrella carrier.

"Bury the traitor!" he howled at his sock chooser.

He railed at breakfast and he railed at lunch. He railed at dinner and he railed at dawn. He would wake up sweat-drenched and stomp to the window looking for a sign, any sign, that his men had returned with the head of the child on a stick or with the boy's limbs dragged over the gravel by the hunting dogs.

And on other days he would sit quietly contemplating the future. There were only two moments in his day when no one was allowed to disturb him, when he had a respite from the constant meetings with ministers, inspections of mines and factories, and tours of his lands. The first was when he was doing his ablutions. The second was when he sat repairing his beloved clocks, with his beloved dogs dozing at his feet. In his solitude, he said to himself *the boy will reign. If this is the future, there is nothing I can do.* Sometimes he even contemplated the cost to the people of his family's rule: the bloodshed and violence, the dwindling communities in the farthest reaches of his empire, and he thought about what would happen to Balaal if a poor, uneducated child were to take over. Balaal had known only peace. The Matanzas were strong leaders. No one invaded or even threatened to invade. And this boy from nowhere, and—rumor had it—without even a family to sustain him, would wreck it all. Wars would ensue. Conquerors come. Balaal would fall.

And instead of news of the boy, word spread about the Popcorn Rebellion. These simple fishermen had left Judge Ochiades covered in popcorn in a child's buggy on the road, in the fumes and grime of the city. As the messenger told the story, the mayor spat out his coffee and kicked the Chihuahua by his feet. He said to himself, "I'm going to kill these shrimp-heads once and for all." He could barely stop himself from having the messenger executed on the spot.

"Prepare my horses!" he shouted. "I'll need a retinue of a thousand men. Bring the cannons and the machine guns. Bring the flamethrowers. We'll smoke him out. If the village doesn't cooperate, we burn it down."

Then he had a better idea. *Wait until June 15. The greatest day in Matanza history and therefore in Balaal's history.* The day exactly two hundred years earlier when the first Matanza laid claim to the land by murdering a landowner. This glorious day was celebrated every year by the smashing of a bottle of red wine in the town squares, to signify the spilling of blood, followed by a raucous party. This year would be different. Mayor Matanza would celebrate by routing the recalcitrant fishermen who'd dared to insult his family. Even better, the mayor would have some months to prepare, and he'd need it without his brother, The Butcher, whose disappearance remained a mystery.

News spread fast in Balaal. A stable boy mentioned Matanza's plan to a friend, who had a cousin visiting from Hāzeni, who knew a netmaker from Žalovanje, whose brother was a sleep talker, whose wife overheard and happened to mention it to a waiter in Gashuudakh, who had a distant cousin who knew a fisherman from the Fishing Village with No Name on the outskirts of Balaal. That fisherman was Shadrak.

✳

"Get out now," said Shadrak. Kin looked up from the boat he was cleaning. "My boat no gwon save you this time. He comin' with a thousand men."

Then Shadrak turned to Jesa. "You too," he said. Jesa, in her apron and scrubbing gloves, looked at him. "Matanza gwon kill y'all." She barely paused. She finished swabbing out the boat and sat on the stern.

"You still haven't told us why you left Kin on the island," she said.

"I done tol' you twenty time. They be waitin' for he return. I seen 'em hidin' behind the sand dunes, creepin' about. Them Tonto Macoute be stupid but they be dangerous too. So I call im back off the islan' and he get kill the nex' day, what you say to me, Miss Jesa?"

As was his wont, Fundogu appeared suddenly, dressed in his white robe, fingers ringed. "This fisherman is correct," he said to Jesa. "Go to Bujiganga. You will be safe there."

"I'm tired of running," said Jesa.

"It is not about you," said Fundogu. "You here means we are all in danger. You need to go tonight, in the dark."

"Why don't I take Kin with me?"

"No. You cannot go together."

"Why not?"

"That is not your destiny. That is not what is written in the Great Book."

"What great book?"

"The one in my head. You need to leave."

"When will this attack take place?" asked Jesa.

"We are not sure," said Fundogu. "Some say it is on Matanza Day. Some say tomorrow."

"I thought you could tell the future," she replied.

"Your future is in Bujiganga tonight. Kin goes the other way."

Balaal's outcasts traditionally ran for the hills. Up there lived witches and shamans. All around them were beasts that had succumbed to genetic mutation and were neither this nor that—rats with lions' claws, pigs interbred with tapirs, feathered bats that sang like starlings. It was rough terrain, alien territory. There were invisible pathways that appeared magically out of dense thicket. There were canyons as wide as seas and valleys where the stones sang.

The hills were cactus territory. Great bulbous heads of it, spines like daggers. They sprung out of the earth like death itself, in all shapes and forms: cylinders, spears, globes.

A man could walk for weeks and swear he had not moved. Hills appeared and reappeared. Streams would dry up and suddenly re-form somewhere else. While Balaal was always on the verge of a terrible burning or drowning, an extinction, the hills would be there forever. They were indomitable as gods. In fact, the people of Balaal said the hills *were* gods.

The first thing they had to do was get Kin out of the fishing village and through the city incognito, from where he could reach the hills. They gave him a rucksack and a false beard made of seal fur. A tag team of fishermen and street hawkers planned to take turns to show him the way, but it soon became clear that while they kept getting lost, Kin already knew the way. He'd lived on these streets for years.

"I grew up in this city," he said, and he slalomed past cavernous factories, under bridges, across roads packed with taxi-buses and rickshaws and all of human life teeming.

"Go home," he said to the squeegee man tasked with showing him the way. The man spent his days cleaning the windshields of cars stopped at traffic lights. He was supposed to know the city but all he knew was windshields.

"I can't. I was told to get you to the outskirts of the city."

"We're nearly there. Your street is back that way," and he pointed.

He even remembered to say thank you.

Kin left all of his guides behind and arrived at a street market. Unlike the fish market in the village, this one sold everything from rubber tires to elephant tusk soup. There were stalls selling dolls and bullets and dried insects and a thousand other things. The noise reminded Kin of the old days—the rancor of the city, the clamor and grind. The honking of car horns doing battle with a muezzin's call to prayer over the cries of hawkers and the radios at the stalls tuned to the mayor's propaganda or pirate stations playing all kinds of music, from Indian pop to Puccini.

After the quiet of the Fishing Village with No Name, it was a cacophony to Kin's ears. Bicycle bells and the clucking of chickens, engine growls and children's cries. He remembered his days prowling these markets, looking for a morsel to eat or a length of material to cover himself for the night. And now he was back, alone, the same solitude as before. All his families—the street kids, Jesa, the fishermen—he'd left them all behind again.

Street dogs loped in and out of the shadows, indifferent to the din. They were, he thought, the cousins of those beach hounds he'd seen every day on his morning walks. And even as he thought this, he said to himself, "I could disappear in the city. They wouldn't find me. So many nooks and corners to hide in. Instead, they tell me to go to the hills."

He knew Matanza had spies everywhere in the city and nowhere in the wilderness, and that was why he'd been sent there. But still, what chance would a boy have among the brujas and wild animals compared to the city? What chance when he was alone?

He kept going. He would follow their advice but only because it was Fundogu who'd given it. "Hide out in the hills," said the old preacher. Fate would do as it wished with him. But Fundogu had been right so far, about the danger that arrived just after Kin's baptism and about the abandoned island as his refuge. And who was Kin, a boy not yet fifteen, to argue?

CHAPTER 8

The entry of Jesa into Bujiganga—

Iquique—making plans

THE ENTRY OF JESA INTO BUJIGANGA WAS A BEAUTEOUS THING. THE CAMEL TOTTERED LIKE A drunk in high heels. Jesa, straddled between its humps and wearing three white scarves around her head, swayed, righted herself, and upended a final bag of popcorn into her mouth. The revolutionary had arrived.

Bujiganga was a village of collectors and madmen, tinkers and scrap merchants. The place itself was made of found materials. Houses were constructed of forks and cricket bats and old magazines. Roofs were made of axe handles and broken glass and wooden crates. Everything was used and reused until the residents could no longer remember the original purpose of anything. Windows were mirrors and mirrors were windows. New mothers transported their babies in wheelbarrows.

Bujiganga was the home of improvised electrics. Each corner of every house overflowed with bad wiring. Random filaments protruded from the buildings at all angles. On the roofs were jerry-rigged antennae, metal conductors soldered or taped together and stuck there like fragments of surrealist sculpture. Telephone wires sagged on pylons and went nowhere, dropping into creeks or off ledges.

The place was a mosaic. Streets were awash with glowing bottles, water-filled tires, tin cans, and from every window and on every surface, multicolored squares of washing hung out to dry.

In Balaal they say that every village has its idiot, but, according to legend, Bujiganga had *only* idiots. Or at least a majority. The one doctor in town howled at the moon every night. The barber brushed his hair with the skeleton of a trout. They said the place was run by a cabal of monkeys who lived in a bus shelter.

"We're here," Jesa said to the camel, jerking its neck with the rein—an improvised length of fishing rope.

It was early morning. A wolf whistle went up and dozens of tinkers came out of their houses, rubbing their eyes. As was their custom, most of them had left their goods on the street all night—tarpaulin sheets crammed with pots and pans, knock-off watches, electronics, handbags, hammocks, plastic jewelry, kettles, buttons. Although the people were mad and woebegone, they were not thieves. Swirling among the million pots and pans and tuning forks, the wind twisted its music up and down the scales, a metallic arpeggio that kept the Bujigangans company morning and night.

In the town, there were several soothsayers and clairvoyants in bowler hats, some with their heads on backwards. Because they could tell the future, they had already announced Jesa's imminent arrival, and some had stayed up all night in anticipation.

As she rode through the center, the residents of Bujiganga gawped at the stunning sight: this mangy, lolloping beast of the desert from whose masticating jaws drool dripped and whose legs seemed too bandy and malformed to carry its great cylinder of a stomach. And between those comical, conical humps, a handsome lady in white scarves. Some of the residents pondered: surely this noblewoman of whom the soothsayers speak, this revolutionary, deserves a knightly horse or an elephant, something with stature and poise, not this abomination of yellow fur and bad breath?

The camel pranced through the narrow street. The tinkers, scullery maids, truant schoolchildren, and delinquents applauded and chanted. The people called out to her:

"Matanza met his match!"

"La bruja tiene cojones!"

"The skunk who fought back!"

And whispers went around:

"She sent the judge packing. Kicked him out of court. Made him sit in the traffic."

"I heard she chopped up The Butcher. No one's seen him for weeks. Or his men."

"Rumor has it she set her bats on the soldiers and drowned them in popcorn."

"I heard she fought off eight policeman and fried them in their own fat."

A woman in her sixties, dressed in a nun's habit, approached and the camel stopped.

"Welcome to Bujiganga."

"Thank you," said Jesa.

"Come with me."

Jesa kicked the camel so it knelt. Then she dismounted and the woman led her to a small shack. Inside was a sofa.

"Sit here. Relax," said the woman. "I know you had a long journey. You'll want some tea. I'll be back in a minute."

It was only at this moment, as she was waiting, that Jesa realized she had been riding half the night on the camel's back. She removed her scarves, lay down, turned onto her side, and fell asleep. Outside, where the wind tinkled and chimed, the camel too, tethered to a post, was already snoring.

✳

When Jesa awoke, she realized not everyone in Bujiganga was mad. And neither was the place run by a cabal of monkeys living in a bus shelter. A group of women were alternately tending to her, cooking, and making plans at a table. The nun approached as Jesa opened her eyes.

"We heard you were coming," said the nun.

Jesa sat up and pulled her hair out of her face. "I was told to take refuge here. They're planning another attack on our village."

"So you're in hiding?"

"Yes."

The woman in the nun's habit smiled. "No, you aren't. No one takes refuge dressed as Joan of Arc in white scarves and traveling on an eight-foot camel. You're here to stir up trouble. Or at least we hope so."

Jesa took in what the woman was saying.

The woman smiled again and said, "We welcome you with open arms. Here, the government keeps attacking us. The Tonto Macoute raid our stores, take away our women. Sometimes they kidnap our children. They make us pay taxes, which go into their pockets. Look at the streets: they're full of holes. We go for weeks without running water. Then we hear you defied them with your Popcorn Rebellion."

"It wasn't a rebellion."

"Then what was it?"

"We kicked out a corrupt judge."

"Do you know who that man is?"

"Ochiades. Great-granduncle of Mayor Matanza."

"If you kick out the judge, you kick out the government. It's the same thing."

"Do you have some water?"

"Of course."

One of the women brought a glass of water and placed it on a table beside them. Jesa drank a little and rearranged herself. Her clothes were coated with a film of dust from her long journey across dry terrain. They had moved inland, parallel with the mountains that overlooked the ocean.

The woman in the nun's habit said, "Forgive me. My name is Iquique. We're planning a revolution. People say we're insane, but it's not true. We're just poor. And the reason we're poor is because the Matanza family has stolen everything. All we have left is dry land."

Jesa nodded. "I understand," she said. "But I don't know how I can help you. They have an army. You have what? Bric-a-brac."

"Maybe, maybe not. Come with me."

Iquique led Jesa to the table on which there was a map opened out, and two of the other women shook her hand.

"Look," said Iquique. The map had pencil lines all over it. "The quilombos of Buenavida. One thousand former slaves living in the hills. They hate the government. Sklonište and Bouazizi. Cienfuegos. The miners. Los barbudos. Ghiath Matar and the warriors who kicked out the soldiers in 96. Kakurega. Four hundred ninjas and five dozen samurai who routed a government battalion in 72. Qo'zg'olon. Fought street battles with the riot police and won. These are all towns the government has attacked. They're all sympathetic to us."

"Who is *us*?"

"The people."

"These are stories from history books," said Jesa. "Ghiath Matar in 96. Kakurega in 72. Does anyone remember those battles?"

"We do," said Iquique.

"Times have changed. The Matanzas are stronger than ever. They run Balaal. If you defy them, you die."

"And yet you defied them and you're alive."

"For now."

"You're a courageous woman," said Iquique.

"I had nothing to lose."

"Except your life."

Jesa shrugged. She wondered if these women knew her whole story, how her husband, a fisherman and a rebel and a first-class troublemaker, had died and she'd been tainted as a water widow, Balaal's own form of an untouchable.

She said, "Well, I fear I'm endangering you all by being here. Fundogu told me to come."

"We've heard his name. The healer. The wise man. Anyway, you made a good choice. No one will betray you here."

"May I ask you something?" said Jesa.

"Of course."

"We're here talking about armies and revolutions."

"Yes."

"But you're a nun. Don't you live in a convent? Haven't you taken vows? And also. . ."

"Wait. You're in Bujiganga. Things aren't what they seem. We have monks here who strangle soldiers. Every nun carries a weapon. Knives, machetes. Don't be fooled by our appearance. We realized long ago that the church we served didn't serve the people. It only served the rich. So we rebelled. And half of us were killed for our rebellion. The rest of us hid out in little towns. But things aren't what they seem. The nuns and monks here, we don't spend our lives in prayer. We're too busy building things and organizing. There is much to do."

"What things?"

"I'll show you later. The madmen on our streets aren't mad any more than you are. They're prophets. They rail at the moon because they see the future. Miss Jesa, you're not in the fishing village anymore. You're in Bujiganga. Now will you help us get prepared?"

"For what?"

"The revolution. The battles to come. They've been foretold."

"Yes. I told you, I have nothing to lose."

"Then good," said Iquique. "We just need to hide that camel."

But it turned out the camel had already hidden. The tireless beast had miraculously untethered itself from a post and wandered off, traversing the wastelands of Darvesh and the garbage dumps of Shkarravira, loping stolidly into a wood where only wild owls and the real madmen resided.

CHAPTER 9

Truck ride 1—paisanos—cave
man—ammonite—loopwalking—the
thingness of things—Tanah Mati

Kin tossed the fake beard and walked with his back to the sun, just as Fundogu had told him to. "Head for the hills," said the old priest, and he did.

First, he needed a ride. He saw a likely-looking truck. It was pulled over at the edge of a road that led out of Balaal.

"Where you going, kid?" asked the driver, a young woman with a flower in her hair.

"To the hills."

"Climb in the back."

He found himself huddled with paisanos, children, sheep, chickens, and a bird in a wooden cage. The paisanos greeted him and made space on the floor for him to sit. Their faces were weather-beaten, flat, and lined, and the permanent smudges of black in the creases of their skin gave away their professions— farmhands and miners one and all.

The truck stumbled and bumped along a rutted road and stopped every so often to pick up more wanderers. The jouncing eventually drew Kin into a dreamless sleep, which was soon interrupted because they ran out of floor space. Now everyone stood and held something. Someone passed him a child, a baby girl who whimpered and wriggled and wanted her mother. She was wrapped in a rough brown horsehair blanket that still smelled of the horse. Someone else gave him a flask of tsai, a salty green tea, which he swigged once with his free hand before passing it on.

With the baby still squirming in his arms, he watched the landscape turn from green to barren. The trees grew squat and stumped until there was nothing but cacti and tumbleweed and foxtail agave. He watched the sky turn broad and dark, clouds menacing the remaining stretches of sun, and wondered what he was doing, where he was going. He understood cities. The wilderness was different. Here, the air was clear and thin. The sky went on forever. He looked around and wondered where a man would hide or find food.

They passed the steppes. Vast plains. A herd of horses moved across the land, small and thickly built, almost stunted, made for rough weather.

As the truck went further, the climate turned cold. They passed flat fields and a frozen lake, and then suddenly the truck stopped and began to disgorge a crowd of people. They paid the driver with assorted coca leaves and chocolate and balls of dough. The mother relieved Kin of the baby and Kin turned to her and said, "Where are we?" but the woman didn't speak English and she was gone before he could try another language.

The truck pulled away and he looked back. The people on foot seemed to be walking somewhere but he couldn't see where. There was nowhere to walk to—just endless plains. Somewhere there had to be a fissure in the flatland, a crevice that led to a settlement.

The sun dipped under distant mountains and a bleak wind kicked up motes of dust and sand. The earth began to sing.

Kin folded his arms. He had a rucksack and inside it a woolen coat that one of Jesa's friends had made for him. He put it on now and squinted into the sunset. A pang of fear gnawed at his stomach.

The truck slowed and stopped again. The last few passengers climbed down and proffered their payments to the driver. Kin had nothing to give the woman but a small coin. Two sheep remained in the back of the truck.

"Miss," he said, "is there anywhere I can sleep out here?"

"Sleep?"

She turned to look at him. Despite her youth and the flower in her hair, she too had the face of a herder or a farmhand.

"There are caves to the west." She pointed. "The Manbudhin live over there in the hills, but they'll probably kill you."

"Where do you drive to next? I have another coin. I can pay you."

"This is the end of the line. I'm taking the sheep to the pasture, but you can't come. My brothers won't let you on our land because you're a stranger. Your best chance is the caves."

She got out of the cab. She was dark and broad-shouldered. She wore herder's pants and a thick gilet to ward off the cold.

"Get to the caves," she said. "If you hurry, you'll make it before dark. What weapons do you have?"

"A fish knife."

She looked at him skeptically. "Good luck," she said. "Here." She handed him a small grease-stained packet.

He took it, turned, and then turned back. "Thank you," he said.

＊

A man in a cave is a man unhinged.

The fourteen-year-old Kin had slept in many places—on roofs and factory floors, in packing crates and shipping containers, in a lighthouse among beetles and roaches, and in Jesa's cramped, sea-wracked house, but never in a cave. He knew outcasts lived in caves. Men who disappeared from the world, who learned to live in darkness, to commune with shadows.

In Balaal, cavemen were regarded as people of a higher spiritual order: philosophers and shamans, men and women who might emerge from the dark and found a religion or know how to purify souls.

But still he trembled more with fear than with cold when he stepped through the mouth of the cave. The opening was just a little taller than Kin, and seemed like the opening to a child's grotto, but when he entered he understood why caves were sacred. The interior looked like a cathedral made of dolomite. Even in the waning light he could make out gigantic flutes of rock that stretched thirty feet high. Brocaded walls, stalactites and stalagmites that looked like melted wax. Under his feet were rocks and sand and stones.

His eyes adjusted quickly to the dark. He didn't want to take anyone or anything by surprise, so he called out, "Hello" and immediately heard a dozen hellos in return, receding in volume and in his own voice. He said it again and heard the echo again. Gingerly, he walked forward. He was now completely out of the wind but he didn't want to go too far from the entrance, because an entrance is also an exit.

He tried to remember his ten-year-old self, the king of derring-do, his fearlessness. In those days he would have run through the cave shouting at the universe.

He came across an ammonite, the snail fossil, the size of his splayed hand, and he remembered something Fundogu had said once: "Everything begins and ends in the sea."

A wave of hunger came over him and he pondered whether to eat the snack the truck driver had given him. "Food attracts animals," he said to himself. But he was too hungry to wait, so he sat on the floor, opened the paper bag and crammed four doughy balls, one after the other, into his mouth. He still had some water left and now he sipped it, knowing he might not find more for a long time.

As the dark came down, he felt his way to a corner of the cave and buried himself in the coat and a thin blanket Jesa had given him. He fingered the coral necklace around his neck and said, "You will protect me all my days."

He slept fitfully. He was out of the wind, but the night brought many noises: a coyote howled and the sky rumbled in the small hours, poised for a rain that never came.

In the morning, he staggered into the sunlight like some Stone Age innocent and took another sip of water. It was like the old days, his childhood, when his first thought on waking and his last thought before sleeping was how to get food. Except Balaal was full of food if you didn't mind scrounging and stealing. But here? Here, he was in the wilderness, banished to a place of dust and rocks. And he was alone again, all his families shed like leaves in winter.

He looked around. The hills were to the west. That's where Fundogu had told him to go. "The tribes will take care of you," he'd said. "They have animals. They fish the rivers. Their warriors are so fierce and the land so inhospitable that the government soldiers never go there. You'll be safe. Hide out for a while."

He bade farewell to the cave, taking one last look at the necklace of spiky stalactites that hung from the roof, a cluster of organ pipes with no music in them. Below the stalactites, forming the bottom row of the monster's teeth, was a line of stalagmites, tapered tubes of crystallized rats' urine.

He began walking. It was early. The sun was still dallying and a cool wind teased the dust of the plain. Kin made good ground. He began to ascend the hills, looking for signs of humanity. There were none.

From the top of the first hill he saw more hills. He descended and climbed again. Cacti and sharp stones. Surfaces worn by time and bitter winds. He heard himself breathing. He reached the top and looked out. Nothing but more hills and the plain. And the sun rising.

Soon he was lost and hungry. The food was all gone and there was barely a drop of water left. At midday the heat began to assail him. He stripped down to his shirt and pants, stuffing the coat into the backpack, and kept going. Up hills, into valleys which led to more hills.

Where were these tribes? "They will take care of you," said Fundogu. But he had to find them first.

He came to the remains of either a deer or a horse, now a xylophone of bleached bones stripped down by vultures and wild dogs.

As the sun hit its zenith he found another cave hidden at the foot of a hill. He called "hello" as he had done before and the echo was exactly the same as it had been at the previous cave. He went inside. He saw the stalactites and stalagmites. Then he saw the ammonite, the fossil with its snail-whorl. *This is the same cave. The universe is playing a trick on me.*

He went deeper into the cave to feel the cool of its breath and recognized everything. All day he'd walked a perfect loop and ended where he'd started.

His thoughts turned to practicalities. Where to go? What to eat? Where to find water? He thought of retracing his steps to return to the truck driven by the woman. She'd helped him. She'd been the last person he'd seen, shown him the way to the cave.

Then he vowed to keep moving: to shout his name to the hills and find succor. To note the landmarks so he wouldn't go in circles again. He would move at night instead of in the dreaded heat of the day.

He summoned his mantra, *control your fear*, and said it to himself again and again until he said it so often it lost its meaning and all that was left was the final word *fear*. It wasn't the same fear he'd felt in the city: the flashlight beams of the Tonto Macoute, rats the size of badgers scampering around his feet, hulking drunkards entering the shadows where he hid. No. It was a new fear. Something alien, unknown. It was the absence of signs he could recognize. A blankness so vast he couldn't name it. Although the words were familiar—hill, sky, cave, desert—the sensation of being among them and the sensation of infinite solitude made him afraid.

When he felt the cool of the evening, he went outside and began walking. In front of him and behind him were identical hills. He couldn't remember from which direction he'd come.

As the dark came down, he found himself stumbling. The terrain was craggy and full of cacti. He feared wild beasts would emerge, protected by the night. Mountain lions. Coyotes. Wolves.

He stumbled on until he came to another cave, only to rediscover the ammonite and the stalactites and the stalagmites. He sat and wondered how he could have walked another circle and not known, not recognized anything. Up and down the same hills. Then he lay on a flat patch of sand and fell asleep.

When he woke it was still dark.

He peered outside the cave. He was in a vast valley of dead land that kept repeating itself. The shamans called it Tanah Mati. Kin said to himself, "I'm a ghost."

He sat up in the sand. I should have stayed in Balaal, laid low, worn the seal fur beard, changed my name.

Now he became feverish. It happened within minutes, something brought on by the air inside the cave. Despite years living on the streets of Balaal, he'd never been ill before, and soon he was too weak to get up. Instead, he clung to the coral necklace.

Days passed.

He began communing with his shadow, holding conversations on life and death. He enacted scenes from the earliest days he could remember, his days scrounging for food or telling jokes with the other homeless children.

He saw scratches on the walls that he hadn't noticed before and concluded that these were tracts in strange idioms, written by ancient philosophers for him to decipher, although it was the cave itself that confounded him. He couldn't understand its language, which is to say he couldn't understand its silence. Outside too, the rough grasses had stopped singing.

He thought of *things*—fishing rods, cardboard boxes, sea shells—and the *thingness* of things: how they felt in your hand, how they came from factories in the east or were made by the hands of those he knew or washed up in the swell of the ocean. He thought of Balaal and the smell of fish. The damp air, and wood rotting in the heat.

In lucid moments he remembered *white* things: Jesa and her skunk-streak of white hair and Fundogu's white robes.

His mind rarely wandered far from the fishing village. He saw the cloud of smoke in front of the face of the black fisherman with the paunch. Shadrak! The old fool who helped everybody if he could, except for stranded whales.

He hallucinated. Sometimes he hallucinated himself hallucinating. After a while, he began to lose track of what was real. He saw a demon on the cave ceiling, who, depending on the time of day, appeared in the shape of a harp or a lobster or a pencil.

Delirium came and went.

He began talking aloud. He conducted debates with himself on the nature of fish, what they knew and in which language. What does a fish understand when it's caught in the net? Does it whimper or yowl or ululate? Does it know it's dying?

He philosophized on every subject he could think of, constructing arguments and counterarguments until he'd looped his mind full circle just as his feet had walked in loops always back to this godforsaken cave. And then he became Stone Age man again, scrabbling around in the dust.

He began talking to Jesa every hour. He asked her about household chores, about the height of the waves that morning, about the state of the roof or whether the door hinge needed oiling.

He would sit with his back to the cave wall, and when he wasn't talking he listened. His ears became so attuned to the cave that he heard spiders spinning webs and detected the infinitesimal rustle of an ant colony deconstructing a dead scarab beetle. He listened for the flapping of birds' wings. He listened for the sound of horses' hooves and sheep's bells. He listened for the wind. Above all he listened for human voices. None came.

At one moment he heard whistling. It sounded like two birds, some kind of call and response. A conversation that went on for several minutes. Then silence. Maybe he'd dreamed it.

He had never been religious, but now he found himself bowing before stones. He saw heaven in the ridges of the ammonite. He discovered a crack in the cave's ceiling, which let in the light, a crevice the thickness of a finger, and he stared at it for hours. He began to think of it as God, until in the dullness, in the silence of this blackened cave, he told himself *either God is dead or I am.* But he was alive. Unbeknown to him, he turned fifteen in that cave, although he might have been fifteen thousand, because he lived as the earliest men had lived: in fear and with no certainty that there would be a tomorrow to wake up to.

In the depths of his sickness, he suddenly became lucid. He saw the faces of the drowned soldiers in the *other* cave, the one on the island where the lighthouse stood. He saw their bodies squirming in their final throes and he saw The Butcher struggling furiously to hold onto the last tenuous strings of life, the final breaths before the water took him. But he didn't see Hormigonera going under. Instead, he saw her clambering onto the bowrider, gammy leg and all, and he saw her switch on the engine and ride the massive wave, the boat bucking and lurching in its maw, and righting itself, and her huge nose cocked to the wind as she sailed into the eye of Nazaré and, unable to cling on to the boat's railing, flew—yes, *flew*—from the boat back toward the lighthouse where she sailed through the window—the recorder's tone hole—and landed in an anteroom smack against a wall.

He thought of Fundogu's prophecy: Kin would lead the people. Now he knew what he would lead them against. Among his visions was that of Balaal's dictator, Matanza, dressed in a shiny suit, observing and applauding a massacre while six dogs cavorted at his feet. The women throwing water from buckets at the stranded whale transformed into women throwing bucketfuls of blood onto the streets, their families decimated, their houses upturned. Kin had to unseat the dictator. And just as the visions came, so too did a new mantra, a verse from nowhere: *I am the ocean. I am the four winds. I am the stars that guide the living. I am the memory of the dead.*

✳

In his lucidity, ten days after he'd entered the cave, he realized he'd starve if he didn't leave. He was emaciated and broken, his mouth parched, his tongue the size of a shoe. His skin was a waxy sheen, strangely pallid, and his hands shook like the hands of the Ecstatics he'd seen at religious festivals—women who danced themselves into a frenzy till they fainted.

He hauled himself up and staggered into the light. It hit him like a hammer blow. Blinded, he blundered into the day. *There's always a way out. Even if it's death, there's always a way out.*

Then slowly, almost imperceptibly, he heard the earth singing. It wasn't only the wind. It wasn't only the stones. It was everything in concert. The cactus began it—a B minor chord—and the wind came in with a counterpoint. The stones only started singing when the wind had found its rhythm, and they, being frivolous and small, sang delicate harmonies. Meanwhile, the cave behind him hammered out great organ chords on its stalactites, deep and sonorous, like something from the beginning of time. There was music in them after all.

He began walking again, guided by the sounds of the earth's song. This land was far from dead. The agave trilled like a harp. The saguaro honked like a bassoon. The devil's claw thrummed like a zither. The ocotillo and cholla shared manic cimbalom chords between them. The music shifted, sometimes quieting to an austere gagaku and then rising again to a symphony. It stirred Kin's blood and propelled him forward. He walked and walked, forcing himself to go against his instincts, go the opposite way to where he thought he should be going, because that's what had confounded him before. Do everything backward and upside down and the wrong way round, and above all, *listen*.

He came up a hill, guided by the stones' singing. As he neared the top, he saw patterns etched in a rock: parallel lines, a spiral, a curve. He passed it and saw others: lines and dots carved into the flat stones.

At that moment, he thought again of Fundogu, who had christened him Kin das Ondas, Kin of the Waves. He understood that no ocean wave would save him this time, but the waves in his name weren't only from the sea. The noises of the night and the music of the day were made by the vibration of air. "Sound waves," Jesa, his one and only teacher, had called them. The *other* waves. Half-blinded as he was, if anything would save Kin das Ondas, it would be his ears.

He looked over the edge of the hill and saw a cluster of trees. Beside them, barely visible, was a stream.

CHAPTER 10

Los barbudos—rabbit stew—

The Professor—the hat and the

cat—the library—the history of the

Matanzas—the Bruja of Laghouat—

Chinese zither—entrenamiento

KIN STUMBLED ACROSS THE LANDSCAPE TOWARD THE STREAM. HE MOVED DOWNHILL, blinded by the sun, and heard los barbudos—the bearded ones— before he saw them. They were in front of him, tramping down the highland like the three musketeers, whistling and singing folk songs, which carried on the breeze. On hearing his footsteps, they turned around.

"¿Quién es este?" said one of the men.

"Hey!" shouted another.

They approached. Kin raised his hands.

They were longhaired and bearded, carrying rifles, one of them with a great Zapata bullet chain making a cross over his chest. They wore military uniforms, but Kin saw that they weren't government soldiers. The tallest of them wore a pair of patched-up glasses and a Palestinian keffiyeh around his neck, another a vast sombrero which cast his face in shadow, and the third, open-shirted, had bright blue eyes and a tattoo of a bullet over his heart. This last one carried a string of freshly killed rabbits tied together by their tails.

Kin fell to his knees and begged for water.

A man-child at the end of his rope. A cave dweller. Feral. The kid wasn't sun-wrecked, like most of the strangers they encountered in the wilds, but he looked like a desperado, unkempt, unfed and unwatered, half-crazed with need and thirst. He didn't appear to be an agent of the government, so—as was their custom—they saved him. The one with glasses tipped a metal canteen of water into Kin's mouth, then lifted him by the arms. The men led him toward the settlement.

"¿Que haces aqui?" said the one with the tattoo, who was holding him by the elbow.

"Hey," said the sombrero-wearer, a pace behind. "You don't understand Spanish? He asked if you're a spy."

"Que diciste?" said the first one.

"Nada."

The tallest one, with the eyeglasses and Palestinian scarf, didn't say a word, but he held Kin by the other arm, supporting him down the rocky face of the hill.

"¿Tienes hambre?" said the tattooed soldier.

Kin was too exhausted to speak, so he nodded.

"We'll give you food, don't worry," said Sombrero. "Hey, man, you understand me? El muchacho no habla ni español ni ingles."

The one with glasses looked over his shoulder at Sombrero, but said nothing.

"¿Eres una mujer?" continued Sombrero. "Are you a boy or a girl? Where's your beard? You look like a girl. Are you alone, muchacho? You didn't bring no soldiers with you, right?"

"Déjalo en paz," said the man with the tattoo.

"Sure," said Sombrero. "Next thing you know, the army's here and we're all dead."

Within minutes, they were in the valley. A community lay in front of them: twenty rondavels—circular houses made of thatch—with smoke rising like frayed rope from the chimneys. An array of trees stood behind the houses, and in front of them, near the foot of the hill, the winding stream Kin had first seen.

He'd been so close. Thirty minutes' walk and he would have found them ten days ago. He'd missed the sounds made by the hunters. He'd missed the houses in the settlement. He'd missed the smoke spiraling up the sky. The mountain hideout wasn't camouflaged. Any fool could have walked over the hill and found the inhabitants immediately.

They took him to a shady patch under a tree and made him bathe in a porcelain tub which stood on four metal bear claws in the open air. The hunter wearing the keffiyeh, who'd previously been silent, said, "Lie down. Don't try to talk."

While Kin was in the tub, an old woman approached and applied a layer of sheep's fat to his face, which was cracked from the days lost in the wilderness, rubbing it in roughly with her calloused hands. He soaked in the balmy water, eyes to the heavens watching the clouds pass by. What he wanted more than anything was food.

The man tossed Kin a set of clean clothes—a pair of ill-fitting jeans and a ragged gray t-shirt—and took him into one of the rondavels. They sat on the bare mud floor in semidarkness, and soon a woman brought in two plates of rabbit stew and rice and a jug of water. They ate in silence. Kin finished his in minutes. The woman brought more.

"They call me The Professor," said the man.

Kin tried to say his name but it came out as an unfamiliar croak. His tongue was still swollen and his throat hurt.

"It's OK," said The Professor. "Don't try to talk."

Kin focused on his food. He hadn't eaten in over a week. The rabbit was stringy and salty but he savored every scrap. When it was gone, he drank so rapidly The Professor removed Kin's cup and put the jug in its place so Kin could swig straight from it.

Without saying another word, The Professor got up and left. Once he'd drunk all of the water, Kin lay down and curled up like an embryo. His body craved sleep but his mind wouldn't settle. Was he safe? Who were these people? He looked upward. The thatched, slanted ceiling of the rondavel led to a small hole in the center, the chimney. It reminded him of the light that shone down from the roof of the courthouse-that-wasn't-a-courthouse. And then it reminded him of the crack in the roof of the cave where he'd been holed up for days on end, the sliver of light he'd thought was God. Now he lay still and listened to the sounds of the mountain hamlet—footsteps across the scree, chatter in English and Spanish, a lone dog whining—till they coalesced into white noise.

✳

Twenty-four hours later, Kin woke up. The Professor, propped up against the rondavel's wall in his military uniform topped with a red and white keffiyeh, was staring at him.

"Kid, if you can talk, tell me something. What are you doing here?"

Kin cleared his throat. His tongue was no longer badly swollen, but his face was as numb as a rock.

"I'm running away. . ." he said. His voice was raspy like metal scratching stone. He cleared his throat again. "I'm running away from the mayor's men. They're searching for me. I don't know why."

"The Tonto Macoute?" said The Professor.

"Yes."

"Then you're one of us. How old are you?"

"Fourteen," said Kin. "Maybe fifteen. I don't know."

Sombrero appeared at the door of the rondavel.

"It talks!" he said. "You're not fifteen. Where's your beard?"

"Hey, Sombrero," said The Professor. "Don't you have chores to do?"

"How was my rabbit?"

"Very good. Now why don't you leave us in peace?"

"¡Si, profe!"

The Professor poured two glasses of water from the same jug as before, which had been replenished, and handed one to Kin.

"Where are you from?"

"I live in a fishing village. It has no name. There's a port nearby, but we don't go there. We have a couple of. . ."

"Wait," said The Professor. "Which fishing village? Do you know Fundogu?"

"Of course."

"Are you the ones who kicked out Ochiades? Who started The Popcorn Rebellion?"

"Yes."

The Professor drank his water and scratched at his sparse beard.

"Everything is beginning to make sense," he said. "You aren't here by accident. You're part of the revolution. Did Fundogu send you here?" he asked.

"Not exactly." Kin coughed again. His face ached. "He told me to go to the mountains. What revolution?"

"Did he tell you who you'd find here?"

"No. Well, he said there were warriors."

"He sent you here to be trained," said The Professor.

"No, I was lost. I've been in a cave."

"Yes." The Professor inclined his head. He had a distant look in his eyes as if he was doing a puzzle. "Which cave?"

"I don't know. I was lost."

"Was there an ammonite fossil by the entrance?"

"Yes."

"You were in the cave of Zugarramurdi. You were safe. The spirits kept you safe and only released you when you were ready. You have some blisters and sunburn. The woman will keep treating you. You'll need a few more days to recover, maybe less as you're young. Then we can talk some more."

"What revolution?" said Kin.

"Just rest for now," replied The Professor. "The revolution can wait."

The Professor stood up. He was lean and wiry like everyone in these hills. His glasses were held together with thin strips of sellotape bunched like a badly applied bandage and his beard was threadbare. And now he was thinking about the old priest Fundogu and about who exactly this child was, because he too knew some prophecies, had heard of a boy and a whale and the rebellion in the fishing village, the first stirrings of something. And now the boy had been in a sacred cave, a place frequented by brujas and spirits.

✳

For three days, Kin barely moved except to sit up when food arrived and when the old woman put sheep's fat on his face. He spent the rest of the time sleeping. His world became the baked mud floor of that rondavel, just as it had been the floor of the cave. At night he dreamed of the beach and the sounds of the fishing village: the waves washing over the shore, the squawking gulls, the cries of the fishermen in many tongues.

On the fourth day, The Professor came back to see him.

"You're looking better. Do you know where you are?" he said.

"In the mountains," replied Kin. His tongue had shrunk to normal size and his skin was no longer dried and cracked like a crater.

"You're on Mount Naranco," said The Professor. "It's named after a giant. He was a tyrant. He treated his servants so badly that after he died they put huge rocks on top of his mausoleum because they were afraid he'd come back to life. They wanted him buried forever. Those rocks were so big they eventually formed this mountain range. And we're next to the biggest mountain of them all: Naranco."

Kin was sitting against the wall of the rondavel and The Professor joined him.

"Here, everyone reads," said The Professor. "If you don't read, you can't stay with us. The one with the hat, Sombrero, and the other one that you met, El Gato, they read all the time. If you want to be a soldier, you have to think."

"A soldier? I'm a fisherman," said Kin. "I was just baptized. . ."

"You have to know why you're fighting and what you're fighting against. And that means you have to know history and politics and philosophy. Follow me."

They stood up and The Professor led Kin toward another rondavel. It was the first time he had been outside in four days, except to do his ablutions, and he squinted against the sun and tried to find his bearings. They passed several men and women, who all greeted Kin. They passed the blue-eyed soldier too, who paused to shake Kin's hand.

"Me llamo Gatillo. El Gato. Mucho gusto."

"Mucho gusto," said Kin.

As they walked on, The Professor said, "That man, El Gato, he's the best shooter in these mountains. He used to be an army sniper. Now he hunts rabbits for *us*."

The second rondavel was the same size and type as the first, except it had piles of books on the ground and a homemade shelf of cedar wood stacked every which way. There were paperbacks and hardbacks, skinny pamphlets and books the size of bricks jammed together or leaning diagonally or with their spines horizontal. There was barely a space to sit.

The Professor said, "This is our library. There's only one rule. Everyone reads every day. At least an hour. No excuses. Do you know how to read?"

"Yes."

"Yes?"

"Yes."

The Professor paused. "You said you were a fisherman. Who taught you to read?"

"A woman called Jesa."

"Then look through these and choose one."

"Where did you get all these books?"

"We're librotraficantes. Book smugglers. We get them on our excursions to the city, or Silmiya brings them."

"Who's she?"

"She's a farmer. Goes into the city in her truck and gives people rides."

"Maybe I know her. I think I came here with her. There were two sheep in the back of the truck. She said her brothers don't like strangers, then she showed me where the caves are."

"That's her."

Kin touched the spines of the books.

"They're books, not bombs," said The Professor. "Get comfortable. This is your reading hour."

Among the books was a history of Balaal. It was thick with dust and contained sepia photographs that took up whole pages. Kin sat against the wall, laid the book on his lap, blew away a patina of dust from the cardboard cover, opened it at page one, and began to read.

✳

CHAPTER ONE
The Beginnings of the Matanza Family Dynasty

The history of modern Balaal began with a remarkable discovery made by a six-year-old girl named Miranda. The girl, described by contemporary sources as plain and strong-willed, hailed from a family of illiterate farmers. The young maiden was out playing by the river one summer day when she discovered and brought home a six-gram nugget of metal. She said the nugget had caught her eye while she was washing her favorite doll, also named Miranda. The metal turned out to be gold. Miranda's parents, who owned the land, had the gold weighed and valued.

Soon word spread that there was gold in this little freehold and in the surrounding areas. A gold rush ensued. Opportunists and adventurers from many regions descended on the farm. Within weeks, they had dug several large holes in the ground. As more gold was discovered, hundreds more men arrived and set up camp on or in close proximity to the farmer's land. Among them was Porfirio Matanza, a poor, uneducated herdsman known for his large nose and the fact that he had six fingers on each hand and six toes on each foot.

Due to the uneducated nature of those scrambling for gold, unseemly behavior and disturbances were common. Violence broke out regularly in the encampments. Several murders were recorded, among them the death by strangulation of one Günther Erdrosseln, the stabbing of Joacyr Esfaqueado, and the drowning of Juan Manuel Respiro. The problem lay in the fact that whenever someone claimed a nugget or a seam of gold, someone else contested it. As the violence escalated, the herdsman and opportunist Porfirio Matanza gathered a group of men to police the mines and serve as foremen.

At this stage, the farmer who owned the land was entitled to 50 percent of whatever anyone found. One night, Porfirio Matanza broke into the farmhouse, shot the farmer dead, expelled the farmer's family from their home, and laid claim to the land. With the help of his gang, Porfirio Matanza took over the running of the newly dug mines. He avoided the same fate as the farmer by handsomely rewarding some and killing others whom he suspected of coveting his newfound wealth. And the 50 percent became 90 percent.

Within six months, Porfirio Matanza had a militia of three hundred men and a small fortune. He began investing his wealth in businesses in the center of Balaal. He then bought the title of mayor, which was conferred on him in a public ceremony in a square in the center of the city. Within a year, the square would be renamed Matanza Square. On learning that elsewhere there were kings, queens, and emperors, Porfirio Matanza became discontented with the title and named himself His Mighty Highness, Conqueror of Balaal and the Surrounding Towns and Lord of all the Beasts of the Earth and the Fishes in the Sea.

Porfirio Matanza ruled Balaal for forty-six years. It was a period of peace, and prosperity for the Matanza family and friends. In this time, the mayor commissioned several buildings for the exclusive use of the ruling family, which stand to this day, and a number of statues. Thirty-two of the statues depicted Porfirio Matanza on a horse waving a sword, although there were no wars documented at the time. The other sixteen statues depicted him dressed as a statesman, although there is no record of him ever meeting other leaders or indeed leaving Balaal. The statues' hands appear to be five-fingered, contradicting contemporary medical records which state that Porfirio Matanza was six-fingered, while the nose is only slightly bigger than normal, allowing for artistic license.

In the garden of Porfirio Matanza's palace there was a magnificent zoo which contained dozens of rare wild animals in cages. The animals included a lion, a giraffe, an elephant, two camels, a tiger, several penguins, and a number of birds with multicolored plumage. It is believed that these beasts had never been seen before in Balaal and their provenance was unknown.

On the other side of Matanza's garden was another set of cages. Inside them were his enemies. These included scions of wealthy families, generals who were rumored to be plotting against him, and a few writers. The latter had written nothing about Porfirio Matanza but were suspected of harboring subversive attitudes. By way of explanation for their imprisonment, a mayoral assistant explained that two of the writers had failed to praise sufficiently a number of poems written by Porfirio Matanza and published in the national newspaper the Matanza Daily.

The cages of the zoo were hosed down once a week, and the enemies of the regime were treated with the same courtesies as the animals. Guests were taken to viewings of the zoo while Porfirio Matanza's personal orchestra played Beethoven and Mozart in the background. Periodically, the mayor would free a dissident in a show of magnanimity. Contemporary sources also say that despite the adequate treatment of the animals, one of the camels escaped and was never found by the regime.

Porfirio Matanza was renowned, at least in his own writings, for being a man of the people. Despite a number of unfortunate massacres, public executions, and assassinations of critics, the mayor frequently expressed his desire for an open, free society. He sometimes walked the streets, closely followed by his retinue of armed guards, and he liked to go to markets to receive gifts from his many admirers among the tradesmen there. These gifts included ink pens, rugs, maps, works of art, and young girls.

In middle age, Porfirio Matanza, sometimes known as Matanza the Elder, married a commoner named Eliza Fernandez, who bore him three sons and two daughters. The eldest of the boys was Anastasio.

Anastasio Matanza grew up in the Matanza palace surrounded by dozens of servants. He was born with four fingers on each hand and four toes on each foot. At the age of eighteen, after a bout of strange behavior with a capuchin monkey, he was declared clinically insane. Rather than being locked away, as was common for the insane, Anastasio was given the title Head of Security of the Mayoral Entourage and Guardian and Savior of the Marsupials of Balaal. After the death of his father, from intestinal complications following a lobster dinner, Anastasio was named mayor of Balaal.

Anastasio Matanza was known for his unorthodox views and original mind. He made enemies with ease, one of whom was the Bruja of Laghouat, a witch and fortune teller. When Anastasio Matanza found out that La Bruja had prophesied his early demise, he placed her under a death sentence and offered ten thousand rahats to whichever police officer killed her.

Contemporary sources inform us that in order to avoid Matanza's police, La Bruja turned herself into a black dog. On hearing this, Mayor Matanza ordered a purge of all the black dogs in Balaal. They were to be shot on sight. Economic records of the era show that sales of fur dye went up 22,000 percent. Thousands of previously black dogs were painted blond or brown. Some of the police officers and soldiers obediently shot any black dog they saw. However, many of them owned black dogs themselves, so they hid their pets in attics until the purge was over or they purchased fur dye that was now selling at the all-time-high price of 100 rahat an ounce. Fur dye was officially banned, but it was sold openly on the Anything-But-Black-Market.

When the purge was two weeks old, a rumor spread that La Bruja was no longer hiding in the guise of a black dog but had transformed herself into a mango. Mangos were summarily pulped in the markets, by mayoral decree, usually by the feet of the soldiers. This caused consternation among many fruit sellers and led to the short-lived Mango Uprising, which was crushed within twenty-four hours.

Shortly after the Mango Uprising, the papers printed a story saying that La Bruja had transformed herself into a cloud. Anastasio Matanza, now commonly known as Matanza the Mango Masher, was unable to destroy the clouds by decree. Instead, he lay low in the winter months to avoid being attacked by a thunderstorm. It is believed that he eventually forgot all about the Bruja of Laghouat.

The mayor, also commonly known as Matanza the Mad, still in his early twenties, decided on a policy of conquest. He marched with his men to the farthest shores of the province and killed everyone who refused to submit to him. On one skirmish, he was gored by a ram and contracted gangrene. He returned to the palace to have his leg surgically removed by the finest surgeon in the land, a woman named Maraya the Wise.

Once Maraya the Wise had done her work, the mayor's leg was given a full state funeral. It was measured for its coffin, neatly shaved and painted with a bronze burnish, and Matanza himself, seated on a throne, delivered the famous "Eulogy to My Left Leg." The leg did a final triumphal tour of Balaal, and the people were press-ganged into appearing in the streets with flags and portraits of the leg. Contemporary illustrations render it as a shapely limb bearing the hallmarks of the leg of a Greek god. At this time, several recently commissioned public statues of Anastasio Matanza lost a leg overnight.

The loss of a leg slowed down Matanza the Mad but did not cool his temper. Archives recount that he was known to smash windows, rage at passing squirrels, and shout at the woodworms that took root in his wooden leg. The latter became so pernicious that he sent the leg to jail on a charge that the woodworms had attempted a coup d'état. Woodworms were now enemies of the people and officially outlawed. The wooden leg languished in its own cell, condemned to rot away in perpetuity.

Anastasio Matanza fathered a son with his nanny, a woman named Claudia Dummemaus. The boy was named Eloy. Court diaries tell us that Eloy was a strange and nervous child, born with seven fingers on each hand and seven toes on each foot. When Anastasio Matanza died of intestinal complications following an oyster dinner, Eloy became mayor at the age of eighteen.

The new Mayor Matanza's nervousness continued. His night sweats were known to drench the bedclothes. He feared that one day the people would rebel. He feared that his generals would turn the army's guns on him. He also feared that the sky would fall on his head. Court papers tell us that he believed every meal to be a concoction of seven types of poison, undetectable to the eye or the microscope, and he consequently employed a pair of food tasters, twins by the name of Dumblewit and Dinglecock, whose job was to take a bite of every meal Eloy Matanza was to eat.

As Matanza's paranoia grew, the twins were tasked with trying on his clothes in case someone had poisoned the lining. Next, they began taking the first puff of his cigars. Then they were to sit on the toilet before him in case someone sent a snake up the sewer. They were ordered to test the bed before Matanza would lie in it. They were tasked with taking his walks and standing in for him when the dentist or doctor visited. Contemporary sources tell us the doctor explained to the twins that this was not how medicine worked. However, after some cajoling, the doctor was persuaded to publicly state that the mayor was in excellent health.

With his paranoia now out of control, Mayor Matanza chose increasingly to stay in his bunker. No one saw him for twenty-six years except Dumblewit and Dinglecock. He died at the age of sixty of intestinal complications following a shrimp dinner. A rumor suggested it was either Dumblewit or Dinglecock who had poisoned the mayor, but this was unconfirmed. In any case, by the time of the mayor's death, according to newspaper sources, barely anyone remembered who he was. This was because, without his knowledge, his son had taken over as mayor of Balaal. This son, named after the first Mayor Matanza, was called Porfirio II. He was the only male in four generations to be born with five fingers on each hand and five toes on each foot, closely followed by his brother, a man universally known as The Butcher. Neither brother ate seafood.

✳

Kin read until his eyes were heavy. The more he read, the more he understood Balaal. Starving workers, aimless wanderers, desperadoes, desaparecidos, escaped camels, and ragged armies of street children, of which he had been one. They were nameless masses, huddled in corners of mines or put to work in factories. Occasionally they appeared in protest marches, chanting slogans and waving their fists, but nothing ever seemed to come of these marches. The chapter would always end with "and then the soldiers sprayed them with water cannons and the crowd dispersed." Or "then the mayor made a speech and everyone went home." Or "the worst of the dissidents were rounded up and shot by the Tonto Macoute." Or "the protesters were arrested and sent to prison."

On finishing the history book, he turned to the first chapter and began again. He'd got as far as chapter 3 when The Professor came in, wrapped in his thick cotton scarf.

"You've read this book already," he said.

"I'm reading it again."

"There are other books," said the Professor. And he handed Kin a heavy hardback called *The History of War*.

✳

For another week, Kin was given no chores and his food was brought to him on a wooden tray by an old woman who never spoke or smiled. She wore a dark scarf around her head, which meant she was a widow, and her hands were wrinkled like old parchment, mottled and blotched and as delicate as scrolls under glass. Every morning, she woke him with a feast: a slice of bread, an egg, apples in honey, or figs.

He became so accustomed to her silent intrusions that he began to hear the music of her approach before she'd even moved. It was the sound of a Chinese Guzheng zither. Its earthy twang didn't resound like a cello or a violin but it hinted at a secret life, a life of hide-and-seek and bees and tree bark.

Occasionally, he would hear whistling. Not the whistling of a contented worker or a songbird but something stranger and distant that echoed over the hills. It was too staccato to be the wind, too controlled to be a coyote, and too loud to be a wild rock hyrax. One day he asked The Professor about it, and he told him, "We whistle across the mountains. It's how we communicate with the other settlements. It's a language. That's how we know if we're going to be attacked or if someone's delivering something."

As part of his recovery, Kin would go on walks, sometimes alone, sometimes with The Professor. After the walks, he did his ablutions, tried to avoid Sombrero, and returned to the rondavel to read again.

Every day, The Professor stopped by the rondavel and always asked Kin the same question: "What did you learn today?" Kin's answers varied little. He'd read about Porfirio Matanza/Anastasio Matanza/Eloy Matanza/Porfirio Matanza II/The Butcher/the massacres/the murders/the assassinations/the slaughters/the imprisonments without trial/the insane decrees/the absurd proclamations/

the massive statues/the gargantuan palaces/the colossal castles/the browbeaten masses/the bullied underclasses/the cowed communities/and so on and so on and so on almost until the present day except for the fact that The Butcher's whereabouts were unknown. And The Professor would always ask him the same question next.

"What else?"

"That's all."

"What else?"

"There's more?"

"Read this."

And it was seldom poetry or novels that the straggly-bearded Professor placed in Kin's hands, just as the religious tomes, travel books, romances, and assorted pulp was also left on the shelf. All The Professor gave him was history books. From morning to night he read.

Weeks passed. They passed so peacefully that Kin no longer pined for the fishing village, for the smell of brine and seaweed and the rhythmic wash of the waves on the shore. The memory of his morning walks on the beach faded a little and he began to forget about the objects he'd found there, the inventory of his days, the city's junk and detritus: dolls washed up on the shore, a de-stringed lute. Even the notes and songs of the water and the ships began to dissipate under the sound of the Chinese zither of the old woman and the sounds of cacti and stone.

One day, The Professor came in and sat down next to Kin on the rough rug where the boy did his reading. He adjusted his glasses and said, "We know who you are. Kin of the Waves. You're the boy who pushed a whale back into the water. And then you escaped from the trial with Ochiades and emerged alive. You kicked the regime in the teeth. And we know about the woman Jesa. She will support us."

"How do you know all this?"

"We're gathering our strength. When the revolution comes, it has to be final. It has to work first time. We won't get a second chance."

"So there will be a revolution?"

"That's right. It's been foretold."

"That's what Fundogu used to say: it's been foretold."

"Yes, well he would say that. He's the one who foretold it," said The Professor. "All of us on the mountain, we're here because we couldn't stay in the city. Matanza would have had us killed or sent us to prison. In fact, some of us *were* in prison and managed to escape. We came to the safest place we knew: the hills. You've read about them now."

"Yes."

"Fundogu hates the Matanzas just as we do," The Professor went on. "He sends dispatches through Silmiya, the woman who drives the truck, the one who gave you a ride. So we know the time is coming. We heard it from Fundogu and from our contacts in the city. We're going to train you. You're strong enough now. You've recovered. It's time to earn your keep. El Gato will teach you how to shoot, Sombrero will teach you how to fight, and I'll teach you everything else."

✳

For several hours a day, Kin underwent training. At first, he learned how to survive in the wild, to make things using his surroundings and his wits: fishing rods, tents, canopies, animal noises. He learned how to divine water. He learned how to recognize the tracks and scat of bears and mountain lions, ibex and tahr.

When he'd mastered these things, los barbudos taught him how to be a soldier. He learned how to load and fire guns of many kinds, dress wounds, and fight hand to hand. As they taught him, they glanced at one another. They had never seen anyone learn so fast. They found him rugged and disciplined and afraid of nothing.

His final test was the study of maps and documents smuggled in by Silmiya. He was to memorize lines and contours and ratios, the schedules of guards, the angles of walls, street addresses, the position of lamps by the side of the road. Once he understood what each symbol on these hand-drawn maps represented, it was easy. The streets of Balaal contained no mysteries for Kin.

After two weeks, El Gato, the blue-eyed sniper, told the boy he was already a soldier. After three, The Professor told Kin he was already a professor.

Sombrero said, "Hombre, you became a mountain man."

"No," said Kin. "I'm Kin of the Waves."

"Whoever you are," said The Professor, "you're one of us. It's time for a coup. Get some sleep. We leave tomorrow."

CHAPTER 11

Los barbudos in Balaal—

reconnaissance—the art of war—

I am the ocean

SILMAYA'S TRUCK CAME SKIDDING AND JOUNCING TO THE EDGE OF THE CITY, SPITTING STONES and kicking up dust. The truck's headlights shone on hoardings and rubble and a half-collapsed fence. Balaal at dusk. Eight men jumped out the back and with a muttered farewell to their driver picked up the ammunition she'd provided and took to the alleyways in a staggered line, rifles strapped across their shoulders or revolvers concealed in backpacks. They dispersed, two by two, like the animals of the ark, each pair to a safe house.

Kin and The Professor slipped into a disused storehouse on the outskirts of the city. They snuck in through a side door and squinted at the cavernous space, a cave drizzled with spiderwebs. There were wooden pallets for beds and cockroaches for company. At eleven o'clock, they emerged in their skivvies and walked the backstreets, leaving their guns behind.

When they arrived at the wide boulevards, they took the shadowy side of the street and turned their collars up to hide their faces. In the night breeze, Kin smelled cedar. The trees in the garden of the Matanza Palace. They headed for an apartment block and stopped at the entrance. A lightbulb illuminated the doorway.

"It's too bright for a break-in," said Kin.

"We can smash the bulb," said The Professor, looking up. He glanced around. A few people were milling on the street.

"No. Wait here."

Kin walked to the back of the building and returned to The Professor.

"There's a drainpipe. No one will see me. It's better than forcing this door."

"You're going alone? I can't climb a drainpipe."

"I'll get inside and let you in."

"How?"

"There has to be a skylight. I climb the drainpipe, get inside through the skylight, and let you in. Then we go to the roof together," said Kin.

"How do you know we can get to the roof?"

"Look. There are plants up there. Someone must water them. Just wait here. But stay out of the light."

Kin shinned three stories up the drainpipe and clambered onto the roof. He found a skylight half open, pushed it all the way and jumped down into the building. The interior was dark and empty and smelled of garlic and cigarettes. He listened for footsteps, heard none, and took the stairs down, avoiding the elevator. He got to the atrium and let The Professor in. They climbed the three floors, hauled themselves up through the skylight, and lay flat on the roof. The Professor pulled out a pair of binoculars and aimed them at the mayor's palace.

"That is one big house," he said. "They'd need an army to protect it."

"They have an army," said Kin.

Across the street, Kin made out the squares and rectangles of the mayor's home, like the assemblies of random boxes and crates he'd seen at the port. It was a palace made for a mayor, all concrete and glass. The money from the mines way out in Bocadelin had paid for the land, and indentured servants had done the rest. The main building was a walled monolith with gardens stretching out on every side, built for the very first Matanza. Later Matanzas had added offices and annexes, so now the palace sprawled.

At night, it emitted an evanescent glow like phosphorous, from the lights of the guards' towers, from the sentry boxes, and from the palace itself, a glow that radiated over the center of the city and could be seen from the hills.

In addition to the glow, there were searchlights that swung till midnight in slow arcs around the walls both inside and outside the property. These Kin and The Professor watched, calculating the circumferences of the pools of light, where these overlapped, and where there were blind spots.

"I read about it," said Kin. "The compound has two parallel walls that surround the main building. Both walls fifteen feet high, and between them a no-man's-land."

The outer wall bordered the street, which was lit with tall lamps. But here too, there were blind spots, parts of the wall a revolutionary could straddle in the dark without being seen if he were quick and agile. Or he could climb a tree on the street, tiptoe along an overhanging branch, and make the leap over the wall into the unknown.

"What else?" said Kin.

"Four guard posts, one on each corner, overlooking all four walls."

"That's what the map showed."

"It was accurate," said The Professor, and he moved the binoculars in a slow arc.

A man on the inside—a palace lackey—had provided the rebels with a rough map. He'd smuggled it out to them, a map scribbled in pencil, handed to a contact who gave it to Silmiya, who'd folded it tight and stuck it in her boot. Precious contraband, just like the scribbled schedule of the guards, the diagram of the surrounding grounds, the traced images of padlocks. All of these had fallen into the hands of los barbudos, and they'd studied them like scripture.

The Professor said, "I can't see the other sentries. They must be behind the walls."

"The map said there were four other sentry posts, not including the towers and the one at the main entrance. And that one is heavily guarded day and night. And it said there was a blind spot."

"But only at midnight," said The Professor.

At midnight, the guards turned the searchlights off because Mayor Matanza was a poor sleeper and couldn't bear the moving aurora that daubed his curtains yellow and cast shadows on his ceiling.

At the same time the guards switched off the searchlights, they ended their shift and a new group replaced them. This was the moment Kin and The Professor waited for, to see it for themselves. They lay stock-still and The Professor passed Kin the binoculars.

"Take a look," he said. "I make it two guards in every tower. That's eight guns. And the sentries are probably the same. So sixteen guns."

Kin peered through the lens and turned the focus wheel. The image clarified.

"Two men per tower," he said, "but we don't know how many on the ground and we don't know how many in the palace itself."

At midnight, a church bell chimed from an adjacent street. As the twelfth chime sounded, the searchlights went dark, and Kin and The Professor saw flickers of flame and movement—guards lighting cigarettes and heading home to their sweethearts, while others arrived in dribs and drabs through the main gate, yet to get into position for their shift. A window of nearly two minutes.

"This is our moment," said Kin. "We go in at midnight."

The beating of an owl's wings disturbed the air and the creature landed on the roof a few feet from Kin and The Professor. Unmoving, it stared at them, its fierce eyes orange and black like some harbinger from another world. Then it raised its wings and flapped away.

"Was that one of Matanza's spies?" said Kin.

"We may need a distraction."

"What do you mean?"

"At midnight," said The Professor. "Say we get fireworks. Someone lets them off near the front entrance. A big bang and lots of color. To get the guards' attention. And while that's going on, we climb over the wall."

Kin nodded. "Tell you the truth," he said, "It's not getting in I'm worried about. It's what happens next. How do we get out in one piece with Matanza?"

"We kidnap him, hold a gun to his head."

"I know the plan. I just don't know if it'll work."

"None of us know if it'll work. That's why we're the suicide squad. We remove him. We get him to a radio station, and he makes an announcement, disbands the Tonto Macoute, disbands the army, and stands aside. But that's not your problem. You pick the lock, get us in, and then you disappear. You're the mayor-elect, and you're still a kid."

Kin returned the binoculars.

The Professor said, "Let's go find some fireworks."

✳

They spent the night on the stone floor of the disused storehouse. All around them were the sounds of the city: car tires and dogs barking and once the wail of an ambulance Kin heard as a high C till it faded.

In the dim and quivering light, The Professor pulled out a tiny dog-eared paperback edition of *The Art of War* and held it close to his eyes, reading but not reading. The words washed past him because all he could think of was the downing of the mayor. He visualized the scene—a cacophony of barking dogs and himself hauling Matanza by the collar through the ranks of the soon-to-be-disbanded soldiers. When the light grew too weak, he placed the book by his head and closed his eyes.

Meanwhile, Kin went through the plan a hundred times in his mind: scaling walls, dodging sentries, picking locks in the belly of the beast, the heart of Matanza country, where the monster's troops amassed, where the Tonto Macoute did tricks with flick-knives and awaited orders.

Lights blinked through the broken windows and invaded the dreams of the two rebels: torches, street lamps, car headlights, and a fire lit by a tramp to keep the bats away. They slept uneasily. Several times Kin awoke and thought he was back in the shipping container, the metal coffin of his childhood. Once he dreamed he was in the cave with the ammonite and the stalactites and the pinprick of light he'd thought was God. The words came back to him: *I am the ocean. I am the four winds. I am the stars that guide the living. I am the memory of the dead.*

It was only in the small hours fatigue finally overtook them both as the wind ruffled the nests of the pigeons on the roof and a slice of the moon like a sickle cut through the dark.

CHAPTER 12

The attack

THEY SPENT THE FOLLOWING DAY LAYING LOW. KIN BOUGHT KOFTA AND SWEETBREAD FROM a vendor with The Professor's remaining coins, and they ate sitting on wooden pallets and went over the plan a last, hundredth time. In the heat, the storehouse turned into a furnace, so they skulked outside in the shadows. The hours dragged. Finally, night came, and at eleven they left.

✳

The assault on Matanza's palace happened at night under a starless sky. With only a handful of men, los barbudos had rejected a full-scale attack. Instead, Matanza's end would come swiftly and silently, from an undercover invasion. They would cut off the head and watch the body die. Los barbudos had men on the inside. They had courage and they had discipline and safe houses around the city where they could retreat or get supplies. But no one thought of retreating. This was the day Matanza would fall.

Armed men stalking through the city was nothing new in Balaal, but eight of them in uniform counted as a militia—an enemy of the regime. So some of los barbudos wore jeans, only a few came in fatigues, and Sombrero wore his sombrero, at least until the palace came into view, at which point he hung it on the high branch of a tree and swore to himself he'd return for it.

They came from their safe houses through streets they'd memorized from the maps. Kin led The Professor because he knew the city better than any map reader. Every trashcan and boarded-up bodega was his. Every curve in the road, every tasseled awning, every jerry-built tenement they passed was his. He knew where and when a dog might bark or a security guard might stir in his sentry box, and he steered The Professor through the quiet shadows.

They skirted street lamps and dodged the burning lanterns that kept Balaal safe from evil spirits. They passed a mélange of city odors—car fumes, rotting mangoes, trash, lagoons of urine, and fetid canal water—and in the dark Kin's sixth sense led them away from the random clusters of Tonto Macoute patrolling the big roads.

They took a side street past Matanza Square, where stood a huge bronze statue of a Matanza mayor on a horse. Kin glanced across the open space, saw a few soldiers milling and a cluster of mendicants in their cardboard lairs, and moved on.

He turned a corner, caught the scent of cedar from the trees in the palace garden, and heard the collective buzz of the palace's electricity—walkie-talkies and generators, TV sets, radios. They were back to where they'd been the night before.

Kin and The Professor stood in the shadowed doorway of the building across the way from the palace. From there, they could see the road but couldn't be seen.

The Professor looked at his watch. "We're early."

"How long?"

"Ten minutes."

A motorbike spluttered its way past them, then a truck. In the humid air, Kin sweated and listened. He picked up the high-pitched whine of a mosquito and a song playing distantly on a radio. He wanted to tell himself *control your fear*, but he had none and instead touched the coral necklace around his neck. He glanced at The Professor, who was gazing steadily at the palace, his face a mask of stillness.

"Are you ready?" asked The Professor.

"Of course. Are *you*?"

"This is the day you become king."

"Mayor," said Kin.

"You know what I mean. We keep him alive if we can. . ."

"And kill him if we must. I know. We've been over this a thousand times."

"We need him to abdicate publicly," said The Professor.

"I know. And if he doesn't, then we need him to die. Either way, he's gone."

"And remember," said The Professor, "after we break in, you wait in the safe house." The Professor glanced at his watch.

"How long?" said Kin.

"Five minutes. Get ready."

Kin adjusted the strap of the carbine on his back. He pulled out the knife from its holster at his side and felt the blade, then returned it. The Professor placed a rucksack on the ground in front of them. He untied it and took out a rope ladder with two metal hooks covered in rubber.

"You know your spot?" said The Professor.

"Right between the guard towers. I climb, you watch over me. Then you climb, I watch over you."

"Like we practiced."

"Like we practiced."

"And if we shoot," said The Professor.

"We shoot to kill. Trust me."

"Three minutes."

Even with his keffiyeh around his neck, The Professor didn't sweat. Half his life he'd been waiting to attack Matanza and had spent years in the mountains gathering his strength. He was readier than ready.

"Remember," he said, "we don't go on the first chime of the church bell."

"We go on the last," said Kin. "That's when the guards move and when those fireworks explode."

"You know the plan better than I do."

Canned laughter erupted from a television, and a flicker of wind flipped a scrap of paper in the road. This was boulevard territory. Thick trees planted on the sidewalks. There was ample shadow, but they had to get across the street to the palace wall first, a five-second dash.

Suddenly the church bell sounded. Kin and The Professor counted out the chimes. On the twelfth, they ran, and simultaneously there was the muffled thud of a firework detonating. Not a hundred yards from the palace's main entrance, a panoply of sparks whizzed into the air. Every guard at the palace turned to look, and some came running. Another erupted into the night sky, this one higher and whistling and dissipating in a scintilla of red and yellow pinpricks.

As the first fireworks jumped, Kin and The Professor reached the wall. It loomed over them, fifteen feet high. They had a window of one minute, maybe two, as the old guards left and the new ones arrived. The Professor looked up and down the street quickly. All clear.

"Go! Go!" he whispered.

Kin threw the rope ladder. The hooks latched onto the wall first time, the sound cushioned by the rubber covering and by the fizz and flare of fireworks. He scrambled up, reached the top of the wall, and peered over. He was still in shadow. No sentries in sight. He swung his legs over the top, gripped the edge of the wall with the fingers of both hands and dropped like a cat. He landed silently on concrete.

The Professor followed. He reached the top of the wall, unhooked the ladder, threw it to Kin, and then he too dropped silently, landing on his toes.

Kin placed the ladder under a tree and he and The Professor commando-crawled to a padlocked gate in a second wall. Behind this wall stood the palace, a black rectangular silhouette darker than the night sky.

Still on his stomach, Kin pulled out a nail from his pocket. It took him thirty seconds to pick the lock. But before they could open the gate, they heard voices and saw the tiny flicker of a flame at a sentry post barely fifty feet away and Kin caught the scent of cigarette smoke. The firework show was over. Kin eased open the iron gate, silently praying it wouldn't creak above the sound of the guards talking.

They were in. Trees and hedges dotted the palace grounds, just as they'd been told. Now they crouched behind a shrub. Kin peered over it and saw the sentry post near the front door of the palace, six guards milling. The two barbudos crawled again, heading for a side entrance to the palace. This was where the trash was deposited—outside a narrow door by the kitchen.

Kin and the Professor made it to the trashcans, large dark buckets on wheels. Another blind spot. Kin felt his way to the door and turned the handle. One of the chefs, who was in on the plot, was supposed to have left it open, but something had gone wrong. It was locked. Kin pulled out his nail again and tried to pick the lock. But he couldn't get the nail in. He tried the second nail he'd brought, but it didn't fit. He bent down to The Professor, who was crouched among the trashcans, and whispered.

"I can't open it."

"What?"

"I need another nail or a hairpin or something."

"I don't have a hairpin."

"We have to find something. Or we break down the door."

"We can't break down the door. They'll hear us."

"I know. So find me something to use."

The Professor looked from side to side and then opened a trashcan. The stench hit them immediately.

"Close it," whispered Kin.

The can was waist high to The Professor. He looked at Kin, then began to rummage.

"Close it!" said Kin again. "They're going to smell us from a mile away."

"We have to find a tool to get the door open."

He found nothing in the can but old food, so The Professor closed the hinged flap of the lid.

"Think!" said Kin.

"Your knife."

"I can't pick a lock with a knife. It's too thick."

They heard footsteps and lay flat on the ground among the wheels of the trashcans. A guard wandered up and stopped. He was twenty feet away. Kin saw the man's shoes. A few seconds passed and the guard walked the way he'd come. Kin breathed again and felt the concrete around him, hoping against hope to find a piece of sharp, loose metal, anything he could fit in that tiny lock. The Professor handed him his watch.

"There's a spring inside."

"I can't open your watch without a tool," whispered Kin.

He looked around. On the wall next to the door was a sign saying Trash Pickup. Kin gripped the edges of the metal plate and pulled the sign off the wall. It made a noise—the creak of iron on stone—so he lay flat again, waiting for another guard to appear. The sign brought with it four thin, rusty nails. He picked up one of them and inserted it into the lock, twisted and wrenched and poked and pressed until he heard a click. He turned the handle of the door, and pulled it open.

"We're in," whispered Kin.

"Now go back," said the Professor. "I'll meet you at the safe house."

"Where are the others?"

"I don't know. But stick to the plan. Get out of here," said The Professor.

"No," whispered Kin. "You can't do it on your own. Where the hell are the others?"

The Professor looked around urgently. There was no time to argue.

The kitchen was so dark they had to feel their way in, touching slabs of metal, trolleys, and counters. Somewhere inside this building Mayor Matanza lay asleep. Perhaps he was dreaming his final dreams in this lifetime. Kin touched the coral necklace and visualized the map of the palace.

He counted out footsteps, and The Professor followed. The Professor's night vision was bad. He'd tied his taped-up glasses to his head so they wouldn't drop in the leap over the wall, but now he squinted against the dark and trusted in Kin's sight. *Where were the others?*

The kitchen had a swing door. Beyond that was a small atrium that led to the formal dining area of the palace. As Kin led the Professor toward that door, he felt a change in the air. Something barely perceptible. Something telling him to get out. But by the time he realized what was happening, it was too late. He felt a blow to the back of his head and all went dark.

CHAPTER 13

Truck ride 2—tennis ball—the Magi—

bread and water—roof

EVEN IN THE HAZE OF HIS PAIN AND FALLING IN AND OUT OF CONSCIOUSNESS, KIN REGIStered details. He knew he was in the back of a truck. The Professor was slumped opposite him. Their wrists were tied. And there were two others in there with them: armed guards, he reckoned, soldiers of some kind.

As they passed by, he heard the sounds of the night outside the truck: the thrum of a bass in a club, old men laughing, a receding siren. Through the slat window in the side of the truck, he glimpsed a shred of the moon. Then he went under again, swooning into unconsciousness.

When he came to, someone was hauling him and The Professor out of the vehicle. They could barely stand. Two men, one on either side, dragged Kin across a courtyard, through gates that clanged open, up and down stone steps. The Professor, similarly accompanied, followed close behind.

Finally, their wrists were untied and Kin and The Professor were thrown into a cell. The Professor collapsed. Kin sat against a wall and tried to appraise his surroundings. No beds or lights. No furniture. One high window. A bucket in a corner.

He felt the back of his head—a lump the size of a tennis ball—and listened to his own breathing. *I am alive.*

It was the dead of night and all around them were the sounds of grunting and honking, men talking in their sleep. In the corridor outside their cell, a ghostly swathe of artificial light glowed. The Professor didn't move or speak.

"Are you OK?" said Kin. He crawled over to his mentor, who was lying on his side. Kin looked for signs of damage: bruises and blood. He put his hand on The Professor's shoulder and felt the rise and fall of the man's shallow breaths. He went back to the wall and waited for his eyes to adjust to the dark.

We were inside the palace. We were in the kitchen. It was a

few minutes past midnight. Then the world disappeared. There were others. Los barbudos. Where did they get to? Are they here? Were we betrayed? The fireworks sounded and I climbed the wall and The Professor climbed the wall and I picked a padlock and then another and the other barbudos were to follow us and El Gato was on a roof and then the world disappeared.

Kin tried to recall the details of the truck ride: the sounds he'd heard just minutes before. He sniffed the air and tried to work out where they were. All he knew was they were far from the sea. The tang of brine and salt was nowhere. Here was men's sweat and mold, rancid fruit, the stink of feet. He tried to gather his senses because he was already looking for a way out, and for that he needed to know how they'd gotten in.

Eventually his body shut down and he fell into a distracted sleep, half-waking every few minutes, the throb of his head wound pounding like percussion.

＊

When he awoke it was to the cooing of pigeons, three of them, which he christened The Magi, on the narrow ledge outside the bars of the cell window. It was a small space near the ceiling, too small, he calculated, for a man to crawl through even without the bars. The pigeons turned and turned in a little dance, the morning sunlight behind them.

The Professor finally flinched. The side of his face was swollen and his eyes were dead with pain or grief; Kin couldn't tell. He struggled to his knees and hauled himself against a wall so he could sit opposite Kin.

The cell was ten feet by ten feet by ten feet, a perfect box of gray concrete. In the morning light they saw its shape and the shape of the iron bars that formed one wall, a door built into it and a rusty padlock holding that door locked.

"What happened?" said Kin.

The Professor raised his eyes at him. He tried to talk but nothing came out besides a guttural croak. Kin tried again. "Were we betrayed?"

The Professor again tried to speak and again failed. His ear was covered in congealed blood.

They stayed in the same positions, one across from the other, in silence, until they heard footsteps. Then the clang of a baton on the bars of their cell. A man passed two pieces of bread between the bars and placed them on the floor, and then he did the same with a plastic canteen of water.

The Professor and Kin ate and drank and waited. What would be their fate? Kin wondered if this time there would even be a trial in the old disused warehouse or somewhere else, or if this time his fate was sealed. After all, they'd been caught in the palace. Two armed revolutionaries. A discarded ladder. And maybe the other barbudos were stuck in a cell or worse. Dead or blabbing to the Tonto Macoute right now: *It was the one with the glasses and the beardless one.*

And so they waited. Around them, in adjacent cells, they again heard indistinct chatter, grunts, occasional howls. Was this a prison or a madhouse? And where were they in Balaal? Who were the other inmates? From the tiny window high in the wall they saw the light of day and heard the shuffling of the three pigeons. But the sounds of the city were absent. Kin wracked his memory to trace that journey the night before, to find a route in his mind through the night streets, to locate the prison, but it was unclear. All he knew was they were on the outskirts of Balaal.

The day passed. Chatter rose and fell and one man along the corridor yelped like a dog. Another cried loud and long. The Professor maintained his silence save for occasional moans of pain as he touched the side of his face. Later, a guard brought more bread, and later still Kin and The Professor did their ablutions in the bucket in the corner of the room.

Some time before nightfall, they heard footsteps again—this time two men—and heard the jangling of keys. The men unlocked their door.

"Get up."

Kin stood but The Professor remained slumped against the wall.

Kin said, "We have to move," and he tried to pull his friend to his feet.

The two guards remained outside the cell.

"Suit yourself," said one of them and beckoned Kin outside with a gesture of his hand.

"Where are you taking me?" asked Kin.

"Outside. Your friend can stay here."

Kin shuffled into the corridor and one of the guards snapped the padlock closed.

"This way."

The guards, one in front of Kin and one behind, led him past a line of identical cells. Men lay or sat in a litany of poses, tortured and lugubrious, like some medieval fresco of hell. One inmate stood at his bars, a soothsayer with his head on backwards. The guards took Kin to the end of the corridor, unlocked another iron door and led him up a staircase. Shortly, they were on a roof.

"You have ten minutes," said the guard with the keys. "Don't get any ideas. It's a fifty-foot drop."

In the waning daylight Kin stared at the roof courtyard. Like everything else he'd seen there, it was bare concrete. There was no other soul on the roof except him and the guards. He looked at the view. Three-hundred-and-sixty degrees of sky, and as he neared the far edge, which was protected by a metal perimeter, a view of distant Balaal with its jumble of roofs and spires. In the other direction, he saw the hills changing color. Now he knew where he was.

As he approached the perimeter and looked down, he saw miles of wasteland stretching out like distended parchment, barren and cracked, a few hummocks, some patches of green, but no place to hide even an eagle's egg let alone an inmate on the run. He walked still closer to the edge. The prison was nothing but concrete and a giant fence forty feet high and topped with barbed wire.

❋

The first few days they fell into a rhythm. Three pigeons on the ledge. Bread and water twice a day. The hoots and jabbering of the other inmates. Ten minutes on the roof accompanied by two guards who barely said a word. The changing of the bucket at the same time, when the cell was empty, for The Professor had made it to his feet by the second day and was able to walk down the corridor and take the steps to the roof. No sign of other prisoners while they were there. A morbid heat in the cell, dead air which made them sweat. Another bucket for washing.

The Professor still couldn't speak. Instead, he shook. Kin watched him trembling and understood. Would they be tortured? Would they be executed? Would they be left here for the rest of their lives? What was being planned for them right now?

❋

The Professor couldn't talk and he could barely walk. He shuffled like an old man. The light had gone from his eyes but Kin would keep him alive, just as The Professor had kept Kin alive in the mountains.

Kin focused on finding an escape route. Could he and The Professor overcome the guards? A surprise attack, some fancy move, and Kin would have a gun and the keys. But he didn't know how many other guards there were and he didn't know how they would get beyond the giant fence. And after that? Flatlands for a mile, maybe two. They'd be sitting ducks.

At night, hemmed in by gray concrete, he lay awake stroking the coral necklace around his neck. If he knew one thing, it was this: there was always a way out. Of caves and guarded warehouses, off islands, out of shipping containers, if you got in, you could get out.

❋

The strangest thing was that the soldiers and guards hadn't even checked the pockets of The Professor or Kin before throwing the two of them in the cell. Kin still had the nails he'd used to pick the locks, and The Professor still had *The Art of War* in his breast pocket. They hadn't been strip-searched or even washed. Kin figured they probably didn't look like anti-Matanza plotters, what with The Professor's patched-up glasses and Kin still a boy. This meant that maybe they were under Matanza's radar.

But all that mattered was escaping before they starved to death. Or before The Professor broke down completely. His face was healing—the swelling had gone down—but he had become the ghost of his former self. With only bread and water, sleep interrupted by the noise of the other men, and ten minutes of air a day, there was no way he would recover. Kin too felt himself growing weak. It was a blessing to see the horizon every day from the roof, but because he was Kin of the Waves, he needed the sea to imagine his escape. Giant waves to come to the rescue.

It took him two weeks to figure his only way out.

CHAPTER 14

Feathers—pandemonium—hunger

THE THREE PIGEONS KEPT APPEARING. BALTHASAR, MELCHIOR, AND GASPAR. THEY HAD cloudburst and tree branch in their eyes. Roof shingle and telegraph wire. They knew vistas and sky. And when they appeared every morning, Kin beseeched them to bring gifts. They had what he needed to escape. There was no other way.

"Hey," he whispered to The Professor. "We need to build wings. Look." He opened his hand to reveal a cluster of feathers. "These pigeons leave feathers on the ledge every day. And on the roof. They're shedding for us. They've started to bring tree sap from branches. We turn this into wax. You remember that book you made me read, up in the mountains, the story of Icarus?"

The Professor was seated with his back against the wall.

Kin went on. "Then we fly out of here from the roof. I can pick the locks with the nail. I already tried. I can get us to the roof. But then we need to fly."

The Professor raised his eyes to look at Kin. His voice had begun to return, and now he spoke quietly. "You're dreaming."

"There's no other way. I saw it from the roof. This place is crawling with guards. Even if we got out, there's a forty-foot wall and No-Man's-Land. We can't dig a tunnel through concrete. We have to fly off the roof."

"You've gone mad."

Kin jumped to the tiny window high in the wall and clung to the ledge with his fingers. He hauled himself up, reached through the bars with one hand and swiped at a feather, which came floating down to the floor. He too dropped and landed.

"Every day they bring us something. Yesterday it was new twigs with resin. And there's a corner of the roof—I've seen bigger feathers there. We need to collect them without the guards seeing."

The Professor put his fingers to his lips, shook his head. "Do you remember. . .?" he said, and it came out as a croak. "Do you remember how the story of Icarus ended?"

"We don't have to fly close to the sun," said Kin. "We just have to fly over the wall and across No-Man's-Land. Then we run."

The Professor went silent again, still shaking his head.

✳

More days passed. The other inmates continued their cacophony of moans, yawps, whimpers, and whines. Every time Kin and The Professor were led out for their ten minutes of fresh air, there was a rattling and a banging on the cage bars. Once an inmate threw a bucket of urine at them and got a beating later from the guards. The strange soothsayer stared, for he knew who Kin was and he knew his fate.

In the cell, Kin began constructing a set of wings. He gathered the feathers the pigeons left daily. They were gray and white, downy wisps soft to the touch, and as he felt them he felt the air and the clouds and the warmth of the sun. From the fresh twigs left by the birds he teased out sap with his fingers and stuck the feathers together in lines. He hid the whole thing under The Professor's keffiyeh in a corner of the room. And when it got too big, he folded the growing wing and took solace from touching it.

The food got worse. One day the bread came green with mold. On another, the water was flecked with drowned ants. The professor became sick, then recovered, then became sick again, and the guards ignored Kin's protests.

"He needs a doctor!"

The other inmates howled with laughter. One barked. Another wept.

"He needs a doctor!" cackled a pickpocket.

"Save his soul!" shrieked a graverobber.

"Rub his tummy!" bawled a murderer.

Kin learned to keep his counsel. There was nothing he could do to help The Professor except tell him they would be out soon. Once these wings were complete, they'd wait for a moonless night and sail the skies to freedom, to the foot of Mount Naranco, and walk back to the rondavels and start again. And even as he said it, he felt his ribs jutting through his shirt and thought his wrists had grown thin. He hadn't seen his own face in weeks but out of the corner of his eyes he perceived the ridge of his cheekbones and now felt a pang of hunger gnawing permanently at his flesh. Bread alone. It was all they'd eaten.

"We need food," he said one day to a guard leading him to the roof. "We're starving."

"Shortages," said the guard. "Haven't you heard?"

"Heard what? We're in prison. We hear nothing."

"Shortages. No food. No water. No uniforms. Maybe you should've saved something from the mayor's pantry and shared it around."

Kin sucked in the air and looked at the horizon. The Professor was at his side, his beard bedraggled and his eyes dark-ringed like a panda's. Some of the inmates had night tremors. They would yell out, cry for their mothers, and then the others would tell them to shut up or start banging on their bars. *Pandemonium*, thought Kin. *All the devils. That's why they let us out two at a time, like Noah's animals.* No one slept a full night.

Across the city, during his ten minutes of air time, Kin saw a plume of smoke ascending. It curled above the minaret of a mosque, obscured a factory tower, and evanesced into a sheet of white cloud like a ghost. A squadron of black birds swooped by, dipping and turning in unison. He watched their gait, tried to catch how they tucked in their legs, spread their wings, and glided on air currents. He had never envied creatures as much as he envied those birds.

✳

After another week, he knew they had to go. The rations had grown smaller, the inmates more unruly. And the guards had taken to bashing heads. It was only a matter of time before the heads were theirs. Worse, The Professor was fading away. He had barely muttered a sentence since they'd been caught in the mayor's kitchen, and Kin feared he wouldn't last much longer.

But the wings weren't ready. The feathers had frayed in the heat, turned to hair-like wisps, and were barely enough for one man, let alone two. Icarus would never use this. The glue had melted and hardened, melted again and hardened again till it resembled dried soup on a plate. Were a man to dive down fifty feet and spread his arms with these wings on his back, would he not drop like a stone to his death? Would he not be a fallen birdman, a legend, a tale told by an idiot to be passed down the generations of inmates?

Kin didn't know what to do. He pondered and pondered until one morning something strange occurred and gave him his answer.

＊

Balthasar, Melchior, and Gaspar appeared on time. They did their tap dance on the ledge, babbled a while in bird language, and then stopped so sharply Kin looked up. In a kerfuffle of feathers they were gone, replaced by a sharp-beaked seagull with an evil eye.

This seagull was twice their size, bright white, and still as a rock. It looked into the cell and let out an ear-piercing squawk which Kin recognized immediately.

"You," he said. "You were at the cave on the island of the abandoned lighthouse. What are you doing here, so far from home, so far from the sea?"

The bird stared him in the eye. It jerked its head, opened wide its yellow beak, and squawked again louder than before. It twitched, flapped its gray wings, inclined the white hood that stretched down to its powerful chest so its head came between the bars on the window and into the cell. It unleashed a third ear-splitting caw, withdrew its head from between the bars, turned in pitter-pattering steps and flew away.

Kin knew it was a sign and so did the soothsayer down the corridor, who began banging at his bars.

"Hey," Kin whispered to The Professor. "We leave tonight. We go at midnight."

"You understand bird language?"

"You could say that," said Kin. "She's an old friend of mine."

CHAPTER 15

Padlocks—fly boys—la bruja sabe

todo

KIN PICKED THE LOCK. IT WAS ONE OF THE EASIEST. A FAT LUMP OF RUST WITH A LEVER that clicked. All around them the usual night plaints, sobs, lamentations.

They moved fast and in silence through that deranged corridor. If the other inmates saw them, they would wake the dead with their hollering. Kin and The Professor were on tiptoes, the wings in their hands. They'd nearly reached the steps to the roof when they both noticed one inmate at the bars of his cell. The soothsayer, his face backwards, inscrutable like a mask. Kin put a finger to his mouth and the soothsayer nodded.

Kin handed his wings to The Professor and picked the second padlock. He used the same nail as he'd used for the first and slipped it open like cracking a nut. The door creaked but no one heard and they took the steps fast and reached the roof. It was a moonless night. Stars glinted in their constellations.

It was at this moment Kin realized the wings he'd built were nothing but toys. A fancy dress uniform for a child. The feathers were light as cotton and the glue would disintegrate in the night wind. The wings would carry them nowhere. They had more chance building a ladder to climb to the moon.

In his despair, he sat down on the concrete roof and breathed deep.

"What is it?" whispered The Professor. "We're dead men, aren't we?" He held up his wings. They were already falling apart.

Kin sat and waited. He was an escape artist. He'd squeezed through the eyes of needles. Sometimes at night he would lie awake and think about every moss-fringed wall he'd scaled to get free of some child snatcher, every half-jammed window he'd forced open, every shadow he'd hidden in. He thought of Nazaré and sea beasts and the distended snout of Hormigonera sniffing at his skin. He was a born skedaddler, and now he sat on a concrete roof hemmed in by a perimeter and a fifty-foot drop. The hundred yards from freedom may as well have been a hundred miles or a hundred years. Those wings weren't going to fly.

But in the blink of an eye something came across the heavens. It moved slowly and soundlessly like a great planet haloed in its own light. It was the shape of an orb and it drifted toward the roof where the men waited. Kin and The Professor looked up.

A yellow glow. On its side a word painted in black: Freedom. The hot air balloon, all the way from Bujiganga. Hanging from its basket were two ropes. Kin and The Professor discarded their wings, took hold of the ropes and climbed. They were weak from all those days of moldy bread and dirty water but they scrambled and hauled themselves up and into the balloon's basket, where Iquique and Jesa awaited them.

There was no time to talk. They had to rise. The guards would see the hot air balloon, if they hadn't already, and gun it down. And so it rose as Iquique turned up the propane. And it rose and it rose far from that concrete roof until the compound lay below them, a giant rectangle surrounded by desert. Then the prison and its surroundings became a blur, a receding mass of dark and shapeless land.

✳

From their vantage point in the sky, Kin, The Professor, Iquique, and Jesa could see Balaal laid out before them—a circuit board of tiny lights that at its farthest reaches gave way to an expanse of black ocean. The air swirled around them and the gas of the balloon sounded in chalky breaths as Iquique turned the valve.

"You look terrible," said Jesa. She held Kin's face in both hands.

"This is The Professor," said Kin. "We were together in the mountains."

Jesa nodded at him. She was wearing her black scarf again, hiding the mark of zorrillo. "I'm Jesa. And this is Iquique. You must tell us everything."

The Professor was still panting and unsteady.

"I will," said Kin. "We were in the mountains and then at the mayor's palace and in the prison. I lost count of the days. How did you find us?" asked Kin.

Iquique interrupted. "It was *me*. A little bird told me."

"A seagull?"

Iquique smiled. "She's no seagull. La bruja sabe todo."

The night air was cool. Gentle gusts jolted the balloon as it soared.

"And you?" said Kin to Jesa. "You escaped from the Tonto Macoute."

"As you can see, shaman. I found refuge with the nuns." She gestured to Iquique, who was wearing her habit. "I'll tell you more later. We have to get out of here."

"Where are we going?" asked Kin.

"Wherever the wind takes us," said Iquique. "And then home to Bujiganga. We have work to do. A revolution to start. But first you two look like you need a good meal."

"And a good sleep," added Jesa. "How on earth did you end up in this prison?"

"It's a long story," said Kin. "But we were in Matanza's palace."

Iquique glanced at Jesa. "I told you," she said. "It's started already."

Seated on the floor of the basket taking them across the night sky, The Professor spoke quietly, so quietly the others didn't catch what he'd said.

"I need to find my men," he repeated. "There were eight of us in the raid on the palace. I don't know if they're dead or alive."

"We'll find them," said Iquique. "We're going to need every man, woman, and child we can get."

It was then that Kin understood The Professor's pain. It wasn't the man's swollen face or any other injury the eye could see. It was that he'd lost his brothers-in-arms.

✳

The days dragged. Jesa and the nuns made Kin and The Professor rest and fed them three meals a day, although all Kin wanted to do was sit in a fishing boat and listen to the waves lashing the wooden hull. He told Jesa everything: the cave of Zugarramurdi, the village in the mountains, the failed attack, and the days stuck in that dismal cell.

The Professor wanted to leave as soon as he had the strength to walk. He needed to return to the mountain village, to find out what had happened to Gatillo the Sniper and Sombrero and the others. To find out if they had been betrayed.

"You aren't ready for a journey." said Jesa. "You can barely put one foot in front of the other, éstupido."

"I have to go," said The Professor, and he said it again and again until it became true.

The nuns arranged an escort for him through the city and planted on his face a thick seal-fur beard to increment his sparse whiskers, to give him a disguise, for he was, after all, an escaped convict.

"We'll come for you soon," said Kin.

A few days later, Jesa spoke to Bujiganga's soothsayers. They had consulted cards and the patterns made by fallen leaves, birds' entrails, and the movements of stars. They foretold upheaval. "It's now or never," they said. "Gather an army and overthrow Matanza before Matanza Day. If you don't, he will destroy you and hundreds of others. The fishing village will burn."

CHAPTER 16

Gifts—Jesa, Kin, and Iquique recruit

an army—the fairground—cockfight

in Bouazizi—Kakurega—Sklonište—

the basher—the temptation of

Cienfuegos by a slug of aguardiente

Jesa, Iquique, and Kin prepared to leave Bujiganga. It was time to recruit an army. They were packing supplies when there was a knock on the door. The soothsayers again, three clairvoyants in bowler hats, each carrying gifts. Three men, wrinkled as Methuselah, one blind, one deaf, one dumb, none with his head backwards. The first knelt in front of Jesa and handed her a large cloth bag. She took it and felt heat emanating from its contents. She peeked inside the bag and saw thin slices of bread heaped one upon the other.

"Thank you," she said, "but this is too much. This. . ."

The clairvoyant had already bowed, stood, and turned. The second, a blind man, felt his way toward her. He too knelt and offered her a bag, this one clinking and clanking. She looked inside. A dozen small glass bottles of some clear liquid. She looked closer and saw the bottles were all the same: a label proclaiming Red Horse Aguardiente, A Taste of Heaven, a liquor like fire.

"I thank you also, but. . ."

I don't drink, and surely Iquique and Kin don't either. The third clairvoyant was small and squat even by the standards of Bujigangans, and the band of his bowler hat was adorned with cockatoo feathers. He knelt and gave her a box of cigars. By now she knew to say nothing but *thank you.* The three old men backed out of Iquique's shack with a final nod.

"Here in Bujiganga," said Iquique, "the one thing we never ask is why."

✳

Minus the camel, which had again wandered off on an epic pilgrimage through a mushroom-filled wood, they had to walk. Bujigangans didn't have cars. It was the bleakest day of the year, a day when an unseasonal frost had kicked in for no reason but a whim of the weather. And when they arrived at the disused

fairground, they blinked into the mist and took in a sight so deso-
late their spirits flagged.

The skeleton of a rollercoaster stood stark against the sky.
Matchsticks and pipe cleaners on a grand scale. Spindles of rust.
A disused Ferris wheel and a half-collapsed shooting range came
into view. And a merry-go-round choked with weeds that pierced
the wooden floor and grabbed at the legs of the painted horses.

Here lived a group of rough-edged travelers. They were knife
merchants and experts in the wielding of their tools. Rumor had
it they could hit a bullseye from fifty yards, slice up javalina in
minutes, sever an ear clean as a whistle.

Jesa, Kin, and Iquique were there to recruit them as weapons
suppliers and trainers in hand-to-hand combat. After all, these
people had been persecuted for four generations by the Matanza
family and they knew how to fight.

Throughout the reign of the Matanzas, these men and women
had been kicked off their own lands and harassed constantly by
the Tonto Macoute. They'd stood on trial for running the fairground without a license, for refusing to pay the Matanzas' bribes,
for holding animals captive, and for practicing unauthorized
religions. Every charge against the travelers had been invented
to harass them, and their trials were presided over by Ochiades,
the oldest living Matanza, the same Ochiades who had been
harassed himself by flies, bats, and a wandering camel in the
courthouse-that-wasn't-a-courthouse.

As Jesa, Kin, and Iquique entered the fairground, the first
thing they noticed was the silence. This place had once pulsed with
children's cries and organ music, vendors of candy corn and lottery
tickets. Now all they could hear was the wind straining against the
creaky Ferris wheel.

They walked through dried-out mud and rigging lines which
still held fairground tents and which reminded Kin of the ropes
on the jetty of the Fishing Village with No Name. They came to a
row of caravans. Kin knocked on a door and soon a man appeared.
He was half-asleep, lank hair down to his shoulders, and naked

from the waist up despite the weather, a tableau of tattoos across his chest: faces and figures, ancient symbols, runes. He rubbed his eyes. Three people he didn't know: a nun, a boy, and a witch. Was it the first line of a joke?

"We need your help," said Kin. "We want to end the reign of the Matanza family."

The man cleared his throat and spat a wad of phlegm at the foot of his caravan. He was whiskery as a wild animal, somewhere between forty and sixty years old—it was impossible to tell because his face was a map of inflexions: creases, scratch marks, unhealed bruises. He squinted into the morning light, scratched the back of his neck, and nodded rhythmically.

"The Butcher," said the man. He paused to spit again. "And Matanza. He killed my parrot, Madrugada. Strangled her dead. I been waiting ten years to put a knife in his guts. We have a secret weapon."

Then he led them to a huge tent and pulled open its flaps. There, inside a cage, was an enormous sleeping tiger.

"We ran a circus before we were a fairground. Now we're nothing. But we still have this beautiful baby, and he still has claws."

Before leaving the fairground, Kin handed the man six bottles of aguardiente. "To warm your cold nights," he said, and he was glad to relieve his back of some weight.

*

In Bouazizi, they came across a hundred men at a cockfight. These were the last remaining warriors of the insurgency of 98. They'd shacked up in the one building the government hadn't razed: the church.

The outside was Gothic. Every niche and buttress was lined with gargoyles of all kinds: chimeras, monsters with snake necks and lion heads, gurning grotesques, and evil monks. Bird's nests littered the gables and the crocket.

Inside, the godless soldiers were huddled in the chancel yelling at two cocks strutting in circles.

As Kin, Jesa, and Iquique entered the church, they first felt the vastness of the interior and then a sense of unease. A madman was hammering away at the church's organ: Bach's Toccata and Fugue at double speed, and one of the church's pillars, near the entrance, seemed to be moving. Kin got closer and saw the pillar was so covered in cockroaches you couldn't see the stone beneath. The hundred men were all shouting at the same time. A voice rang out: "Kill him!"

The cockfight. Every now and again the two proud pugilists would attack one another in a mad whirr of rancor and feathers. Then they would desist and stroll a while. They preened like harlots, primped like dandies. Then they would go savage again, take wing, climb, and swing. Then they stopped again, took stock of the situation. Remembered how pretty they were and pranced for the crowd.

The shouting increased until finally one cock killed the other in a rasp of blood and screech and dead marble eyes.

Kin looked up. Carvings of angels and devils. In the prayer rooms, which shone with the glow of candles, ancient relics lay in boxes.

"It's just a trick of the light," said a voice. Kin, Iquique, and Jesa looked around but saw no one. A painting of a saint was talking to them from the wall.

The Bouazizi took some persuading. They'd been camped out in the church for months. They stank of sweat and soot. Some had gone mad. Some found that their faces had begun mimicking the gargoyles outside: rictus grins, bulbous eyes, the horror of all they'd seen. A few had become pious, kneeling before the altar day and night. The survivors of Bouazizi were known as The Fanatics.

"An army needs fanatics," said Jesa.

"They look more like lunatics," replied Iquique. "These people cannot fight with us."

But once the cocks were done scrapping, the men dispersed, melting into the transepts or the towers with an air of mourning.

"This is when you take revenge on Matanza," said Kin to a group of the men gathered in the pews.

"With what? We have a stack of Korans and Bibles and a prayer mat."

"You're fighters. So fight."

The sun burned in through the rose window and a kaleidoscope of color hit the wooden Jesus hanging high on the altarpiece. The saint in the painting whispered to Kin again, "I told you. A trick of the light."

Suddenly Kin was blinded by a sunbeam. When he opened his eyes, the men were transformed into soldiers. Their jaws turned square, their rags took on the hue of military fatigues, and their wooden sticks appeared to him as guns.

"You will have your vengeance," he said to them.

Kin and the women left with a promise ringing in their ears that fifty men would join the revolution, and they in turn left the remaining bottles of aguardiente—all but one, for luck—with the Bouazizi.

※

Kakurega was altogether different. The warriors lived in a circular temple on the edge of the city, hidden by huge rocks and trees. Iquique knew the way and she led Kin and Jesa down a stone path and across a wooden bridge suspended over a stream.

"I thought this place was a myth," said Jesa.

The temple had no door. Incense burned and the place was so quiet Kin heard his feet echo.

The warriors sat in small clusters, facing inwards, meditating or reading. Some walked with bare feet across the stone, almost gliding. *How can these be the same men who routed the army in 72?* thought Kin. *They look like monks. They are monks.*

One of the Kakurega invited the three visitors to tea in a garden behind the temple.

The men lived lives so austere they had no temptations. They trained their bodies in the morning and their minds in the evening, and slept with no covers on stone floors. They washed in the stream, hunted and foraged in the woods, and did their ablutions in designated parts of the wilderness behind their temple.

Their silence reminded Kin of the fishermen. Except those raggedy crews on the water would drink the village dry, cuss and brawl when the wine ran out, and wend their way to Balaal's brothels half-cut and reeking. These men in the temple didn't touch alcohol or tobacco. They barely touched the floor when they walked. They were already an army, and the man looked quizzically at Jesa when she said, "Help us to overthrow Matanza."

"Why?"

"Because the family is a cyclone. It sucks up everything in its wake. It kills and robs. It throws the people to the four winds. If we don't stop them, they'll destroy everyone and everything. So we're doing it for liberty and justice."

There was a pause. The man sipped on a glass of water.

Jesa looked at him uneasily. "Isn't that a good enough reason?"

"It is good enough. I just wanted to hear you say it."

"So now you've heard me. What's your answer?"

"Here we live in a circle, madam. You may have noticed the shape of the temple. We gather in a circle. We sleep in a circle. Each man forms a part of the whole. There is no head of a circle. Everyone is equal. Our decisions are made together. So I alone cannot tell you whether we will fight with you to rid Balaal of the Matanza family. But I know this: when we routed them in 72, they came back and burned our homes. They murdered our families. They persecuted us for years. This is why we came to live here, where they could not find us. We remember everything. We do not forgive those who do not ask our forgiveness. And the Matanza family has never asked."

Kin and the two women camped on the grounds of the temple and the following day they left with a promise of support from the warriors of Kakurega. They tried to give their hosts the bag of bread, but one of the men said, "We thank you, but you must keep it. We take nothing from outside our own lands. And you may need it."

✳

Sklonište was a war zone. A mountain of rubble and red dust. The houses had been bombed. The schools had been bombed. The hospital had been bombed. The library had been bombed. The market had been bombed. The bomb shelters had been bombed. And all by their own leader, Mayor Matanza. And all because the people refused to pay a tithe to the very same Matanza. The very same Matanza who told his brother, The Butcher, to set his attack dogs loose. "We cannot have disobedience. We know where that leads." But as there were no attack dogs (the only dogs in the Matanza family were of the cuddly kind sitting at the mayor's feet), and as his soldiers were busy busting heads on the other side of town, The Butcher sent in his air force, which consisted of one little Fokker.

This little Fokker—originally acquired to transport members of the Matanza family to various outposts of their fiefdom—had been rigged up by an aviation mechanics expert called Slikta Caureja. Caureja added a bomb stowage unit and a set of levers to open it from the cockpit. And so the little Fokker dropped bombs on the mayor's enemies.

Everywhere you looked, craters punctuated the roads of Sklonište, great gouges filling up with debris and rain. The tenements were ruins, stripped inside out with their guts and bones showing: rebar and window frames, wiring and pipes. The walls were black with flame soot and the streets choked in piles of brick and ash and timber.

Somehow, in the midst of this wreckage, there lived a race of feral scavengers. They blended into the rubble, slipping in and out of crumbling doorways, ghosting through the urban scree, rummaging through the remains for usables. They were pickpockets, rat-men. Some were scrappers, stripping the buildings clean of metal to resell. Others were black market runners, trading found goods. They combed the wreckages and rescued old books, carpets, watches, cabinets, lamps, wine glasses, grandfather clocks.

And some of them were fighters too. Bare-knuckle bashers and insurrectionists. Club wielders and slingshot virtuosos. They'd stayed alive under bombardment and they'd stay alive against Matanza's troops.

"We're building a force to remove the Matanza family," said Kin.

"Who's Matanza?" said a scavenger.

"He's the one who did this to your town."

"Never heard of him."

"He rules Balaal."

"Not here he doesn't." And the man took Kin, Jesa, and Iquique to see Bashir, King of the Rats.

Bashir, King of the Rats lived on a throne of rubble—six-hundred bricks atop a twenty-foot-high trash heap—from where he surveyed his kingdom. Rodents ran wild through the garbage and a triumvirate of wise vultures stood guard on the perch of a half-demolished tower block. From sunup to sunset Bashir, King of the Rats puffed on Macanudo cigars and sipped stolen brandy and read with his one good eye the books his minions rescued from the bombed-out library, about war and peace and about battle tactics. He had a chest the size of a cement mixer and a look in that eye that said, "The world's in ruins but I'm untouchable."

"We'll help you kill Matanza," said Bashir. "It's our civic duty. And besides, what's it the scripture says? An eye for an eye. He plucked out mine." Kin handed him the soothsayer's cigars.

✳

Kin and the two women heard the mine of Bocadelin long before they saw it: the sound of five thousand men digging a hole. It was a roaring and a rumbling. It was a hacking and a ranting from the tower of Babel, with every language and dialect under the stars. Above all, it was the witterings of an everyday hell on earth: men-become-automata soaked in sweat and grime. Hatchets in the ground, digging for gems like dogs digging for old bones.

The mine was bathed in sunlight. It reminded Kin of a poet he'd read in the mountains who'd asked, "What is gold but a piece of the sun? A lick of fire made solid." In search of this piece of the sun, those men dug into the ground and they dug and dug and they dug so hard they dug a grave for themselves a thousand feet deep. Even if Matanza's men hadn't pointed a gun at their heads, even if they weren't so poor they couldn't afford a bunch of bananas, even if they hadn't been men with no past, no present and no future, they'd have stayed and dug anyway. Because once you've seen gold it remains in your eye like a fleck of dust.

In and out of that vast cavern the miners flowed. They were lean and brown-skinned and some looked as if they'd been hewn from the very rock they were gouging. In age, they ranged from fifteen to fifty, although it was hard to tell because boys were as ragged as grown men and grown men were as wiry and gangling as boys.

By day, they were machines. At night, they would drink and cavort with the whores in fishnet stockings. The men slept six to a bed in makeshift cabins or under tarpaulin tents or in hammocks strung up between poles and trees. They found any space a body could fit in and slept side by side with their mining tools, the only possessions they had. Some slept on roofs or in the rutted road-ways where the stray dogs lingered.

"So how do we approach them?" asked Jesa.

"Think of something," said Kin.

"They'll think we're whores," said Jesa.

"Of course they won't. Didn't you notice? I'm a nun," said Iquique.

"Can you preach?" said Jesa.

"Can you darn a net?"

"They eat in shifts," said Kin.

Iquique scratched her chin. "They do everything in shifts. I think they sleep in shifts. I heard there aren't enough beds."

Kin said, "So we talk to them in small groups."

And so it was that the nun who was no longer a nun and the witch who had never been a witch and the beardless boy approached the biggest, roughest-looking miner they could find and they tempted him with a midnight whistle and a slug of aguardiente from the bottle while he'd wandered out to piss.

He was a giant black man with dreadlocks down to his waist. Once he'd recovered from the shock of seeing two women who weren't whores and a boy who wasn't a miner, he swigged deep and tried to return the bottle.

"Keep it," said Kin. "We're starting a revolution. Will you join us? Will you and the other miners fight the guards and the Matanzas?"

The man looked at them, puzzled.

The miners had been on strike several times and had always been repaid in their own blood. Surely it was time for them to claim what was theirs, to take back the mines and the city.

"Will you join us?" Kin said again.

The man looked them up and down. Several seconds passed. Then, in a basso profundo, he said, "Give us this day our daily bread."

They stared at him. Jesa wondered if he was another madman along with the Bujigangans howling at the moon and the Fanatics of Bouazizi holed up in that decrepit church with their fighting cocks and open sores.

The man went on, "Give us bread and we'll follow you to Jerusalem or Jakarta or the bottom of the sea. Feed us and we'll fight. Matanza's a cockroach. We call him Escarabajo like the beetles we find in the mines. We stamp on them till their spines come out their guts. We'll do the same to Matanza if you find us food every day."

"Will the miners trust us? We're just a boy and two women," said Iquique.

"We don't care if you're women, men, or lizards. If you feed us, we'll fight. Do you know why this town is called Bocadelin?"

"No," said Jesa.

"Boca del Infierno. The mouth of hell."

The bear of a man began to slink off into the night. Kin called out to him: "What's your name and where can we find you?"

"Cienfuegos. Named after the rebellions. I'm either here or in the mine. The day I'm not is the day I'm dead."

He walked toward the shadows that were his shared sleeping quarters, but then paused.

"Hey," he said. "If you want to rise up against Matanza, try there. But you need to bring bread." He pointed at a dilapidated building. On its roof were two pieces of wood strung together to form a cross. "Tomorrow at 10:00 a.m. I'm not sure what kind of nun drinks aguardiente, but you should be at home there," he said to Iquique.

The following morning, Kin, Iquique, and Jesa went to the makeshift church and talked to a gathering of thirty miners, including Cienfuegos and six clones who were his brothers. The men were a mixture of roughnecks, born-again desperadoes, and illiterates. Some were from religious families. Others were there praying to God to send a crock of gold their way.

Iquique stood up and said, "The church supported rich land-owners throughout history. It propped up dictators. It kept poor people poor by telling them they'd find riches in heaven as long as they served their God and their masters on earth. We don't believe that anymore."

The miners looked at one another, dumbfounded. The church was crumbling. In summer, the walls sweated in the heat. In winter, icicles dripped from the ceiling. Someone called them the tears of Jesus.

Iquique continued. "We believe those who work should receive the fruits of their labor. The church exists to serve the poor, not the rich. And we're here to tell you to fight. Take what's rightfully yours."

This nun who'd ascended the pulpit, which meant she was standing on a wooden crate, was five-feet-two-inches tall, and she had the face of a grandmother. Somehow the miners listened.

They coughed and scratched at their scars. Suddenly, at the front of the room, one of them stood up. He was the oldest man there, bent-backed and rheumy with the years. His voice was little more than a rasp.

"I remember the Night of the Sixteen Daggers," he said. The congregation gazed at him in silence.

"I was there at the Slepvak Massacre. They killed everyone but me. The Butcher was there. He pointed his gun at me and said they always leave one alive to tell the story." He rubbed his elbow. "This lady is right. Let's rid the world of the Matanzas. Let's start with the guards. Strangle them like puppies. We should have done it years ago."

Applause broke out, and the men began talking among themselves. Jesa, head covered again in her black scarf, was at the front, near the old man, who had sat down. She could see his hands trembling. She stilled them by proffering a slice of bread. He looked at her in wonder and took it. Then she and Kin moved around the congregation and handed out the rest of the bread in the holiest of communions.

Iquique called out, "We'll be back in a week with more bread. Be ready. A change is coming."

✳

And thus was the bedraggled, ragtag army recruited. The fairground travelers would bring knives and wits and a massive caged tiger. The Fanatics of Bouazizi would bring dreams of revenge and a whispering painted saint. The warriors from Kakurega would bring discipline and battle strategy. The men from Sklonište would bring street smarts and Bashir's command. The miners would bring muscle and old grievances.

There was just one part of the army that still needed recruiting. At that exact moment this part would be out hunting rabbits or chopping wood or reading books in rondavels. But los barbudos would be ready and waiting.

CHAPTER 17

Jesa, Kin, and Iquique discuss the

odds—home—the return of the

prodigal camel—Fundogu has a

vision

Kin, Jesa, and Iquique began the long journey home. They caught rides in trucks and rode smoke-belching buses and walked when they had to. When they reached the outskirts of Bujiganga, Jesa and Kin turned to Iquique.

"We're leaving you here. We have to go home to the fishing village," said Kin.

"It's not safe," said Iquique.

Kin wiped his brow. "We'll manage. I need to go home. I've been in the mountains, then prison, then on the road with you both. I'm done in."

Jesa said, "Me too. I'm going home, just for a few days. I need to smell the ocean. And check my house is still standing. We'll visit you in a week."

"So be it," said Iquique. "Then we'll get word to our recruits. Build an army."

Jesa paused. "Do you think we can win?"

"Against Matanza?" said Iquique.

Jesa corrected her: "Against *the Matanzas*. There are more than one."

"You heard Cienfuegos, the miner. He called the mayor a cockroach. Cut off its head, even a cockroach dies eventually."

"But do you really think we can win? We don't have an army or weapons."

"History is on our side," said Iquique. "And so are the numbers."

"What do you mean?" asked Kin.

"Once the people of Balaal realize what's happening, they'll join us. And we'll outnumber the mayor's army."

"I'm not so sure," said Jesa.

"Who works for Matanza? Cooks, gardeners, cleaners. Who looks after his horses? Feeds his dogs? These are our people. They're all on our side. Kin and The Professor said we already contacted them and they're with us. They provided maps and plans, remember? We're stronger than you think. We have the miners and everyone else the Matanzas persecuted. Once the revolution begins, they'll be with *us*, not him."

"How do you know?" said Kin.

"I don't," said Iquique. "But this is our moment. They say The Butcher disappeared. There are rumors the Tonto Macoute has gone soft without him. All they do is drink and gamble. Decay begins from within. All tyrannies fall, all empires decline, and they usually start to rot at their core. This is what will happen to the Matanza family. Go home. Get some rest. See you in a week."

Jesa and Kin waved goodbye and began to walk. There was so much to tell, but they were too tired to talk. Instead, they thought of the fishing village. Kin imagined what Shadrak and the others were doing. Some would be preparing for night fishing. Jesa thought of her washerwoman friends. They would have already hauled in the clothes from the lines and put away their brooms and scrubbing brushes.

After a while, Kin and Jesa bought dough balls with the last of Jesa's money, hitched a ride to the village, and went home.

✳

And with perfect timing borne of its ancestral wanderings across vast deserts, the camel strolled into the Fishing Village with No Name. It had seen the best and the worst of Balaal, lost a clump of fur to a pack of dogs, been wrangled by a wrangler with a lasso, escaped, got caught up in a traffic jam, been shot at by a drunk with a catapult, and found a path that led to the village via Bujiganga. A string of drool dangled from its lower lip and a Persian rug sat on its back hump. It perused the courthouse-that-wasn't-a-courthouse, strolled past Fundogu, who was sitting in a tree, doubled back on itself, and collapsed in a heap beside one of the iron cannons that faced out to sea. The beast closed its eyes and slept for forty-eight hours.

When it awoke, it found Shadrak staring at it and smoking a stinky hand-roll.

"You go see Jesa," said the fisherman, and he looped a length of string around its neck.

※

That same morning in the Fishing Village with No Name, Fundogu levitated between the two cannons, the smell of the camel lingering all around. These cannons were relics from the days of conquest and plunder. They'd been removed from a warship and placed there to protect the people. Somewhere in the village was a stash of cannon balls.

Fundogu, six feet in the air and listening to the waves, suddenly spoke in a low whisper. His eyes were closed and he was holding the skeletons of starfish in both hands.

"There are bones in the cave by the lighthouse."

CHAPTER 18

Mountain village—the camel's

cargo—a burnished throne

THE PROFESSOR HEARD WHISTLING FROM ACROSS THE MOUNTAINS, THE CALL AND RESPONSE—messages being passed and received. He felt a change in the air. The ground was humming. Someone had arrived.

He stood up and looked out of his rondavel. A giant camel. And sitting on top of it: Jesa and Kin. He leaped up and thought of a painting he'd seen in a book: Cleopatra entering Rome—either a queen or a goddess.

Jesa's burnished throne was an Egyptian rag rug woven by a team of blind seamstresses from Khaliyat, Land of the Dead. She was dressed in her customary black, but with a covering of dust that lined her mantle like dull silver. She had swapped her washerwoman espadrilles for a pair of boots which had belonged to a drowned soldier and which had been dredged up from the stream that ran through Bujiganga. Her hair was down, revealing the white streak, the pattern of the skunk. Behind her sat Kin, impassive, barely recognizable as the half-dead wretch first seen in these hills. His skin had turned copper from the day's ride in the sun.

The camel itself was perfumed with all the smells it had picked up on its peregrinations. These lingered on its skin and on its fur: sweat and rancid meat, car fumes and rotting vegetation, the scum of river banks and the fetor of the shanty towns that lined Matanza-beaten Balaal.

The Professor took one look at the camel and thought of the battles of Thymbra and Qarqar, the Achaemenid Persians riding their beasts to victory, of Xerxes and Gindibu and the smell of the camels scaring the enemy's horses. Here was a weapon he could use.

Jesa and Kin descended. The Professor clambered out of the rondavel and embraced them in turn.

"Where are your shoes?" said Kin.

"Inside."

"You'll need them. We're going to war. You look well, brother."

Around them gathered a smattering of women from the mountain settlement. They were of all ages, from the paper-skinned grandmothers to six-year-old girls with sullen faces and hair tied up.

"You weren't followed?" asked The Professor.

"No. We took a winding route and laid some traps. There was no one. And what news of the others?"

"Come into the shade. I'll tell you everything."

They drank tea and ate biscuits smuggled in by Silmiya, the truck girl with the flower in her hair.

"Four of our men were killed during the raid on the palace. They never even made it into the grounds. I don't know why the soldiers imprisoned us. Sombrero and Gatillo escaped. They're here, out hunting rabbits and waiting for you to arrive. We have unfinished business with Matanza."

"So we weren't betrayed?" said Kin.

"No. Just unlucky. But we can't make the same mistakes again. What's our plan?"

Jesa sipped at her tea and began. "We have men from five towns. Some of the miners will be with us. But apart from the Kakurega, none of our soldiers are disciplined. I call them soldiers but they aren't. They're drunks and desperadoes. But we think they'll fight."

"Weapons?" said The Professor.

"Some old rifles. Swords, stones. And a catapult."

"A catapult? Like the giant ones that fire boulders?"

"No. Like the child's toy that fires peanuts."

Kin said, "The Bujigangans will bring other weapons."

"Like what?" said The Professor.

"Inventions," said Jesa. "Pipe bombs."

The Professor looked downcast. "What else? Magic spells?"

"Yes," said Kin. "The Bruja of Laghouat is with us."

"I was joking."

"I know."

"We may as well rub a lamp and hope a genie comes out. You said we have some of the miners, right?"

"Yes," said Jesa.

The Professor stroked his beard. "That's where it all started. It all began when they discovered gold. They call that place Bocadelin. It's short for. . ."

"Boca del Infierno," said Jesa. "The mouth of hell. We know. We met one of them. Cienfuegos."

"Cienfuegos? Like the rebellion? A hundred fires."

And he thought to himself that they would need a thousand fires to finish off the Matanzas. That family was like those Russian dolls. You killed one and another popped out the same or worse.

"We have plans," said Jesa.

The Professor looked at her skeptically. Without an army, how would they do it, this peasants' revolt? His own sneak attack had failed and resulted in four deaths.

Jesa went on, "We have people on the inside."

"So did I," said The Professor.

"This time will be different."

Outside, the villagers marveled at the camel. It stretched its neck, peed a spattering torrent into the earth, and wandered through the brush in search of fine grasses to chew. And as it wandered, it passed Sombrero and Gatillo, who were returning bearing rabbits just as Kin had first seen them.

Jesa and Kin ate with the three barbudos and explained the plan to topple Matanza. They drew diagrams with sticks in the dust and explained when and where to meet, how to find the regime's weak spot, and how to circumvent the Tonto Macoute. This time, there would be no sneaking in over the wall. This time they had an army.

As the sun began to wane, Kin and Jesa mounted the camel and bade farewell. The Professor and Kin embraced again.

"I'll return in one week," said Kin, "to lead you and the others to the safe house. Be ready."

They rode home in silence along the backstreets and winding paths, for they were still wanted by the regime. It took them all night.

Finally back in the fishing village, they lay in their old beds, Kin asleep and Jesa lost in a reverie.

She imagined Kin at the front of a procession, facing down a hail of gunfire, falling like a rag doll. Then she saw in her mind's eye the kings of chaos from Bouazizi marching to war and getting distracted by a passing cockerel. They would chase after it in ever-widening, feather-strewn circles while all around them Matanza's bullets cut down the revolutionaries. The whispering saint in the painting would whisper and whisper and never be heard. She imagined Bashir on a trash pile twenty feet high, lighting a cigar while Kin was dragged through the blood-drenched streets by the mayor's yelping Chihuahuas. She prayed her dream was not a premonition.

CHAPTER 19

Bowrider—they be drowned

men—days of blood and war—

two cannons—Bujigangan war

machine—the revolutionaries cause

a commotion—monkey business—

barbudos—the wrong battle

Back in the fishing village, a months-old mystery was solved. A bowrider, the boat commandeered by The Butcher to hunt down Kin, drifted to the shore. Several people said they had seen The Butcher "borrow" that bowrider and sail away with a handful of his men and the mythical hag Hormigonera, but none had seen him return. And because this was Balaal and because this was the fishing village of Balaal, where people believed anything could happen and where frequently anything *did* happen, rumors began circulating. The people said Hormigonera had bewitched The Butcher, turned him into an anteater that was currently roaming the island of the lighthouse. Or they said he had sailed over the ocean and docked at a port in the Indies. Or he had been taken by the spirit of the sea and transformed into a fish.

The Butcher's brother, Mayor Matanza, sent investigators and more police. Nothing. They combed the whorehouses and pleasure domes of all of Balaal and found nothing and now the mayor was planning a full-scale ransacking of the fishing village.

But Fundogu, levitating between the two cannons that faced the ocean, had had a vision. He'd seen The Butcher's bones turning and turning in the low tides of the cave.

"Take me to the island, Shadrak," said Fundogu.

And once again Shadrak's little skiff wended through the waves, as it had done earlier, that time at the hands of the boy, this time at the hands of its owner.

In the shallows of the cave where Kin had hidden from Hormigonera and The Butcher, the old priest Fundogu waded barefoot, hitching up his white robe with his opulently ringed fingers. Behind him walked Shadrak, puffing on the nub of a cigarette.

"There!" said Fundogu.

The two men went deeper into the cave.

The Butcher's military uniform had been ripped ragged by the salty water so all that was left were scattered strips and fibers undulating in the current. These clung to The Butcher's chalky bones that lay in eternal repose, the thrashing and writhing of their final minutes having passed into history. The skull was contorted in a rictus grin. The tormentor had become the tormented.

Fundogu stood over the skeleton.

Shadrak said, "He The Butcher?"

"Yes."

"How you know?"

"This pendant round his neck. Gold from the mines of Bocadelin, the family treasure chest. This man was. . ."

Fundogu raised his head and looked beyond the skeleton in front of him. There were four more toward the back of the cave, each stripped bare.

"What have we here?" he said.

Shadrak followed Fundogu's eyes. The back of the cave was dark but the two men approached slowly and saw the remains.

"They be drowned men," said Shadrak.

"Leave me here a while," said Fundogu.

"Sure. I wait in the boat."

"No. Go back to the fishing village."

Shadrak paused.

"You want me pick you up later?"

"No. Just go. I need to stay on the island a while."

"Then how you get back?"

"I will find a way. Now go."

Before Shadrak left, the two of them swore silence. If the mayor of Balaal knew his brother was dead near the fishing village, he would immediately wreak havoc on the villagers. No waiting until Matanza Day. Everyone would die and the village would burn.

Shadrak turned on his engine and sailed back to the coast.

Fundogu went to the lighthouse, which, known only to him, was the home of Hormigonera. She was hiding in an antechamber.

Because she was half-animal, she had sensed the coming of the wave that killed The Butcher. To avoid it, she had escaped to the lighthouse before Kin. She had gone to a different room and he hadn't seen her. And although she had smelled him, with the wave buffeting the building she had been too afraid to move. By the time she emerged, he had gone. So now she was alone and stuck on the island. Then Fundogu appeared.

"Kas tas ir?!" she shouted, on hearing footsteps.

"I am Fundogu. Don't be afraid."

When she saw him, she bowed.

Fundogu knew she was the devil, but he also knew she came from a line of healers and shamans. She had once known spells and incantations. These he tried to tease out of her, but on turning into a monster who served the Matanza family, she'd forgotten them.

Fundogu gave her the talisman in his hands—the skull of The Butcher with its orifices filled with flowers—which, because it was her former master's skull, had special properties. But her own secrets were buried inside her and she could remember no spells. And for reasons known only to himself, he declared her queen of the island, even though it was not his island to give.

He told her, "You will have one chance of escape. Soon the water will recede and this island will cease to be an island. You will walk across the sand, across the sea bed. You will do it at night when no one can see you. If you stay here, you will die. There will be no more fish to catch and the vegetation will dry up. You will walk to the fishing village, and from there you will escape. The Butcher is dead. You have his skull in your hand. You will be in enemy territory and your only chance is to disappear. I tell you this only because your ancestors are my ancestors. Even though you have forgotten your inheritance, which was all the spells you were taught, even though you have done untold evil in this world, I am unable to abandon you. If you touch another child in this life, you will die in agony. Your skin will turn to flames and your bones will become ash. Your eyes will melt and your fingers turn to cinders. You will see a dozen sunrises from this island and then you will leave and never return."

✳

Later, at night, Fundogu was spotted walking onto land. The drunks and the rascally kids who were still awake would later swear he'd walked across the water all the way from the island of the lighthouse, and no one would believe them for they were drunks and rascally kids. The rangy dogs, for their part, did a double-take and categorized him as Not-Dog-Not-Man-Not-Fish. A cast of crabs hunkered down and asked one another in crab language *who is this water-walker?*

*

Across Balaal now, in all the pueblos and townships, villages and shanties of mud and brick that sprung up on the hillsides, revolution was in the air. The people stockpiled arms and made placards from cardboard and string. They organized themselves into battalions. Would-be revolutionaries, led by the Bruja of Laghouat, took over the radio station. She appeared at the studio door one morning in the shape of an enormous crocodile and scared off the regime's propagandists, and now the station belonged to the people.

All across this city where everyone lived in fear of everything—thugs in uniform, outbreaks of disease, water shortages, food shortages, storms that could level a skyscraper—there was a rumor of new days to come that would involve bullets and blood.

In Balaal, the lights had stopped working. Like in Stone Age times, when the sun went down, the world went dark, only illuminated by the stars or by fires. So people began to chatter and they talked about the stories coming out of that fishing village, where a boy who had moved a whale was now going to make history, where a bruja with the hair of a skunk had put down her water bucket and her iron and faced down a Matanza in court.

The roads were thick with traffic fumes which half hid the men, women, and children who wandered between cars selling bottled water or umbrellas or prayer beads or condoms. And in those traffic jams, word went around. A change is coming. There's something in the wind. Those soldiers there, those policemen, those corruptos waiting to catch you and take a bribe, their reign will soon be over.

For a week it went on, this rumor of revolution. No one knew what it was exactly or where it would start, because no one had seen the boy, and the woman seemed to appear and disappear like a ghost even though, apparently, she was traveling the land by camel. And surely nothing would really change unless Mayor Matanza decreed it, for who was this boy and who was this woman? They were nobodies from a nowhere village, a village full of illiterates and octopus grabbers, dunces and fishmongers.

In the mines, word went around. The big bear Cienfuegos, as dark as a shadow, and his six brothers rounded up their friends and explained a plan to take control of, first, the mine and then the city. They knew how to swing a pickaxe and they knew how to dig. Now they would dig a hole for the guards and one for the mine owner who'd kept them starving in shacks and sleeping on roofs.

Days of blood and war were coming. Cienfuegos and his brothers knew it. Jesa and Iquique knew it. The Professor knew it. Bashir, King of the Rats knew it. The travelers knew it. The Kakurega knew it. The Bouazizi knew it. Fundogu and Shadrak knew it. And now half the peasantry of Balaal knew it because they'd heard it on the radio. Everyone knew it. Everyone except Mayor Matanza, Escarabajo, who spent his days fiddling with his clock collection and walking his dogs. And none of his lackeys thought to mention the rumors for fear of being shot.

✳

At 3:46 a.m., June 5, a tin can rolled down Salamurhaaja Avenue for sixteen feet before it came to a halt outside Lilly's Bakery.

At 4:14 a.m., a mouse came dashing through a sewage grill on Cacique Street and shot along the shadows like a bullet.

At 4:29 a.m., a guard sitting at his post outside the National Bank of Matanza cleared his throat and went back to sleep, chin leaning on his rifle butt.

At 4:42 a.m., cross-legged, white-robed Fundogu levitated 3.6 feet in the air outside the courthouse-that-wasn't-a-courthouse in the Fishing Village with No Name on the outskirts of Balaal. His eyes were open.

At 5:00 a.m., with the first rumors of sunlight, the village began to stir.

Many years later, the historians in the fancy academies would say the insurrection began here not once but twice: first, when a washerwoman incited the Popcorn Rebellion and the people took to the streets with vuvuzelas and trash can lids for drums or shields—they didn't know which because they didn't know whether it was a street party, a protest, or a cortege; second, when the people stirred from their rough horsehair hammocks in their little fishing shacks and pocketed their knives and slingshots and said goodbye to the old folks and the young and knew they might never return.

They came bleary-eyed in their dozens down the salty roads, led by Just Jesa on a camel, past the shuttered fish market and the cankerous wooden stubs of the jetty, where the fishing boats jostled among buoys and seaweed.

Some glanced sideways when they saw the wreckages of houses leveled during the last ransacking—piles of scuffed timber and broken glass—and not yet patched up, their residents gone to live in packing crates or shipping containers, or the lucky ones with kind neighbors just for a while, just till they could get back on their feet.

They passed the warehouse-courthouse where Fundogu was still levitating, and some bowed as he came to earth and joined them on their slow morning march.

All of the village was represented: the skinny Somalians and the Japanese, the Eritreans and the Guyanese; washerwomen and net-menders; acrobats and Believers. Beside them all, with their sixth sense of where to find the action, the beach dogs loped in gangs: old friends, tail chasers, bone diggers.

At 5:28 a.m., the Bruja of Laghouat flew over the crowd in

the guise of a seagull. She squawked twice, perched on a roof, and trained her yellow eyes on the growing mass.

At 5:36 a.m., the elongated figure of Lambu, court lackey-turned-fishing villager, arrived wearing dungarees and fisherman's boots and wiped the sleep from his eyes. He was a head taller than the rest of the villagers and held a rope in his hand. On the end of the rope was the ancient turtle, Abacaxi, another court lackey, now grown to the size of an armored car. In its two hundred and fifteen years it had witnessed scores of protest marches, street battles, ran-sackings, massacres, and revolutions, but never taken part in one.

At 5:50 a.m., the sun rose. At first it flirted. It raised an eyebrow above the ocean. Then it lifted half a head and turned the air blurry. In the new light, a pair of hook-billed cormorants cut across the sky and plunged into the dark water.

With the ascent of the sun, the marchers' spirits soared. One began banging out a rhythm on a trash can lid and another let fly with a flurry of vuvuzela buzz, echoes of the Popcorn Rebellion. A trio of acrobats, way out in front, essayed a series of tumbles and arabesques, at which a group of stray cats, hunkered down in a packing crate, gawped and yawned.

Because Abacaxi, the turtle, was too slow to keep up but too good an omen to leave behind, the marchers procured a farmer's cart and horses. Twelve of the strongest men in the village lifted the turtle onto the floor of the cart and two giant Brabançon horses, white-maned and shaggy-tailed, neighed and pulled their load down the street. Abacaxi reclined on his throne, ancient head turning like a periscope.

As they reached the outskirts of the Fishing Village with No Name, Jesa dismounted her camel, called a halt, and gave some orders. Something had caught her eye.

"Those! There!" she said. "We need them!"

"They've never been used!"

"I don't care! We need them!"

And thus the two cannons which had faced the sea for three centuries and never been fired were loaded by twenty strongmen onto another cart pulled by four horses. The cannons were altogether heavier than Abacaxi and altogether harder to move, but Jesa insisted and the men unscrewed a few rusty bolts and ripped the cannons from their moorings. After all, there was no way a revolution could take place without a pair of three-hundred-year-old cannons even if no one knew where to find cannon balls.

The procession passed Irfan the Ironmongers and Samuela the Seamstress and a smattering of bodegas that sold everything from Russian shampoo to Chinese fans. A newspaper stall opened up at 6:00 a.m. and closed at 6:01 a.m. when the owner remembered today was the day for making news not selling it and ran to change out of his pyjamas and slippers.

At 6:27 a.m., there was a crack like gunfire and the marchers stopped dead. Then someone said, "It's just a firework." And sure enough it was a group of nighttime revelers letting off skyrockets on the beach. Both revelers and fireworks were commandeered and absorbed into the march, for fireworks were, after all, explosives, and who knew when a diversion might be needed, such as the one Kin and The Professor had tried during that first raid on the palace?

Bujiganga was a revelation.

Two of the nuns diverted the procession to a small field. There, from behind a clump of trees, rose the hot air balloon called Freedum. It slowly climbed up the sky, vast and rotund like a second sun. It had been repurposed, kitted out for war.

One of the Bujigangan women said to Jesa, "From the balloon we drop bombs."

"Tell them to get down to earth," said Jesa.

"Why?" said the woman. "This is a weapon of war."

"Tell them to get down now. This balloon can be seen from miles away. It'll alert Matanza's men and we'll lose the element of surprise."

The woman reluctantly pulled out a child's walkie-talkie. Inside the basket three warrior-lunatics stuck out their tongues and goggled their eyes and returned the hot air balloon to earth.

But the balloon was just for starters.

The tinkers and scrap merchants were inventors, and the clairvoyants in bowler hats, some with their heads on backwards, had instructed them to invent something fit for a revolution.

From the monastery there emerged twenty-five knights in suits of armor and a whole cache of deadly weapons made from recycled metal: halberds, tridents, maces, and all manner of daggers. There were throwable axes, war hammers, chain metal nunchucks, and long-handled spears perfect for poking a hole in some unsuspecting sentry.

But there was more.

From the bowels of a ditch, the Bujigangans next wheeled out two giant tanks made of found metal. The tanks creaked and lurched and the brakes screeched like vultures, but the things moved and they had the menacing schnozzle of a Panzer and revolving turrets like owls' heads. They were children's toys on a massive scale, complete with fake cupolas, drivers' hatches, tow hooks, and glacis plates. They were made of melted down metal parts, banged together and soldered, and inside them were tractor engines powerful enough to propel the tanks all the way to the palace and back. None of the armaments worked and the side armor wasn't fit to withstand a hammer blow, but the tanks *looked* like weapons of war and the madman behind one of the wheels was giggling like a toddler at the thought of driving slap bang into the heart of Matanza territory.

But that wasn't all.

From behind the monastery of Bujiganga, a strange breathing could be heard. It turned out to be gaslit fire. And the gaslit fire turned out to be the breath of an enormous mechanical dragon. It moved smoothly on wheels, which carried the weight of its metal scales, recycled from trashcan lids and medieval shields dredged up from a swamp. Although the beast couldn't roar, it could breathe fire, which came out in searing bursts from its gas tank belly every time the women inside it lit the flame.

Jesa's camel was spooked by the fire-breathing dragon. She calmed the beast by talking into its ear. Thus the procession was able to continue, knights already sweating in their armor and tanks near the back, just behind Abacaxi on his cart. Behind them both was the cart with the two cannons, and behind it all, the shiny dragon on wheels.

The procession picked up more warrior-rebels from Bujiganga and wended its way out of town, past the tarpaulin sheets with their hundreds of objects lined up outside the tiny houses. Those who didn't join the marchers waved them on and cheered.

As the sun rose and the morning clouds dissolved, the procession passed through tiny pueblos—smatterings of adobe and straw and wandering goats. The roads ran out and one of the tanks got stuck in a rutted pathway and had to be pushed by hand. Jesa turned back and found an easier route that could accommodate horses and carts, tanks and mechanical dragons.

They traversed a steep hillside, passing the rickety houses of indentured landworkers, who came out and gave them water from a stream.

Then they passed No-Man's-Land, a ghost town. The silence was so eerie that Jesa became suspicious of a Matanza ambush and asked one of her fellow marchers where they were.

"The town has been abandoned for fifty years," said the woman.

They kept moving along the weed-choked roads, past semi-collapsed buildings. They saw a signpost carved from wood, but it was so scratched and defaced by rain and termites that it was now illegible.

As the camel slowed down, Jesa saw a dilapidated shack, and on it someone or something was moving. A thin tail swinging in a wide arc, and then the face of a monkey. It moved to the roof's edge—brown fur, the size of a child—and stared at the procession. It bared its teeth, then carried on with what it was doing: sharpening a stick. It dropped a stone, swung down the side of the shack, and leaped through a hole that had been a window.

A moment passed and suddenly ten monkeys emerged on the roof. They began gesticulating in a mad choreography, one scratching his balls, another waving circles above her head, another hooting like a train horn, another bending over and exposing his buttocks, another mock slapping her mate, another stamping her feet. The sounds of shuffling and snorting carried to the procession and the whole obscene pageant went on for five minutes—a variety show, a living tableau, monkey vaudeville—while the marchers walked past.

Two of the creatures began masturbating at the procession and a third pissed a perfect parabola of yellow urine onto the earth below, his face contorted in monkey joy. Besides the ten on the roof, more now emerged from the shack: bigger and darker and not leaping but prowling. Bruiser monkeys, scrappers and thugs.

"This was a human settlement," said Jesa. "It's been colonized."

And she whispered again to the camel to keep it calm while outside the monkeys lit a fire. They sat around it, fidgeting with wooden sticks, and on the roof of the shack others emerged, did a tango, a foxtrot, a samba, a waltz.

"Are they dangerous?" asked Jesa.

The washerwoman beside her said nothing. The monkeys began to pound the roof with their feet, stamping in unison.

Jesa went on, "Because that looks like a war dance."

Fundogu appeared next to the camel, his gait leisurely but his eyes on the monkeys.

"Fundogu," said Jesa, "can those monkeys do damage?"

"Damage? Monkeys can ransack a city in one hour. You have never heard of Xadina D-dar? Or Matekino? Or Scimmia? There were human heads on sticks, armies overrun. They dammed up the water supply with rocks and trees. It took a hundred monkeys ninety minutes to take over Matekino, a city of ten thousand."

"I'll tell the Bujiganga to get the dragon ready," said Jesa. "If we need to, we'll fight fire with fire."

But the marchers passed by, staring at the monkeys just as the monkeys stared at the marchers, and a stalemate ensued. The sun beamed down and cast every living creature in shadow while the monkeys hooted and swooned and basked in the glow of their charade.

✳

Kin, The Professor, Sombrero, El Gato, and ten others—the last of los barbudos—prepared to leave the mountain holdout. They ate a final meal of rice and beans, loaded their guns, jammed their backpacks with dried figs, ammunition, and clean underwear, and said goodbye to their families. They left behind the women, the children, and the elderly. It was a battle for barbudos. No beard, no action. All except Kin, who barely had the first wisps of a moustache. But he was different. This was his revolution.

They came to a mountain pass and waited.

The Professor said to Kin, "What now?"

They were both laden down with a backpack and a rifle.

"We wait."

"For what?"

"Silmaya."

Soon a familiar truck pulled up. Silmaya, a flower in her hair, wound down the window and said, "Need a ride?"

Kin climbed into the bed of the truck just as he had on the journey to the mountains months earlier. He pondered all that he had gone through in that time. Bouncing in the back of that same truck now, he remembered the cave with the ammonite and stalactites, the crack of light he'd thought was God. He remembered the hunger and thirst and the sickness that had made him retch and hallucinate. The walks in circles across barren terrain. Sores on his face. Tongue dried up and swollen. The failed raid and weeks in prison, and the nighttime escape thanks to a seagull and a balloon. And now the second raid, this time with Jesa and an army, a raid, he told himself, that would become a revolution.

The truck bumped and clattered across the mountain pass. The sun burned off the cold of the morning, and the sky was streaked blood-red. The men huddled together, mostly in silence.

The Professor sat next to Kin. Even in the gathering heat of the day, his neck was swathed in his red and white keffiyeh.

"You know the plan," Kin said.

"I know it," The Professor replied.

"Jesa and the others are marching. Then we. . ."

"I know it."

Silmaya had driven or walked in every nook of the mountains and never took the same route twice. She figured that if the truck wore down the ground so much that it created a road, it would make it easier for Matanza's soldiers to discover the mountain hideout. It made for a bumpy ride, and Sombrero told the rest of the men to hold their guns so they were pointing into the air.

The truck passed a frozen lake and then wide-open plains. It passed saguaro and prickly pear and thick clumps of cholla, and the landscape turned from dust-yellow to green. A dozen wild horses stood around, still as rocks in the morning light.

Now that they were out of the mountains, Silmaya was able to get service so she switched on the radio in her truck. After the takeover of Balaal's radio station, anti-Matanza propaganda ruled the airwaves. Matanza's henchmen had tried to reclaim the studio only to find the rebels had skedaddled. The soldiers ransacked the place and destroyed the equipment, but still the propaganda continued, recorded and disseminated on the run, and broadcast from mobile studios. The speeches of former Matanza mayors, which had been played on a nightly loop for decades, disappeared from the airwaves.

Now the radio announcer said a street party had begun in the fishing village that morning. Silmaya slowed down, leaned out of her window, and called to the back of the truck, "The party's on its way! Started this morning!"

Kin wondered if he would see the residents of the fishing village alive before the day was done.

✳

The procession passed through towns that were on no map of Balaal. They had sprung up overnight—tent cities or dwellings of adobe and bamboo. At other times, the marchers expected to come across towns but found nothing but a gust of wind and a ball of tumbleweed rolling down the road. They discovered whole villages had been submerged by nature: trees and weeds and massive leaves choking the buildings till they collapsed, or great folds of mud twenty feet deep which had come sliding down the hill in the rainy season and buried everything.

The Bujigangan knights began to flag in their heavy armor. The horses too, pulling the weights of the cannon and the giant turtle Abacaxi, needed to stop regularly for water and feed. They were farm animals—huge and strong—but this was unfamiliar terrain.

The marchers kept up their spirits with music, banging makeshift drums, blowing their vuvuzelas, and breaking into song. Three lapsed nuns, like the Three Graces, joined the acrobats at the front and began doing the mambo.

At 9:32, a chant went up: "We are the Boo!" It was a group of Bouazizi who had joined the procession.

The Fanatics of Bouazizi responded with "Boo! Boo! Bouazizi," but then the Bujigangans reciprocated: "Boo! Boo! Bujiganga!" It seemed as if a fight would break out between the two groups, but the painted saint, who was held aloft like a placard, whispered to the Bouazizi, "wrong battle," and Lambu the lanky lawyer stepped in and explained they were on the same side, and everyone calmed down.

Wherever they passed, the people came out of their homes and proffered water or bread or fruit and cheered them on. They received fresh milk from a farmer, who offered to slaughter a pig but was rebuffed.

"There'll be enough slaughter later, and in any case we need to keep moving," said Jesa.

At 9:56, the Bruja of Laghouat joined the procession in the guise of an ambling dog. Fundogu saw the creature and nodded his respects.

And soon enough they entered the main thoroughfare of Balaal, the pueblos and back roads now behind them.

CHAPTER 20

The Place Where the Four Roads

Converge 1—inventory of weapons—

roster of rebels

KIN AND LOS BARBUDOS ARRIVED AT THE PLACE WHERE THE FOUR ROADS CONVERGE, THE heart of the city of Balaal. They climbed out of the truck, dispersed according to their plan, and melted into the traffic so as not to arouse suspicion. They slung their guns over their shoulders and took the back roads memorized from maps, the same routes Kin and The Professor had taken on their first attempt to overthrow Matanza, and the same sounds: the cries of street hawkers, the motley traffic. In those same shadows, somnolent street dogs barely stirred.

Thirty minutes later, the men reunited at a safe house behind a market—a disused depot, cavernous and empty. Kin picked open the padlock with a nail and ushered the men in through the sliding metal door. There they let their eyes adjust to the darkness.

After a while, they heard a banging at the entrance. The Professor slid it open again and the gargantuan silhouette of Bashir, King of the Rats filled the doorway. He was accompanied by half a dozen followers—furtive and gaunt as fishermen.

"You made it," said Kin.

"I'm Bashir, King of the Rats. I always make it." He lit a foul-smelling cigar to celebrate his arrival and scanned the room with his good eye. "Which of you is The Professor? Let me guess. Four-eyes here."

"Correct, one-eye."

They waited a while in an uneasy pact. Bashir's rat-men weren't used to standing around in empty rooms. They were pro-curers, always on the move. And los barbudos, although they'd slept in rondavels, weren't used to walls and roofs. They'd done everything else outside, some of them for years on end. Only the jailbirds, Kin and The Professor, remembered days hemmed in, surrounded by concrete.

There was another banging on the door and a dozen rough-looking travelers appeared, two of them pulling a cloth-covered cage on wheels. Another two carried heavy sacks, jangling with the sound of jostling metal.

"We are the travelers," said their leader, Suvaco.

He was the same man Jesa, Kin, and Iquique had spoken to at the fairground that freezing day, long-haired and wild-eyed, a tattoo of his people's history on his chest, and a face filled with scars and scratches. He was joining the revolution to avenge a century of persecution and one dead parrot, Madrugada.

"Welcome," said Kin.

The leader raised a hand in acknowledgement and helped relieve his men of their burdens. All eyes were on the covered cage but no one said a word. Each group of warriors took its place against a different wall and each stared at the others, remembering ancestral feuds, grudges so old no one could even recall their origins.

Bashir dropped his cigar and crushed it underfoot. "Nice tea party. Who else are we waiting for?"

"The Kakurega," said Kin.

"Of course. The mad monks."

Within minutes the Kakurega, thirty strong, knocked and entered the storeroom. They bowed to the rest of the men and took their place beside a wall.

Moments later, Cienfuegos, the miner, and his six brothers came in muttering and sloughing off dust. They were dreadlocked giants, with shovels slung over their shoulders. As they had done all their lives, they bickered, pushed and shoved one another, and laughed it off with a shrug.

Kin welcomed them all and asked, "What weapons do we have?"

Los barbudos came forward, led by The Professor and Sombrero. They carried their rifles and showed the bullet belts around their waists or slung across their torsos in an X.

"One gun per hombre," said Sombrero, "and a lot of ammunition."

Then Bashir's men stirred. There were no soldiers among them, just pilferers and thieves. They stepped forward and put a collection of objects on the stone floor.

"What's this?" said Sombrero. "A rummage sale?"

Bashir looked at him coolly with his one eye. He lit another cigar, plugged it into his smirking mouth, and walked forward slowly, his chest swelling under his camouflage shirt.

"This," he said out of the corner of his mouth, and picked up a tub. "Nitroglycerine. Smuggled out of the barracks at Zurburan in 49. This." He reached into a holdall and pulled out what looked like a toy gun attached to a cylinder.

"What *is* that?" said Cienfuegos.

"Flamethrower," said Bashir, without batting his eye. "Fifty-yard range. For singeing Matanza's curtains. And this. . ." He pulled out a pair of canisters. "To smoke him out."

"Smoke grenades," said The Professor. "Where did you get this stuff?"

Bashir ignored the question and reached into another bag, this one made of thick canvas. He produced something that looked like a four-pronged mechanical hand.

"Bagh naka," he said. "Indian tiger claw." He slipped a metal loop around his wrist so each finger now had a claw. "For hand-to-hand combat."

"Knives are *our* business," said the lanky fairground leader, Suvaco.

Bashir ignored him too. "Or claw-to-hand. Hold this." He gave his burning cigar to an underling. Then he reached into the bag again, this time with both hands. He pulled out canisters and cans and tubs and jars, showing them and replacing them as he talked.

"Explosives. White phosphorous. Tear gas. Dynamite. Landmines."

Everyone peered. A couple of hardened soldiers exchanged glances. Bashir retrieved his cigar, put it back in his mouth, and raised his hands as if to say *that's all, folks*.

Kin turned to the Kakurega. They had no leader so all of them came forward together. They were dressed in long black cassocks and their heads were shaved shiny. In unison they pulled out long, curved swords which they raised and then set down in front of them. It seemed as choreographed as a dance. Then they bowed. There was a pause as they came upright out of their bow and Kin heard the cooing of a pigeon on the roof.

"That's it?" said Bashir. "You bring a sword to a gunfight?"

One of the Kakurega said, "We have old tradition. We no need gun."

"A sword won't stop a bullet," said Bashir.

"We attack with our brains," said the Kakurega man. Then he bowed again. The Kakurega picked up their swords and silently walked to their wall, never turning their backs on anyone. There was barely a rustle from their cassocks or their feet because they moved like air.

It was Cienfuegos's turn. He gestured to his six brothers to move forward. They stood still, looking as sheepish as a group of two-hundred-and-fifty-pound behemoths could manage. Cienfuegos gestured again. His brothers didn't move.

"Hey," said Bashir. "What do you people do? Sit on your enemies? Where are your weapons? You think Matanza's going to curl up and ask you to tickle his tummy?"

"We don't have weapons," said Cienfuegos, "except our shovels. We came straight from the mine."

"What?" said Bashir.

"Thank you, Cienfuegos." said Kin. "We'll arm you. We appreciate you being here."

Cienfuegos said, "We had to take out four guards to get here. Over at the mine. So they know we're on the run. But we weren't followed."

"How do you know?" said Bashir.

"I just know."

Kin said, "We'll get you weapons. We're glad you're here."

Cienfuegos took a few paces back to his brothers. They stood like Greek kouroi, all muscle and hair.

Kin turned to the travelers.

Suvaco, the travelers' leader, lavishly earringed and stripped to the waist, gestured to his sweating comrades and said something in a medieval language. They pulled off the sheet from the cage. Inside it, an enormous tiger lay quietly. The rat-men and los barbudos approached, open-mouthed. The Kakurega looked but didn't move.

"Here kitty-kitty," said Bashir.

"Is it awake?" said The Professor.

Suvaco scratched at a welt on his neck. "He'll be ready when he's needed."

Then a few more of the travelers stepped forward with their sacks and emptied them onto the floor. The contraband landed with a clatter. They had collected every loose knife, every gut-slasher, every blade and shank within a ten-mile radius at the heart of Balaal's badlands: cutlasses, scimitars, a Japanese tsurugi, Georgian khanjalis, chicken sickles, and a double-edged dangpa that could kill two men at a time.

"Nice work," said Bashir, King of the Rats. "More knives than men."

"Don't you ever shut up?" said Cienfuegos.

Bashir laughed. "You miners. You spend your lives in a hole in the ground, then you die and go back in the ground."

Cienfuegos stared at him.

Kin piped up, "We're on the same side here. The enemy is Matanza. We have one hour before we move, so let's use it."

"Wait," said Bashir. "Who said you're our leader?" He puffed on his cigar. "Have you ever used one of these?" He picked up a stick of dynamite. "Or these?" He picked up a gun.

"We have a plan," said Kin.

"That's not what I asked," said Bashir. "I asked who gave you authority."

"We're all from different parts of the city. We have different skills and different. . ."

"You aren't listening. I said who made you our leader."

Kin looked him in the eye. "We're like the Kakurega. We're equals. But we need to follow a plan. There isn't much time because the procession is approaching the city center now. That means someone has to explain what we're going to do. And that someone is me."

"Ok," said Bashir. "Go ahead, Grizzly Joe. We're all ears."

Kin beckoned everyone closer. They crowded round in mutual distrust as Kin pulled out a piece of chalk and began drawing diagrams on the stone floor while he laid out the plan. He had rehearsed this a hundred times. It would make or break the revolution. He drew maps of the mayor's home and its surroundings and all the streets leading to it. He marked in different colors where the mayor's men would be stationed and he marked where *they*, the revolutionaries, would attack, and when.

The rebels had spies on the inside: gardeners, cleaners, servants, scullery maids, lightbulb changers, door hinge oilers, sock darners. These men and women had already played a part in the first plot, smuggling out plans of the palace, divulging the mayor's routine, whispering the location of the guards. And Kin and The Professor had made it all the way to the mayor's kitchen. This time, the rebels made sure they had all the cooks on their side, because the cooks were the key.

The men in the safe house practiced a series of mountain whistles based on birdsong for communication and fiddled with stolen, malfunctioning walkie-talkies, which they eventually abandoned. Bashir, King of the Rats stank the place out with his cigars but relished a chance to stick a knife in Matanza's guts. The travelers were ready and knew their tiger could unleash chaos. The Kakurega would fight with no malice but total discipline. They understood the plan and would stick to it with their lives. Cienfuegos and his brothers saw a chance to avenge all the dead miners throughout history. They had dug their own graves to enrich the Matanza family and never received a moment's peace, let alone a pot of their own gold.

Kin checked his watch. "Jesa and the others will be entering the city now. It's time to join them. Remember the plan. Stick to the plan and we win."

Outside, the trucks growled and dogs stirred from their slumbers, while across Balaal a murder of crows gathered on the roof of the mayoral palace and cawed in unison. They knew what was coming.

CHAPTER 21

The revolutionaries arrive—horse

and rider—collapse in D minor—

El Gatillo in the palazzo—the Battle

of Matanza Square

In its first hour in the heart of Balaal, the procession stopped the morning traffic and attracted a thousand gazes—some in awe, others confusion.

Onlookers who saw acrobats doing somersaults in front of Jesa on her camel thought it was a traveling circus from Arabia.

Bystanders who saw the dragon and the Bujigangan knights in armor thought it was a medieval pageant.

Eyewitnesses who saw the turtle Abacaxi in the back of an open truck pulled by the two white-maned Brabançons thought it was a coronation.

The shopkeepers gawped. The street cleaners did a double take. The homeless leered and joined in. And the procession arrived in Matanza Square, the center of Balaal.

Matanza Square was the largest square in the city. It was surrounded on all four sides by buildings in various states of disrepair. There were two disused government offices, a private palazzo in ruins, a couple of stores.

In the middle of the square stood a giant bronze statue of a Matanza ancestor on his horse. A brutalist lump of a brutal lump. It had been erected fifty years earlier. Fundogu remembered the headline in the underground newspaper the *Balaal Insurgent*: "Matanza in Matanza Square Unveils Statue of Matanza Commissioned by Matanza." The gloved hands erroneously had five fingers.

The morning dew had long since dried on the cobblestones and now a light breeze carried scraps of yesterday's newspapers across the square. A plastic bag did a cartwheel. A lone feather found liftoff. A pair of pigeons did a tap dance and then defecated on the head of the bronze Matanza.

On one side of the square lay the nests of the dazed homeless: a pungent shambles of cardboard, moldy mattresses, and scraps of cloth.

The procession stopped. Jesa gave an order from her camel. There were to be no speeches from a scaffold. No gasoline bombs or burning cars. A stuffed effigy of the mayor that someone wanted to hang from a street lamp was held back. Instead, Jesa pointed at the statue of horse and rider.

The rebels pulled out a collection of fishing ropes and steel twine, and the most agile of them climbed up and attached the statue to the Bujigangans' faux tanks and the horse-drawn carts. A hundred men and women joined them and began to heave.

Unlike the whale washed up on the beach four years earlier, the dead general didn't resist, and neither did his horse. The whole thing came crashing down with a spray of dust and an enormous bang that was only drowned out by the clamor of the crowd. Even the Bouazizis' painted saint, himself an amalgam of oil, dust, and gold leaf, raised a muffled cheer.

Fundogu said, "Now we must finish the revolution," for the downing of a Matanza general in bronze marked the point of no return.

The chant went up. "Matanza out! Matanza out! Matanza out!"

For years, Matanza's army had been falling into decline. Inaction had dulled them. There had been no invasions except for a few plagues (locusts, cockroaches, frogs, bad breath) or occasional outbursts from troops of monkeys. So apart from periodic ransackings and occasional blunder for plunder, the soldiers/police spent their days smoking, drinking, whoring, sleeping, and watching telenovelas. Their uniforms were half-eaten by moths, their weapons rusty with disuse. Stockpiled guns lay in their crates in musty storerooms. Most of their tanks and armored cars gathered weeds out by the airfields, where the winds howled nightly and stray dogs roamed. Some of the vehicles had been stripped clean for scrap metal, which wound up in Bujiganga. The air force's one plane, a little Fokker, lay forgotten, sprouting shrubs in an overgrown field.

The only thing that had held the army together was The Butcher, but now he was gone the army had lost all volition. He was never replaced because he wasn't officially dead. There were no witnesses to what had happened on the island of the lighthouse.

Kin had disappeared into the mountains. Hormigonera had disappeared to no-one-knew-where. And if any of those stolid, illiterate fishermen knew where The Butcher was, they weren't telling.

Despite the army falling apart, there were still vestiges of viciousness. An ambitious army captain here and there. A brainwashed ransacker or two. A few Tonto Macoute lunatics who liked to swing a baton. Without The Butcher's leadership, they were little more than a mob, but they were an armed mob and some of them liked a fight.

When the call came through that there were people massing in Matanza Square and that they looked like subversives, these soldiers stirred. They put on their boots, located their weapons, shook off their hangovers, and marched into the light.

On their walkie-talkies they awaited orders, but their commander was a pile of bones adorning the sediment of a cave on the island of the lighthouse and the other captains were shacked up in the brothels or asleep in their boots, still drunk from the mysterious shipment of aguardiente that had arrived anonymously the night before, delivered by a young female truck driver with a flower in her hair.

They were a medley of every type of armed official that existed in Balaal: head bashers, riot police, soldiers, and Matanza henchmen. They came in blocks. A squadron from the barracks. A unit from the police station. An escadrille from a garrison on the outskirts of Balaal. They came sweeping in from the side streets, heading like an arrow to Matanza Square. And they came fast, because there was head bashing to be done, subversives to be squashed.

At first, they weren't sure who the enemy was. But once they'd eyed each other and seen uniforms and the great absence where the bronze statue should have been, which was now lying on its side, they knew it was the rabble holding the placards that had to be defeated. They rallied together at one end of the square, made a few plans to defend their patch, and compared baton sizes. Those who had guns searched their pockets for bullets and began loading.

But their task seemed absurd, for at the front of this rebel army was a camel, an abomination of wobbly legs and foul-smelling fur, an unlikely looking beast of war chewing on a clump of quack grass. Atop the animal sat a woman, olive-skinned, with a streak of white in her hair. Surely this wasn't the rebel leader?

Next to the woman, the subversives consisted of several skinny figures in leotards doing somersaults and a bizarre array of fishing folk, washerwomen, and drunks. Many appeared to have all the ailments known to Balaal, from scurvy to scabies to syphilis.

All the better, thought the soldiers. It was easier to bash than to be bashed.

There was a hiatus.

No one moved.

Iquique, standing by Jesa and the camel, quoted an old Bujigangan proverb: "I don't know which is worse: the whine of the mosquito or its silence."

The two parties kept staring. By now the sun had risen and it blazed down on them all, casting them in light.

The first chaos was sonic. A cry went up: "We are the Boo!" At the same time, a group of militant villagers resumed the chant "Matanza out!" And just as they started, the street dogs, led by the Bruja of Laghouat, who had turned herself into a fine-featured, floppy-eared Catahoula Leopard dog, began a symphony of barking.

Inside one of the fake Bujigangan tanks there was a vintage Grundig 505 record player, purloined from the wreckage of a country estate, and the madman inside the tank had rigged up loudspeakers and now played a selection of rowdy Turkish kantos, Bavarian yodelling, and Azerbaijani opera.

The wailing and chanting immediately disoriented the soldiers, who found themselves off-balance and stumbling.

The second chaos was visual. In Balaal, nothing was what it was supposed to be, and sure enough the square wasn't a square. It was an oblong with proportions that kept changing the longer you looked. In the middle was the toppled bronze horse and general—now a street barricade. Some of the rebels climbed on top of it while others hid behind it. Yet others, including the dragon and the knights, had arrived in the side streets which led to the main square.

So the Matanza army, five hundred strong, jostling and preening nervously, couldn't tell how many they were up against. What was behind the fallen statue? Who were those people in the side streets who had followed the soldiers? And was the rebel army ten deep or a hundred deep at the other end of the square? What they needed was a birds-eye view of the square, but the birds, like the bats, dogs, horses, tiger, and camel, had chosen the side of the rebels.

The only person with a birds-eye view of the square was the ex–army sniper-turned-deserter-turned-rebel Gatillo, otherwise known as El Gato, The Cat. The Cat had been sent to the square as part of The Plan. Once there, he'd scaled a crumbling palazzo, rifle tied to his back, and scrambled onto the roof, where now he crouched. Through the scope of his gun he watched the soldiers gathering and the rebels on the other side. His bright blue eyes caught everything. He could make out individual cobble stones under Fundogu's feet. He could see the sculptor's handiwork on the mane of the toppled bronze horse and a pigeon fluttering in a fountain. But his focus was on the soldiers. How many would he have to gun down like all those rabbits in the hills he'd shot for los barbudos?

The soldiers stood side by side, immobile. They were jammed in, pawns on a chessboard, weapons drawn and expecting the worst, for everything before them was a riddle and a threat. What rebel army hatches a cacophony like that without meaning business? What rebel army has dogs yelping and bellowing and a woman on a camel at its head? And who *were* those people in the side street? Why, they looked like monks! And in the other side street, who were those mendicants, heads bowed? Were there really so many beggars and drunks in the city center? It had to be a trick, a ruse to draw them in, smoke them out.

At 11:56 a.m., a cat slunk out of a window and into the square. It glanced left. It glanced right. It yowled and vamoosed.

At 11:57 a.m., Fundogu, cross-legged, levitated six feet into the air.

At 11:58 a.m., a bead of sweat made a trail down Just Jesa's forehead and along her cheek and for a second resembled a tear.

At 11:59 a.m., the rebels began breathing in unison without knowing it. Even their hearts began beating in rhythm. And they found themselves reliving The Night of the Sixteen Daggers and the Slepvak Massacre even though none of them had been there. They found themselves reliving the ritual beatings inflicted on the miners, the farmworkers, the shopkeepers. Blood running through the streets. The cries. Whorls of smoke rising from the villages. In a side street, a fifteen-year-old former homeless orphan touched his coral necklace, closed his eyes, and moved out of a shadow.

And just as the clock in an ancient church struck 12:00, all hell broke loose.

Those men dressed as monks in the side street pulled back their hoods, advanced rapidly from the eastern side of the square, and unsheathed their swords. Then a rifle crack sounded from the roof of the palazzo and a soldier dropped. And then another. And another. From the side street opposite the Kakurega monks, a group of marauders disguised as beggars entered the square. They looked like something dredged up from hell: lank-haired pirates wielding cutlasses and all manner of medieval weaponry. Some were tattooed from head to toe and wore necklaces of human bones. They were led by the most manic of all, Suvaco, bare-chested and berserk and carrying scimitars in each hand. He alone gutted six soldiers.

There ensued an orgy of bludgeoning and slicing. While the Kakurega dispatched the enemy with a balletic swing of their swords, Suvaco's men hacked and stabbed and slashed. There was a wailing and shrieking that hadn't been heard since the times of the earliest ransackings, and the spatter of blood flew in great crimson zip lines onto the cobbles of Matanza Square.

The army turned to flee, but found its path blocked by an enormous tiger on a rope. It roared and arched its back and swung its paws in the air in great threshing parabolas. It was flanked by a line of barbudos, led by Kin, The Professor, and Sombrero, who were on one knee and pointing their rifles as if for target practice. The first volley dropped a dozen soldiers.

The bravest of Matanza's men scrambled and fired back. A bullet thudded into The Professor's chest. He reeled and fell, but there was no blood. The bullet had hit a book—*The Art of War*—that was nestled in his breast pocket, rupturing the cover but not his flesh. Kin pulled The Professor up and they reloaded and fired again.

With the Kakurega attacking on one side, Suvaco and the travelers on the other, and the tiger and los barbudos behind them, the army had nowhere to go but forward, toward the fallen bronze statue and the woman on the camel. And so they charged.

But as they did so, the two ancient cannons, which had protected the fishing village for three hundred years and never been fired, let out an ear-splitting boom and two shells exploded. Someone had found cannon balls. At the same time, six canisters of tear gas landed and erupted among the soldiers, precipitating a bout of mad coughing and choking.

After the dust and stones had settled and the tear gas drifted away, the soldiers found themselves set upon by a group of Bujigangan knights in recycled armor, engaged in hand-to-hand combat. By now, the soldiers were half-blind, limbs falling off, and peppered by the bullets of los barbudos and El Gato on the palazzo roof.

But it was the mechanical dragon from Bujiganga that ended it.

As the soldiers scrambled toward a narrow side street to escape the square, they were met by a forty-foot monster exhaling flames, flanked by two fire-breathing circus performers from Suvaco's fairground. Beside them, four of Bashir's rat-men wielded flame-throwers that blasted yet more fire that singed the beards of the soldiers and turned their faces red. The heat blurred the air and made the street impassable.

The soldiers looked left. The soldiers looked right. The soldiers looked forward. The soldiers looked back. No escape. The soldiers looked up. Above them, a hot air balloon was sailing. On one side of it was a big painted B; on the other side, one word: "Freedom." From the balloon, a group of Bujigangans dropped their missiles on the troops: first, it was irons, then broken glass, bullet casings, stones that landed with a crack or a thud or a tinkling and drew more blood. And then more tear gas. With this load shed, the balloon was light enough to float out of reach of the soldiers' bullets.

Once they'd finished coughing and retching, Matanza's men threw down their weapons and raised their arms.

El Gato scanned the scene from the palazzo roof. Knights in recycled steel. An old man in a white robe levitating. Soldiers writhing and groaning. Black smoke rising from the dragon's mouth. An eight-foot tiger corralled by a group of psychotics. A legion of monks in cassocks. A madman with an eyepatch and a fat cigar, ranting. Other soldiers quietly ripping off their uniforms and joining the rebels. A woman on a camel's back. A painted saint held aloft. A whirling of anarchist bats flying in circles. A cabal of monkeys last seen doing a war dance on a roof, now rogue members of the rebel army.

In all the confusion, Iquique found Kin.

"On to the palace," she said. "We have no time to lose. The people can celebrate their victory here, but we need to keep moving."

"What about the wounded?"

"My nuns will tend to them. How many?"

"At least four of the Kakurega fell. And some of the travelers."

"And Matanza's army?"

"Hundreds. Look."

She surveyed the scene. Soldiers beside her groaned and retched, a shambles of gore and hacked limbs. Waves of smoke dissipated into the sky.

"Tend to them too," said Kin. His face was black with soot. "I'll get the Kakurega to take prisoners. All these soldiers are unarmed."

Kin clambered over the dead and the wounded. Bullet casings littered the cobbles. He thought *I'm a killer*. And the thought passed quickly because there was no time to think. The palace awaited.

Word spread. In all the chaihanes, Arabic tea houses, rundown shebeens with their sawdust and spittle floors, the salsa bars and tertulias in smoky cafes, the whisper went round: the revolution was here. Led by a woman on a camel, a lapsed nun, and a boy of fifteen. It was happening in the streets. Guns, bombs, fire-breathing dragons. It was here.

CHAPTER 22

Cienfuegos digs a hole—the

invasion—Madrugada—Matanza

They'd decided to take the palace by stealth. Kin figured that once word of the revolution had got out, Matanza's best and toughest soldiers, the Tonto Macoute, would be there, loyal bodyguards armed to the teeth and protecting their tin-pot, dog-loving, clock-fiddling dictator with their lives. A full-on invasion would mean more bloodshed and the deaths of citizen-rebels, who were, after all, fishermen and washerwomen, miners and mendicants. The storming of the palace would be left to the true warriors among them, and the occasional madman with an eye-patch or a tiger on a leash and a major grudge. They had no way of knowing if their plan had worked, if the cooks had done their job and poisoned the guards. Now they would find out.

Kin, The Professor, and two of the others circled the perimeter of the palace. On top of the outer wall was a jumble of razor wire that hadn't been there when they'd last scaled it.

"How do we get over that?" said The Professor. "We left the hot air balloon in Matanza Square."

"We don't," said Kin. "Hey!" he said to Cienfuegos. "Can you and your brothers dig under the wall?"

"Can a bear shit in the woods?"

"Wait," said The Professor. "The guards will see us."

"What guards?" said Kin. "I don't see a soul. They're all at the front entrance. Or they're asleep. In any case, we have Gatillo."

At that very moment El Gato was scaling a roof overlooking the palace. He had a box of bullets and he never missed.

"Hey!" said Bashir. "Why don't we just blow a hole through the wall? I have dynamite."

"Too noisy," said Kin.

Cienfuegos and his brothers dug under the wall. They'd been digging all their lives for gold. Once they started on the dried mud, they were in within minutes. Bashir's rat-men, skinny and furtive, crawled through.

They found the guards in every single sentry post fast asleep, so the rat-men grabbed the keys. They tiptoed to the main entrance, found more dozing sentries, and unlocked the main gate. There were no security cameras or snipers on watch. There were no soldier patrols or electrified, barbed wire–topped booby traps. There was no password or sunglasses-wearing, machine gun–wielding officer taking IDs. There was nothing but sleeping guards and sleeping dogs. The scheduled miracle had taken place.

The rat-men whistled. The noise came shrilly through the tops of the cedar trees, over the sounds of the city, and all the way to the outer perimeter of the palace, where the other rebels were waiting.

"Hear that?" said Kin. "That's our cue."

They moved quickly to the main entrance, abandoning Cienfuegos's tunnel. Three of the Kakurega slid in through the gate like black water. Bashir, King of the Rats marched in like a bull. The travelers trooped in like troopers. Los barbudos, led by Kin and The Professor, scratched their beards.

Was it possible the plan had worked so well? Knocked out Matanza's protection in its entirety? The Professor turned to Kin and said, "Did they poison them *all*? Or is this an ambush?"

Kin narrowed his eyes and said nothing. Their group consisted of twenty men walking into the grounds of Balaal's dictator in broad daylight. Hadn't Matanza heard his square was burning? Didn't he know his bronze ancestor had been toppled that very morning and *he* was soon to follow? With his guards poisoned, surely he'd called in reinforcements?

The men walked under the portico that led to the main door. The door was a grand thing: a sheet of oak with a brass handle. Bashir tried it. Locked. He readied himself to kick it down. Another whistle went up. One of his rat-men approached with the keys he'd taken from the sentry. He tried a couple and then opened the front door. The men stared in wonder.

The interior of the palace began as a corridor which led to a broad entranceway. From there the rebels, following Bashir, came across an expansive carpeted staircase, lavish and gilded, and then the main room with its high ceilings. There were rococo tables with legs curved like a greyhound's, silver candlesticks, Chinese porcelain vases encircled with blue dragons, diamond-encrusted letter openers. There were glistening chandeliers and cupboards full of dust-dulled crystal, Louis XV furniture, Doric columns, Islamic tapestries on the walls adorned with curlicues, and clocks. Above all, dozens and dozens of clocks, from different eras and continents. The rat-men eyed all of these and shot through the palace, pocketing the small goods.

On other walls were oil paintings of the Matanza ancestors, a gallery of moustachioed brutes in uniforms or high-collared shirts. They were carbon copies of one another, each ancestor passing on the jowly scowl of cold command and varying numbers of fingers.

Suvaco and two of his travelers, rugged and extravagantly tattooed, bounded into the Matanza kitchen, where they surprised a pair of chefs who gasped and leapt back nearly upturning the scrambled eggs in their pan.

"You're here!" said one of them. "It's really happening."

One of the travelers put her fingers to her lips, made a *shh* sound, and went for the cooking utensils, grabbing the biggest, sharpest knives first. The chefs fled in a flurry of whooping. The travelers then went through the cupboards and pantries, removing all manner of French cheeses, Italian pasta, Iberian ham.

Los barbudos—Kin, The Professor, and Sombrero—were still waiting outside, on the lookout for an ambush. They finally entered the palace, rifles drawn, half-expecting an indoor army to come crashing out from behind the curtains. The Professor and Sombrero hadn't seen a carpet or a wall hanging, an oil painting or a cupboard, for longer than they could remember.

Kin entered gingerly, eyes wide. He touched the coral necklace quickly and padded through the room on the lookout for movement, an ambush, a tripwire, anything. *Control your fear*, he thought, but by now, after the Battle of Matanza Square, he was ready for anything.

The Professor found himself distracted by Matanza's books. There were thick tomes on economics, biographies of historical figures, and novels as fat as cinder blocks, first editions with leather covers and hand-stitched binding. It wasn't the time to admire a library, so he turned his gaze to the shadows and the staircase that led to other rooms.

Like los barbudos, the three Kakurega were cautious. They never entered an enemy dwelling via the front door, so they snuck around the back, searching for an entrance, moving fast, in silence. What they found was a kennel like no other. It turned out the rumors were true. The mayor's six pampered pooches had their own garage-sized room complete with sofas and cushions, gnaw-able desks, and miniature trampoline. On opening the door, the Kakurega assumed these were guard dogs. Then one of the Chihuahuas sidled up to a Kakurega warrior and nuzzled his leg. The men closed the kennel and went on, looking for the back door to the palace.

Suvaco entered Matanza's living room. He walked slowly, steadily, toward a corner. His eyes locked onto something on the other side of that cavernous room. There on a perch: a motionless parrot.

"Madrugada?" he said. "Madrugada?!"

Suvaco's lips trembled. His beloved parrot had been stuffed. Guts pulled out and filled with cotton wool, skin peeled, bones broken and rewired, eyes plucked out and swapped for glass. The monster Matanza had really done it to Suvaco's beautiful, talking, multicolored baby.

Meanwhile, Bashir went up the staircase. He walked straight past a servant, who stood transfixed against a wall, and went quarrying for his prey.

In the grounds of the palace a gardener fled for his life. He'd known the revolution was coming and it wasn't the three monks he was afraid of, nor the knife-wielding, tattooed pirate-traveler who'd appeared without warning. It was that he'd just seen an eight-foot tiger loping past the rhododendrons.

✳

Mayor Matanza was an epic crapper. He would spend hours on the toilet, reading, singing to himself, getting lost in daydreams, reminiscing about those happy days when he'd been able to bludgeon a rebel or two, strangle the odd priest. He was a well-known toilet blocker. Drains would inevitably clog from his log-like productions. Eventually, his household had had to employ a full-time plumber.

And so it was that as his empire was about to fall, he was seated on a golden toilet enjoying his morning ablutions. Because his guards were all poisoned and in any case were not allowed to interrupt him when he was on the toilet, Matanza knew nothing of the rebellion until Bashir, King of the Rats barged through the door. The mayor shrieked. Bashir stood in the doorway, drenched in sweat and smoke-blackened by the earlier cannon fire in Matanza Square. He had a cutlass in his hand and a cigar in his mouth.

Suvaco pushed his way in front of Bashir and Matanza shrieked again. This second was even scarier-looking than the first. His bare chest was blood-spattered, with a patchwork of indecipherable green tattoos under the blood, and his face, already pocked with scratches and scars, was now a mask of new bruises, soldiers' gore, and grime from the street battle. His long hair, released from its ponytail so it hung below his shoulders, was matted and slick with grease. He gritted his teeth and held up the stuffed parrot by its talons.

"Remember my parrot, you son of a whore?"

The mayor, in his terror, dropped the *Matanza Daily News*.

Bashir grabbed him by the neck.

"Me first," he said to Suvaco. Then he turned to Matanza. "Where did you put it?!"

"Put what?!"

"My eye! You took it fifteen years ago! I want it back."

"You're insane," said Matanza.

Kin and Sombrero entered the room.

"Hey," said Kin. "Tie him up, Bashir. No executions today."

Bashir jammed Matanza against the wall. "I'll be taking your eye later. You know what the Bible says."

"Never read it," said the mayor.

At this moment, Kin remembered. The man in the fancy clothes with his dogs in tow. He'd barely seen Matanza between the masses and the bodyguards, the schoolkids and the washerwomen, acrobats and holy wanderers on that beach, barely registered who the man was. But the mayor had stopped by to get his photo taken while the whale clung onto life. And then he'd disappeared with his entourage, the way everyone else had disappeared that day, leaving Kin to push the beast into the water. And it seemed a miracle that the same man was being overthrown by the boy in rags, the homeless kid from the shipping container who'd run for his life not once but twice, first to an island, then to the hills, and flown over the city for his freedom.

Kin stared at the man. Matanza had come alive. He was no longer a vague memory on a beach or a name in the history books Kin had read in the rondavel in the hills. Matanza was in front of him, a trembling wretch in the middle of his morning crap.

They left Matanza to wipe himself, then clothed him in a white nightshirt and led him downstairs, the reek of his unwashed body clinging to him like a curse. They tied him to a chair. Two of the three Kakurega were tasked with watching him. Besides Kin and los barbudos, they were the only ones who could be trusted not to slice him into pieces.

✳

Afterward, the rebels remarked on how disciplined Bashir had been. He could have stuck a knife in Matanza's guts, but he didn't. It was only much later when the rebels did an inventory of the palace that they realized every portrait on the walls had one strange thing in common. Each had an eye gouged out of the canvas, clinically and calmly with a very sharp knife. And only much later, weeks after that tumultuous day, was it noticed that all of the statues of the Matanza family members, which dotted the squares and municipalities of Balaal and were now being pulled down and melted for scrap, also had one thing in common: each was missing an eye—scratched or chiseled out by an unknown hand.

CHAPTER 23

The fall of the house of Matanza—the

rebels convene a meeting—Fundogu

speaks—a leader is chosen

THE RADIO STATION, HEARD ACROSS BALAAL, MADE AN IMPROMPTU ANNOUNCEMENT, "Matanza has fallen." The listeners thought this meant Matanza had fallen over, tripped on his shoelaces, until the radio announcer added, "Balaal is free." And word began to spread.

"Matanza's goose is cooked," said a poultry chef.

"No, it isn't. It's a trap," said a lapsed Trappist.

"No, it isn't. He's popped his clogs," said a shoemaker.

"I heard he's in hot water," said a plumber.

"I think he's bought the farm," said a farmhand.

"What does that even mean?" said the farmhand's dog.

Truth was he was slumped in his chair like a punctured ball.

*

On the street, above the protesters, the bright yellow hot air balloon called Freedum sailed by on its route over the palace. The Bujigangans in the balloon, looking down, saw chaos. Through the palace garden various servants and lackeys were running in different directions, attempting to escape the sinking ship. No one pursued them because they too were part of the revolution, and the rebels on the ground were dispersed into similarly random groups: Cienfuegos and brothers digging up the garden, rat-men scampering, a Kakurega warrior looking for the back door.

On the street, a small group of rebels, led by Iquique, walked toward the palace. Among them was Fundogu in his white gallabiya, fingers clasped together as if in prayer. Close behind them was Jesa on her camel.

A whistle went up and the rebels wandered in through the front gate.

Kin came out of the palace and greeted Iquique.

"We won. We took the palace and we have Matanza. We already sent a message to the radio station."

"And his guards?" asked Iquique.

"Poisoned or deserted. Half of them went home. Some of them are still asleep or throwing up in the garden. Others have already joined us."

"Then it's true," she said. "We won."

"Yes. But what now?"

In all the planning, in all the details and logistics of putting together a revolutionary force from these drunks and illiterates and street fighters, they'd quite forgotten one thing: What happens when you win?

The camel appeared in the garden of the palace, Jesa atop it like a conquering queen. The tiger had been corralled by the travelers and returned to its cage, so the camel was calm even in the confusion.

"We need to convene a meeting," said Jesa.

"Let's celebrate first," retorted one of the travelers.

"No time," said Kin. "Bashir and Suvaco are itching to cut Matanza's throat. And our army is looting the palace. We need to get some order."

✳

With the street party in full flow and the remaining palace guards convulsing in the throes of a mass poisoning, Kin, Jesa, Iquique, Fundogu, The Professor, Bashir, Suvaco, Cienfuegos, and one of the Kakurega met in Matanza's dining room to discuss what to do next. They sat around a huge oak table. Above them a chandelier glinted. Beside them, on the walls, more paintings, still-life works of fruit in bowls, dead fish, and pheasants.

"They must have more troops coming," said the Kakurega. "They have army. Where are they?"

Kin spoke up. "Like I told you all, the mayor's cooks are on our side. They feed everyone who works at the palace. They risked everything to put poison in the food. They took out the Tonto Macoute, the sentries, everyone. Even the guard dogs. From what we can tell, there are no more soldiers and no leadership. The soldiers we defeated in the square . . . that *was* the army. The others deserted. They hadn't been paid for months, ever since The Butcher disappeared. This is it."

"So now what?" said Jesa.

Kin went on: "The first thing is to decide what to do with Matanza. Many will want to see him hanged from a tree."

"I'm one of them," said Bashir.

"No," said Kin. "We put him on trial. Justice, not revenge."

"I'll take revenge," said Bashir.

"It's not your decision," said Kin.

"Wait," said Jesa. "Doesn't justice mean we ask the people? We take a vote."

"No," said Kin. "That's mob rule."

"How the hell do you know so much? You're what, twelve?" said Bashir. "Why are we listening to this schoolgirl?"

"He's not who you think he is," said Jesa.

"He's a child," said Bashir. "Why don't we ask the religious people? The old man." He thrust his chin at Fundogu. "And the nun."

Fundogu and Iquique had been sitting quietly. Fundogu had witnessed this revolution from a distance. His mind was on other matters, for he saw the future. He regarded the affairs of men and women as trivial in relation to the great churning, swirling universe. The tides of the sea, the rise and fall of the sun, which was preparing to consume planet Earth in fire—these were the things on Fundogu's mind. But called into the conversation, he roused himself. He stroked his long fingers down the length of the tribal scars on his cheeks and spoke slowly.

"Matanza will be tried, but not here in the big courts where he has supporters. He will be tried in the fishing village, in the old, disused warehouse. He will receive the same justice as any other citizen of Balaal. He is neither above the law nor the law itself. These things are foretold."

Kin said, "For now, we keep him alive, which means we keep him out of the hands of the people. And then justice will have its day."

"Wait," said Bashir. "The mayor isn't the one we should be worried about. He's an imbecile. It's The Butcher. Where is he? He commands the army. He's dangerous. Until we know where he is, we haven't won."

"I know where he is," said Fundogu. "He's dead. Kin killed him."

"I did?" said Kin.

"His bones are in a cave on the island of the lighthouse by the fishing village. All except his skull. This too was ordained."

Bashir scratched his head. "This boy pushes a whale into the sea and kills the biggest killer in Balaal and doesn't *know* about it?" He turned to Jesa. "And they call *you* the witch. What is he: some kind of magician?"

"He's Kin of the Waves," said Fundogu.

There was a moment of calm. No one except Fundogu knew what it meant to be Kin of the Waves. Even Kin himself was unsure what powers he had, so he too stayed silent. Bashir decanted a finger of whisky from a bottle recovered from Matanza's cabinet and tipped it into his mouth.

Jesa broke the spell. "What else do we do? Who rules? Do we create a new government?"

There was a hiatus and then suddenly everyone began talking at once. Bashir started shouting in his childhood Arabic. The Professor quoted Greek philosophers. Suvaco muttered in an ancient dialect. Fundogu recited verses from a scroll. Cienfuegos started singing. The crows on the roof cawed and rattled. Eventually, Jesa yelled "Shut up!" loudly enough that everyone shut up.

"This isn't going to work," she said. "We need order. And processes."

All faces turned again to the old black man in his white robe at the end of the table. Fundogu sighed.

"Everything happened fast," he said. "There was no debate, no political parties, no speeches, and no plan. That is not how revolutions usually work. The ruler, the one who will lead you, is Kin, the boy sitting beside me. Almost all of you will have a seat at the governing table. A radio station will broadcast the news. Indeed, it is already doing so. And the hot air balloon will fly over Balaal and announce this news through a bullhorn and drop pamphlets in the areas where people can read. Usually a revolution needs a way to control the army, but in this case the army has lost its leader. It no longer functions. The soldiers will not give us any trouble. Many of them have joined us already and more will follow. These things have been foretold."

And so it came to pass that the revolution dispensed with the usual prerequisites. Intelligence systems. Communication lines. Logistics. Succession plans. Instead, the revolutionaries walked in and took over. Their scheme had worked perfectly, all thanks to the palace cooks, who had laced the sentries' meals with poison and fed the guard dogs sedatives along with their raw meat. On top of that, the palace janitor had gone around unlocking padlocks and doors. All the stars had aligned, and now Balaal was free.

CHAPTER 24

The trial—an unexpected guest—

The Plague of Weeping—the Bruja of

Laghouat assumes the form of a fly

THE WAREHOUSE RETAINED ITS AIR OF DECAY AND SEA WRACK, WITH A HALF-WRECKED BOAT in the corner and its mess of buoys and netting. The hole in the roof, through which the sun cast the miscreants in a glorious spotlight, had somehow grown bigger. Meanwhile, the bats in the rafters had doubled in number and carpet-bombed the floor with their zeppelin-shaped pellets. They hung out now, dog-faced, upside down and waiting for the action below to start.

All the leaders were there—Jesa, Kin, Bashir, Cienfuegos, Fundogu, Suvaco, Iquique—as well as the citizens of the fishing village, the usual mix of sailors, cleaners, and people who'd washed up on the beach like seaweed, all scarfing down their popcorn. And for the first time in history, the trial would be broadcast live on Balaal's one radio station, run by a group of young rebels and graffiti artists.

Before anyone had settled, the door creaked open and the crowd gasped. Four men, dressed in black suits, entered carrying a dark-wood four-poster bed. On it, Ochiades was propped up against the headboard. He was all bones. His skin was translucent. His head was as bald as a buzzard. He had shrunk to a child's size except for his nose, which had grown in inverse proportion, a giant red-veined hook, a match even for Hormigonera. From under a moth-eaten blanket, his bare feet, six toes per foot, protruded like the claws of a velociraptor. He appeared to be at least a thousand years old.

No one was quite sure for a moment whether this was a man or a skeleton. He was no longer wearing an oxygen mask but it was impossible to tell if he was still blind, as he had been the last time they'd seen him, because his eyes were unmoving, caged in two black sockets, staring like those of a man in a trance. He was now utterly dwarfed by his military uniform with its epaulettes and six medals that dragged him down, pinning him in place.

The four bearers laid the bed on the stone floor of the warehouse and retreated behind the headboard. The skeletal arm of Ochiades rose, and his voice rang out. "Not guilty!" he cried.

"Ahhh," said the crowd. "Ochiades."

Lambu, his old assistant, stepped forward. As if pulling a lever, he gently moved Ochiades's arm downwards to its resting position, six-fingered hand on the blanket.

"You are not presiding over this trial," said Lambu. "Or any others."

With the slowness of the tides, Ochiades rotated his head to glare at his former assistant-turned-interlocutor. Then he barked like a dog three times and fell asleep.

The four bearers moved the bed to a quiet corner of the warehouse.

Then the real judge entered. Abacaxi, who at two hundred and fifteen years old was the most venerable turtle in Balaal, had also fallen asleep. Exhausted from the all-night post-revolution party, he was lifted from the bed of the truck from which he'd witnessed events and brought in by twelve fishermen, who laid his green-gray mass onto the stone floor.

"Ahhh," said the crowd. "The wise turtle Abacaxi."

Then, for a third time, the metal door of the warehouse opened. The Kakurega came in, leading Matanza by a rope. The crowd murmured. Matanza's wrists were bound and his mouth was gagged. He was still wearing the white nightshirt they'd dressed him in twenty-four hours earlier.

The prisoner lumbered in like an animal, eyes wild with fear. He groaned and hollered his muffled obscenities at this obscure enemy who had rescued him from the wrath of Bashir but then tied him up like a common criminal.

One of the Kakurega warriors led him into the light at the center of the room, in full view of the judge, the jury, and the plain folk, and removed the cloth that gagged him. He let out a series of ragged breaths. The Kakurega, in their black cassocks, sheathed their ceremonial swords and retreated to the edges of an invisible circle.

Lambu approached Matanza.

"Are you Porfirio Fulgencio Melgarejo Trujillo Matanza?"

"You know exactly who I am, you little shit. I employed you for twenty years."

"Please answer the question. What is your full name?"

"Porfirio Fulgencio Melgarejo Trujillo Matanza. Idiot. And I refuse to recognize this kangaroo court."

"You have been treated with dignity?" asked Lambu.

Matanza grunted. His nightshirt drooped to his knees. On his feet were a pair of flip-flops unfit for a fisherman's apprentice.

"You have not been tortured?" said Lambu.

Matanza lifted his wrists, which were still tied. "Untie me, damn you!"

"You have been fed?"

One of the onlookers shouted, "Feed him to the tiger!" The crowd tittered.

Lambu said, "This is a court of law. The defendant will have a fair trial."

A bat swooped down, dive-bombing Matanza, who let out a yelp. Missed him by inches. The crowd guffawed.

"Silence!" shouted Lambu.

Outside, Jesa's trusty camel nuzzled a clutch of dandelion.

"I repeat, this is a court of law. We have established that you have not been tortured or deprived of your rights. Now, what are the charges brought against him?"

There was a shuffling in the gallery. The revolutionary leaders had gathered there, standing or sitting, some with their feet up, others leaning against the makeshift bleachers that had been erected for the largest crowd in the history of the court. The people waved bits of paper, clenched their fists and began their accusations.

One of the Bouazizi shouted, "He bombed our village and murdered our families!"

Cienfuegos hollered, "He exploited the miners for thirty years!"

Bashir yelled, "He destroyed our town and took out my eye!"

Suvaco screamed, "He stuffed my parrot!"

More shouts went up about ransackings and bribes and corruption and assassinations and stuffed animals.

Lambu waved his hands in the air trying to signal "enough" but the shouts got louder. The roof rattled and the bats shimmied. Ochiades stirred and Abacaxi yawned. The Kakurega looked on in bemusement as the crowd bayed. Finally, the people quietened amid a flurry of tossed popcorn.

Lambu folded his arms, stretched to his full, ridiculous height and proclaimed, "We will continue. Now. We'll go one at a time. You. Yes, you!" He pointed at the black, dreadlocked figure of Cienfuegos, hulking and jejune. "What do you have to say against Mayor Matanza?"

"His family exploited the mine workers," said Cienfuegos. "Many of us are starving."

"You don't look like you're starving," said Lambu.

"I'm a freak of nature. My mother and father were wrestlers."

The crowd chortled.

"We were kept working in the mines ten hours a day at gunpoint. When we found silver or gold, we had to turn it over to Escarabajo's men."

Lambu interrupted: "Sorry, who is Escarabajo?"

"Beetle. Matanza."

The crowd giggled.

Lambu said, "You will address the defendant by his name."

"Escarabajo promised us bread, rice and beans, and meat on weekends. We never saw any of this. We were kept like slaves in cockroach-infested dormitories. There were no toilets. Men disappeared if they complained. This happened for decades."

Lambu said, "Mayor Matanza, do you deny any of these charges?"

All heads turned to the mayor, a greasy ball of sweat and frayed nerves in a white nightshirt.

"Who is this man?" he said.

"My name is Cienfuegos. I worked the mines with my brothers for fifteen years. You know every word I say is true. Escarabajo."

"The mine is owned by my family," said Matanza. "The owners of the land have a right to the riches of that land. If a potato grows in your garden, the potato is yours. The same with gold or silver. If there's gold in my land, the gold is mine."

Suddenly Kin shouted from the bleachers, "The land belongs to the people of Balaal! Your family has no rights to it!"

"Silence!" said Lambu.

"Nonsense!" said Matanza. "The land belongs to my family! It has done for generations. We staked a claim and it's ours."

"An illegal claim!" retorted Kin. "And now *we're* reclaiming the land! The miners have already taken it back. Your guards are all dead and the Matanza bank accounts have been frozen. The money from the mines will be redistributed to the miners and justice will be served."

A massive cheer went up. Popcorn flew. The camel, who had finished the dandelion and begun perusing a garbage patch, pushed open the warehouse door with its nose and wandered in. Several bats swooped down and an owl on the roof began to hoot.

Fundogu stared at Kin and knew the prophecy had come true. What unschooled fifteen-year-old raised in a shipping container and fed on scraps, could speak like this, could understand the history of this cursed city? The boy was already the foretold leader.

As the sounds of the trial came crackling out of transistor radios all over Balaal, those who had previously been disbelievers began to believe the rumors. The days of Matanza rule were ending. Across the plains, in all the little pueblos, in the labyrinthine city where Kin and thousands of others had improvised an existence, in the mountains where revolutionaries had set up their camps from branches and bits of tarpaulin, word spread.

When it came to Bashir's turn, the King of the Rats wandered over from his seat, eyepatch secured by black elastic, cigar firmly between his teeth. He stood inches from Matanza, face to face, moustache to moustache, two caciques in a riotous cave.

"An eye for an eye," said Bashir. "Remember what you did to mine? The Night of the Sixteen Daggers. Only you didn't use a dagger." He pulled out a teaspoon. "You used this. And that's not all. When we refused to hand over our money to your soldiers, they ransacked the town and tortured our leaders. In your name. And now you're going to pay."

"Ok," said Lambu. "That's enough. We aren't here to threaten the defendant. We're here to see that justice is served. Bashir, what is your accusation?"

"This imbecile destroyed my town, tortured my people, and stole my eye."

"I did no such thing," said Matanza. "If there were abuses of the law, then I regret it. An army always has its rogues, and if one of my men did that to you, then that is a crime. My intention was to keep law and order and to protect the city. We have never been invaded. We have never experienced a coup d'état until yesterday. Balaal has always lived in harmony. And that is because of my rule and the rule of my family."

"Your family are murderers!" someone shouted from the bleachers.

"No!" said Matanza. "My family kept you safe."

But even as he said the word, a strange high-pitched sound came out of the ether. At first it was indistinct, a wind instrument heard through water. Then it revealed itself: the sound of a woman screaming. The people in the warehouse turned their heads in panic. Where was the noise coming from? Then cries of help rent the air and the sounds of battering, the warp and whoosh of flames, buildings set alight, the cracking of roof beams. Old ransackings. Shouts from the Night of the Sixteen Daggers. Cries from the Slepvak Massacre. The volume rose, some kind of collective memory as all the sins of the regime sounded there in that warehouse-courthouse. It was a recording made and played by the universe, an echo of hell on earth that resounded through time, that was now in the very pores and creases of Balaal—in every building, in every ditch, in every godforsaken pueblo where the regime had ruled. The panic turned to wonder. The music of mayhem was playing in their ears, turning Matanza's pleas to dust.

And when it stopped, Lambu said, "I don't hear much of *safe*."

One by one, testimonies came spilling out. Murders. Massacres. Beatings. There was such a list that a Stygian gloom began to descend on the courthouse. The final testimony came from a tiny chieftain, bandy-legged and in his seventies. He approached to tell his story. On his shoulder, he carried a bag made of woven kauna reeds. He walked straight toward Matanza, stopped in front of him, knelt down, opened his bag and took out eighty twigs, placing each on the floor one by one. He divided the twigs into three piles: men, women and children. Twig by twig, he recited the names of the dead—his tribespeople, victims of a Matanza massacre—returning each twig to the bag as he said their name.

Outside, the building became shrouded in a black cloud that would stay there for years. Inside, the air grew heavy. A bat swooned in the rafters. Several of the jurors fainted and had to be removed from the warehouse. Ochiades, fast asleep, broke into his first sweat for sixty years. Kin, seated near the back with many of the leaders, heard an insistent G minor chord that kept warping out of tune. The noise went from a tremulous vibrato to the incoherence of a crazed wind and grated on his nerves. Even the Kakurega were forced to sit on the stone floor to ground themselves against this pallor brought on by the litany of horror.

From the initial glee of the crowd at finally seeing Matanza in the dock, a quiet, silent shift occurred. With the black cloud enveloping the building, glee turned to anger, which turned to sadness. Soon, the jurors began to weep.

At first, it was just a few salty rivulets let forth by the very old or the very young. But then it became a contagion. Lambu began blubbering. Cienfuegos cried and remembered his grandmother's homemade bread. Bashir wept from his one eye and remembered all the things he'd seen with his other.

Iquique wept so that her nun's habit became spotted with teardrops. El Gato, the deadly blue-eyed sniper, cried so hard his eyes turned gray.

Suvaco held out the longest, his lip trembling for a full thirteen minutes before he too began to wail, and without him knowing it, a tattoo on his chest—the face of an ancestor—began sobbing in sympathy.

The painted saint, propped up by the Bouazizi against a wall of the warehouse, let forth a stream of oily tears from his eyes, down the canvas and onto the stone floor. He wanted to whisper something to Kin but couldn't find his voice in the midst of the testimony of butchery.

Beyond the warehouse, the plague of crying spread rapidly. Men and women in the fishing village found themselves inexplicably blubbering. One fisherman's family bawled so much they produced a basin of salt in which to keep their freshly caught fish.

Soon the plague spread to the whole of Balaal. Traffic stopped while drivers pulled over to wipe their eyes. Shopkeepers closed their premises to avoid the goods being drenched in tears. Lawyers and doctors, acrobats and farmers, no one escaped.

Then twenty-four hours later the sun came out and Balaal dried its eyes and continued as before.

Lambu had been forced to call a halt to the trial, but with the end of the plague of weeping he was able to continue. Only the black cloud that enveloped the warehouse lingered as a reminder of the plague. And once again, Matanza was in the dock.

"We have heard from dozens of witnesses," said Lambu. "The actions of Mayor Matanza and his family have been beyond anything expected. No individual could have known the full extent of this barbarism. What do you have to say for yourself?"

"Nothing," said Matanza.

"Nothing?"

"Nothing."

"This is your chance to defend yourself. Whatever excuses you may have or reasons for your actions, speak now."

Silence reigned. A handful of popcorn flew at Matanza and missed.

Abacaxi stirred and his periscope of a neck extended and retracted again as he nosed the air, caught the scent of salted fish.

Outside, Jesa's camel rubbed its flanks against a wall and stared at the black cloud that had enveloped the warehouse.

Matanza's nightshirt was filthy with sweat. He had a three-day beard and his moustache drooped. His eyes too were hooded and resigned. The weight of all he'd seen and heard—from the ransacking of his palace and the disloyalty of his soldiers to the accusations leveled at him—bore him down and turned him once again into a recalcitrant child. But instead of stomping his feet and bawling, he turned silent.

The crowd was now as sullen as Matanza. Why wouldn't the monster speak? Had the black cloud muffled the world, blotted out its sound? The hecklers went quiet. The victims and the relatives of the victims of the Matanza family, who had come expecting to see the mayor hanged, drawn and quartered, or at least strung up from a tree, now looked on wearily. The bats were morose. Even the popcorn throwers ceased.

All that remained was a judgment. Abacaxi was saying nothing, because he was a turtle. Judge Ochiades had fallen asleep again. Lambu stood alone, all harsh angles, in his black suit and shiny shoes.

"Then we will lock you away forever, a fate worse than death, so you can reflect on your crimes. You will never be released. Just as you snuffed out the light of life from so many, so we now snuff out the light of day from your life. You are condemned to darkness until the day you die. May God help you."

The radio broadcast the verdict. Some were angered. They wanted him shot. Or dismembered. Or they wanted his eyes gouged out with a teaspoon. Others were relieved. A passage of history had ended.

And so it was that many of the heroes of the revolution quietly slunk back to their former lives. Suvaco left the warehouse at the moment of the verdict, clutching his dead parrot Madrugada, without so much as a farewell to the other warriors. Cienfuegos and his brothers whispered to Kin they would continue to fight for the rights of the miners and demand a daily supply of bread, and then they too left.

Most of the Kakurega had already disappeared, gone back to their monastery, and no one knew it because they were as quiet as a trickle of water. They had seen enough. They had played their part. Their world was awaiting them, a haiku of fountains and lawns, low walls and mats, and they had no need to dally in a fishing village so insignificant it had no name.

The rat-men too darted through the village and back to the precious city, with its rich pickings and shadows. They'd seen justice served and that was enough.

The Bouazizi went off arm in arm, shouting "We are the Boo!" Halfway down the street, one of them turned. They'd forgotten the painted saint, who was propped up against a wall in the warehouse. Kin heard the painting whisper, "Beware the one-eyed basher. He wants the crown." And then the Bouazizi retrieved the painted saint, tucking him under a sweaty armpit and lurching out into the sun.

Matanza was led away. He remained as silent as a grain of sand.

The rest of the jury and the crowds of fishing folk gradually stumbled out, finishing off their popcorn and blinking into the light. They strolled back to their scratched-up boats and wooden lean-tos, rickety shacks, and hovels, barely knowing they'd witnessed a historic occasion. Above them, the black cloud hovered, the seagulls yelped, and the hot air balloon called Freedum sailed away into the distance. There were boats to clean and sheets to wash, children to feed and fish to catch. And within minutes they'd forgotten this lark, this blessed revolution, and even as they'd rejoiced in the end of Matanza, the image of him, that devil in a nightshirt, was fading from their memories.

Kin lingered a while. Fundogu had said the boy would rule Balaal. He had just watched his predecessor, Matanza, led away in chains and now, aged fifteen, he would replace the mayor. He stood at the warehouse door and touched the coral necklace. He felt a burden, the whole of the city weighing down on him. He looked up at the cloud that shrouded the top of the building and thought *I must begin again*. Then he left, and walked into the future.

✳

The last figure to remain in the warehouse was Judge Ochiades. His men were no longer his men. The Matanza family had officially been liquidated, erased from the present. Hidden as he was in shadow, Ochiades had been abandoned, lying there in his bed, feet protruding from a ragged blanket.

A fly approached him and landed on his nose. It was the Bruja of Laghouat. She buzzed in his face. He grunted in his sleep. She shot into his ear like a meteor. He awoke with a start. She sat on his eyebrow. He swatted and missed. She returned to the bridge of his enormous nose, looked him in the eye and said in fly language, "Your day is done. You escaped judgment, but not by me. You'll die alone and forgotten."

Then she buzzed off, while he lay in the dark, a living skeleton, a rattle of bones and white skin.

CHAPTER 25

A strange discovery underground—

the silencing of the clocks—Mukashi

Banashi

It was the miners who found it. They'd already dug a hole under a wall to get into the palace garden, but once Cienfuegos's shovel hit something hard, they kept digging. They found a catacomb under the garden of Escarabajo's palace. It was arranged in two rows facing one another, with a walkway in the middle. Cold stone and cobwebs. Each cell ten by ten feet with no windows to let in the light.

When they found the catacomb, they also discovered ancient skeletons slumped against the walls in some of the cells. Political prisoners. And bizarrely, a worm-eaten wooden leg in another. They called coroners, anthropologists and archaeologists, one of whom said the wooden leg had belonged to Matanza the Mad, the earlier dictator long dead.

They dug some more and found instruments of torture. In an anteroom they discovered a Judas cradle, a crushing wheel, knee splitters, and a rack. They saw a row of skin stripping whips made of hemp fibers dipped in salt and sulfur and a shrew's fiddle like a violin that gripped the neck and the wrists.

The skeletons were from different eras. Some dated back over a hundred years. They removed them and buried them in public cemeteries and pondered what to do with the catacomb-cum-torture chamber.

Now they had their answer. It was the perfect place to keep Porfirio Fulgencio Melgarejo Trujillo Matanza. Escarabajo among the escarabajos. A home away from home. Or at least a spot under his own garden.

The remaining Kakurega warriors took Matanza to the palace in a truck. They opened the trapdoor Cienfuegos had discovered, which led down to the catacomb, and ushered Matanza through it. Then they left him in a cell and locked the door.

His night sweats came regularly and his dreams were full of ghosts. His collection of clocks ticked and tocked and chimed in his head until one day even they stopped, fell into silence as Time abandoned him. His dogs too were gone.

His jailer was a retired Kakurega warrior named Mukashi Banashi. He was a small man who trod lightly, but he liked to jangle the set of keys at his hip and he whistled like a bird. The jangling and whistling kept Matanza sane. The scraps Banashi fed him kept him alive.

Once a day, Mukashi Banashi would bring food and a clean chamber pot to the ten-by-ten cell. He never said a word to Porfirio Fulgencio Melgarejo Trujillo Matanza, neither in greeting nor torment. Silence and darkness would be the prisoner's lot.

CHAPTER 26

Visit from Fundogu—Amador

(spitting image)—bury your

enemies—mammoth tusk

KIN'S ADOLESCENCE DISAPPEARED LIKE SMOKE IN THE BREEZE. AFTER THE JIBES OF LOS barbudos and Bashir, now his jaw was grizzled, and he outstripped them all in height, could shoot as straight as Gatillo, and read like The Professor. He spoke all the languages of the fishermen of his youth and knew the streets like he knew his own face. With the help of Iquique, Lambu, and the nuns, Kin would run Balaal.

"So now you'll move into this palace, shaman," said Jesa. "You've come a long way from that shipping container."

"No," said Kin.

They were outside the warehouse that wasn't a warehouse.

"What do you mean no? You're the chosen one."

"Not exactly. We're turning the palace into a museum. The Professor will oversee the work. So I'll stay in the servants' quarters. But first, we're going to fix up *your* house."

※

Jesa's shack was rickety as a stick. The Tonto Macoute had bashed it every which way, and now it swayed when the wind came in from the ocean. Kin and Shadrak, who was handy with a hammer, spent a day repairing the damage and Kin found himself back on Jesa's floor. It was no place for a ruler, but Kin didn't care. After the nights on the island of the lighthouse and in the cave of Zugarramurdi and then in the hills with los barbudos and in a prison cell with The Professor, Jesa's home was paradise. Once again he awoke to the wash of the waves and the screech of seagulls.

That same day, the day after Matanza's trial, Fundogu came to visit him. The old man had aged during the revolution. The march to Matanza Square had hollowed him out. So too the sound of gunfire and the smells of smoke and tear gas. His sparse hair had faded to a layer of white bristles and his torso had thinned so now he stood bent like a sapling in the wind. Jesa was at work, so he sat in her chair, cradling a glass of water Kin had brought him.

"My days on earth are numbered," he said. "You will be a fine ruler, but there is a mystery you need to solve. I must tell you about Amador."

"Who's Amador?" said Kin.

"Jesa's husband. He was a fisherman. But before that, he was other things."

"What other things?"

"He traveled the world. He was the most educated man in the village. He knew about art and books. He went everywhere and saw everything. He hated the Matanza family. You are taking up his work. Somewhere in here, somewhere in this house, you will find a photo of him. Ask Jesa. I know she has kept something from his life. The mystery is how he died."

Kin held his breath. He could hear the sound of a lone cicada chirruping in the underbrush near the beach.

"Ask Jesa about Amador," said Fundogu. "He was a great man. Then find out what happened that night. His boat crashed into the rocks and his body was discovered with it. But he was a fine sailor and he was not a drunk. Jesa will never be at peace until she knows the truth. This is how you will repay your debt to her."

"So *you* don't know what happened to him either?"

"Some things are hidden even from me."

With that, the old man heaved himself up off the chair and stood at the door.

"Meet me tomorrow at sunrise," he said. "I will be at the cannons. And you will be on your way to the palace. It is time to take your place."

✳

When Jesa returned, she found Kin waiting for her. She'd gone back to wearing the black headscarf, keeping her white streak covered. She looked no less beautiful, but she was tired and stank of fish scales and sweat.

"Do you have a picture of Amador?" Kin asked her.

She threw a plastic bag full of cleaning cloths onto the floor and sat down where Fundogu had sat. Water widows never talked about their dead husbands. But because it was Kin, and because she figured it was Fundogu who had told him about Amador, she got up, went to her bedroom, and pulled out from under her bed the wooden chest that was full of Amador's possessions. Its surface was chipped and weathered, and the lid sported a painted shell in blue and black, the paint coming off in flakes, the lock long rusted.

"Take your time," she said. "These were his things. There are photos in there."

✳

At first rummage, Kin saw postcards of European cathedrals and old works of art. Stiff portraits of Renaissance-era dukes and kings. There was no writing on the back, just the pictures themselves.

Under them was a handful of books. They were battered with maresia, the damp air of a seafarer's dwellings, and dog-eared with constant use. Some had cankers of mold discoloring the covers. There were books about art and architecture, myths and legends, novels, philosophy. It was as if he were back in the library in the mountain village of los barbudos, the rondavel at the foot of Mount Naranco. The books were small editions, sturdy but light, published by CJ Derguteleser of Berlin and Jigyaasu Books of Bangalore and Le Corbeau of Paris, the type of books a wise sailor might carry on his voyages.

Kin flicked one open at a random page and began reading. It was a philosophical treatise translated from Surzhyk into English.

Beneath and among the books were maps. Kin picked them up gingerly. There was a seventeenth-century scroll made of hemp and linen that depicted the East Indies and a scrap of vellum and wood pulp that showed the Straits of Gibraltar. Most were seafarers' maps with illustrated mermaids and giant squid and one with a hand-drawn image of an aspidochelone, a giant spiny whale the size of an island, which lived only in myth.

Under the maps, he found a smattering of photographs, mainly black and white, squares and rectangles curled at the edges. They felt like playing cards. He lifted the first he found and thought he was looking at a mirror. A young man of indeterminate race, brown-skinned, straight black hair, Negroid-Asian-Caucasian, a mix of everything under the sun. The man appeared to be eighteen or nineteen, just a few years older than Kin, squinting at the camera, a serious gaze, head cocked to one side. Although the photo was grainy, Kin saw clearly his own features.

"Your spitting image, shaman," said Jesa.

"He died in a fishing accident, didn't he?"

"Yes," Jesa said. "But we don't talk of these things, especially not to a newly baptized sailor. It brings bad luck. There are some who say you shouldn't be staying under this roof even for one night."

"Do you believe them?"

She paused. "No. But you have other things to do. Balaal is waiting. I showed you his possessions because you asked. Now we can leave the past behind."

She packed away the books and maps and old photos. "Go and rule Balaal, shaman. Work your magic."

"Wait," said Kin. He breathed deep. "He's my spitting image. You said so yourself. Is he my father?"

"No," said Jesa. "That doesn't add up. He died long before you were born." What she didn't tell him was that some in the village believed in reincarnation, that Kin might be Amador reborn. Or that some said the boy's mother had been a bruja, a real one, not like Jesa herself.

※

On quiet days, Kin could hear every movement of the fishing village. The keel of a boat oscillating in the water. The sounds of engines and cranes in the distant harbor. Walking the beach before sunrise, he could hear the underwater undulations of the caudal fins of fish. He could tune in to the snapping of a crab's claws, barnacles turning in their shells, the air pulsing through a seagull's syrinx to make that accursed caw.

Now, on his customary morning walk, Kin heard the cooing of pigeons.

He looked up and saw a dozen of them on a telephone wire. He thought to himself, pigeons are deranged. Nodding waddlers. All of their evil was in their talons. The rest of them was pure *tontería*, blessed ignorance.

Near the two cannons, Fundogu sat on a rock facing the water. Like Kin, he was a great listener, and now he heard the boy's footsteps.

Fundogu turned to the boy and said, "A disaster is coming."

Kin stared at him. The sun was rising out of the sea.

"What disaster?"

"I will not be here to help you. Jesa will help. The nun and the Professor too. You will have to organize the people. Some will need evacuating. There will be a reckoning with the past. Things that were buried will rise to the surface. These will be difficult days. It has been foretold. Go to the island. There are secrets in the caves. You are Kin das Ondas. You have one more wave to come. Beware the one-eyed man."

The sun lit up the old man's face and he fell silent. Kin knew instinctively what Fundogu was doing. The old man was listening, but not for the things everyone else listened for. He was listening for the rustle of pampas grasses five hundred miles to the south. He was listening to the rumblings of volcanoes and lava flows in Tzorberter ten thousand miles away and the cracking and calving of glacial ice flutes in Xavanire. Above all, he was listening for an echo—the echo of the breath that heralded the birth of the universe. It was out there somewhere among all the dead stars.

After the silence Fundogu began rambling.

"Day will become night and night will become day and the rivers that ran with blood will run dry and you will walk their beds with leaves and stones, and. . ."

As he rambled, he began to rise off the rock. There was air beneath him.

He kept talking. Half of it was riddles, the other half advice. He said again and again there were difficult times ahead. He told Kin to look in the warehouse. He told Kin to bury his enemies, let them rest among the dust that bore them, lest they come back to life. He gave detailed instructions of how to find a crypt in the mountains, a place Kin would need to visit. And he said evil is like an onion: it grows from the inside.

Kin understood the words—*bury your enemies, go to the island, look in the warehouse.* He made out those words like seeing hidden shapes in a cloud even though the old man's voice commingled with the wind and the sound of the sea.

By now, Fundogu was taking his leave. He was six feet in the air. Then ten. Then twenty and next to the tonto pigeons on the wire, who were jerking their heads like mechanical toys. He seemed to be sailing away from earthly things, the pleasure and pain, although the truth was he'd left them behind years ago. A cabal of conspiratorial street dogs eyed him and pronounced in dog language that he was Undog-Unbird-Unman.

Kin saw him as an angel flying in a white gallabiya. Not balancing on currents of air but on some other substance, something unheard of and unimagined. The last thing Fundogu said was, "Love and honor this world, for you have known no other, and remember: everything begins and ends in the sea."

Then he was gone.

✳

That morning Kin found the tusk of a woolly mammoth washed up on the beach, its surface cracked and mottled by sea erosion. He took it to Jesa's house, but found her fast asleep and dreaming.

He would forever associate the tusk with Fundogu, both ancient things now bereft of life. He left it beside her bed and pondered the words of the wise man. He realized the revolution was just the beginning. Trouble would find him wherever he went. Without touching it, he felt on his collar bone the coral necklace Fundogu had given him. His talisman. He would need it again.

Quietly, he put his few possessions in his backpack and left Jesa's house. Balaal was waiting. And so was Silmiya in her truck.

"Hey!" she called. "They told me you needed a ride to the palace. Get in."

And he did.

CHAPTER 27

Ochiades in the warehouse

For twenty days and nights the Bruja of Laghouat taunted Ochiades in the warehouse. She came to him in the form of a fly, a spider, a scorpion, a snake. She slithered and crawled along his limbs and threatened all manner of torture while he lay there starving. She tormented him so much that on the twentieth day she took pity on him.

He was barely able to talk by this stage and had become reduced to his most basic animal state, and what the bruja saw was not another monster from the Matanza family but a small child. She saw in him the boy he had once been, spindly as a grasshopper and bullied for his big, snotty nose and six-fingered hands. And so she came to him in human form. She brought him water and wiped his forehead with a cloth. She realized he didn't have long for this world and she saw fit to ease him gently into the next. And thus she forgave him his corruption and his part in the Matanza dynasty.

The warehouse was still surrounded by the dark cloud of mourning, which produced an unbearable humidity inside. So the Bruja of Laghouat conjured a breeze to blow away the dull, unceasing heat.

She spoke to Ochiades in Latin, then Ancient Greek, then in other languages Ochiades had known in former lives, and he responded by nodding and saying *ah*. She told him stories involving a Solomon-like judge whose wisdom always saved the day and folk tales he'd known in childhood which always ended justly, with the suffering of the bad, the emancipation of the good, and the martyrdom of the unlucky. Once she sang a canticle in a voice so sweet his twelve fingers began to dance.

The third day of the Bruja's turning, Abacaxi wandered in. He was now the size of a tank and moved at the speed of the great glaciers. He sat at the foot of Ochiades's bed chewing on a fern. In his eyes was the great indifference of all animals to the human realm, but his presence provided Ochiades with succor, and he stayed a while, occupying the far corner of the warehouse, and once the fern was done, he nibbled on the last of the spilled popcorn from all those months ago and listened to the bruja's tales, a diversion, a respite from the usual crime stories he'd heard in court.

The bats in the rafters were long gone. They'd escaped from the profound heat and sadness brought on by the cloud of mourning. Now they returned for one last swoop and glare at Ochiades. They came in through the hole in the roof—although, in truth, the roof was by now more hole than roof—and saw a collection of rattling bones and papery skin, blind, deaf, and half-starving. But they also saw he was changed. His aura was that of Ochiades, but a different Ochiades, one almost purged of sin, one with the innocence of a newborn. With that knowledge, they flew away in chiropteran confusion, leaving the bruja alone with the judge.

CHAPTER 28

Cataclysm—drought—Hormigonera

makes her move—Bujiganga lights

the way

THE FIRST SIGN WAS THAT THE ANIMALS REVOLTED. HORSES REARED UP AND BROKE THEIR reins and bolted into the shadows. An obscure bird clamored all night. Dogs paced long into the small hours and barked at the moon. Scores of fish washed up on the beach, some still floundering. Crabs scuttled inland.

As the sun came up, a crack of lightning sounded, like the snapping of a ship's mast. Gargantuan raindrops followed, first like tears, then lightbulbs, till they anonymized themselves coming down in a squall of gray mizzle that drenched Balaal. Blankets of rain fell like strata.

The people huddled against the storm. In the city, they made lone dashes from canopies to doorways, porches to porticoes. The hawkers suddenly produced a slew of umbrellas as streets went blurry with the deluge. Traffic rolled by, kicking up dirty waves.

The downpour was incessant, blasting through windows or creeping under floors, sousing the houses and bodegas of Balaal.

Across the land, in the pueblos and villages and farms, the people stood imprisoned in their huts, watching bars of rain fall from the roofs like stalagmites. Their animals cowered and shivered in pens. Cataracts and hurricanoes drowned the rocks and drenched the steeples.

The rain was followed by a windstorm, the wildest seen in Balaal in a hundred years. It bent the trees diagonal. It sent roofs spinning, blew down chimneys, and on it carried lamentations and prophecies and strange screams of death. Balaal stood at an angle of forty-five degrees.

In the makeshift harbor in the fishing village, the skiffs turned and turned, bumping one against the other. The houses were closed up, shuttered down, like a child closing her eyes against the dark.

But the worst was yet to come.

Following the deluge and the wind, there came ten months of drought. The earth dried up and cracked. Thick fractures cut across the fields, made a mosaic of the land. Cattle, reduced to little more than a collection of moving bones, lay down and died. Rivers disappeared and revealed hundred-year-old hunger stones. On one was inscribed the message "if you see me, weep." Bushes burned.

In the city, the air went shaky. Heat gripped the roads and the tarmac melted. Birds dropped dead from the sky and cats tiptoed off the tin roofs through the gutters and into shade.

"Things that were buried come to the surface," said Kin to The Professor. "That's what Fundogu told me."

Fundogu was right. A few hundred yards from the shore, shipwrecks poked out of the sand and were stripped clean for treasure by human scavengers, relatives of Bashir's rat-men exiled from the city and now picking the bones from the ocean's carcasses. The wrecks were galleons, centuries old. They were littered with the skeletons of conquistadores and moldy detritus of sea journeys: sextants, compasses, the spines of logbooks.

The remnants of older civilizations began to rise from the underland. Burial plots surrendered their bones. A town long drowned in ash re-formed its shape.

With the ocean receded, Hormigonera poked her head out of the lighthouse window, saw nothing but dry land, and walked across the seabed. It was covered in shells and sea wrack. Her limbs were thin as ever and now her formerly distended belly was shrunken too, from days of hunger. She made it to the harbor at nightfall, where the fishing boats lay aground like disused toys. In the dark, she smelled children sleeping in the shipping containers. Starving as she was, she passed them by. She didn't look back, not once, at her abandoned kingdom, the island of the lighthouse, where she'd been imprisoned. She took the shadows when she could and limped to the port, her gammy leg trailing.

She walked and walked under cover of darkness till finally she wandered into the city and got lost among all the other godforsaken citizens of Balaal with their parched throats and cracked skin.

✳

The people resorted to their old methods to ward off the weather. In Sklonište, a lamb was sacrificed, and its entrails placed in a bowl that was taken to the Altar of the Three Marias. There, the priest delivered an incantation to summon the weather gods.

The alchemists mixed mercury and the venom of a rare scorpion into a gold cauldron and saw in the mixture all the chaos of the world. Shamans whispered in the temples. Someone tried to find the Bruja of Laghouat, but she had transformed herself into a breath of wind passing through the high boughs of trees.

A team of thaumaturgists from Kandisha tried to build a weather machine using springs, levers, pulleys, and a guitar string. A Voodoo priest blew mapacho smoke into the sky and made a spell in archaic tongues.

Thousands across the land began praying to rocks and stones, bowing before tree trunks, and burying talismans: shards of bone, petals, cowrie shells. They implored the gods as their crops failed and begged their children to stop shriveling even as the children's eyes turned hollow with hunger. Some blamed Kin, for such suffering had never occurred under the Matanzas.

Only the Bujigangans were able to combat the drought. They built windmills from junk and constructed solar panels, which were unheard of in Balaal. With these sources of power they diverted underground water and used irrigation techniques learned from their ancestors to keep Bujiganga from extinction. Their engineers then traveled around Balaal advising on how to recycle smithereened materials and access the hidden water.

Meanwhile, the nuns arranged for a fleet of trucks to take water from the mountain lakes all the way down to the towns in the valleys and to the city center. Where there were no roads, they used the Freedum balloon to take water and tools to the city's outposts.

"This is God's own work," said Iquique, and she remembered her first love, the one painted on the church walls, the one on the cross.

Kin was by now in the palace in the heart of the city. There, he met daily with Iquique, Lambu, The Professor, and the nuns.

He oversaw his tasks so obsessively he forgot to sleep. Days and nights passed and he never grew tired. No village or pueblo was left untended. Those who saw him at work began whispering.

"He never sleeps."

"He's a hero."

"He's a brujo."

"He's a shaman."

"He's a whale whisperer."

The nuns themselves were too busy to gossip. Ten months flew by in a blur of labor. With Fundogu gone, they were the guiding lights showing Kin the way. He commandeered a group of ex-soldiers to cement over the cracks in Balaal's roads so the trucks could transport water, and he worked with the mad geniuses in Bujiganga to spread their irrigation techniques. Remembering his lessons from los barbudos in the mountain village, he taught others how to divine water.

Through it all, he tried to remember Fundogu's words: find out how Amador died, go to the island, bury your enemies, look in the warehouse. And when fatigue began to overcome him, he remembered other words, the words he'd heard in the cave: *I am the ocean. I am the four winds. I am the stars that guide the living. I am the memory of the dead.*

CHAPTER 29

Bashir on the move—

metamorphoses—theater—

The Place Where the Four Roads

Converge 2—raindrop

It was during the time of the drought that Bashir, King of the Rats launched a coup.

He gathered his follower-scavengers from Sklonište and told them, "That boy is no more legitimate than the Matanza family. He's on the throne because an old, dead priest said he should be."

Next, he went to recruit the Fanatics of Bouazizi. Their fighting cocks had escaped in a storm and now the men huddled against the weather in the run-down church, bored and hungry. Worse still, their painted saint wasn't talking to them, which meant he was in a huff. Bashir bashed on the door and ascended the pulpit.

"We're taking the palace. There are pantries full of food. More fighting cocks than you've ever seen. The city is ours. Who's coming?"

They'd won the insurgency of 98. They'd helped kick out Matanza at the legendary Battle of Matanza Square. Now they'd take the city with Bashir, because anything was better than drowsing in the musty pews of that church.

✳

The following morning, Bashir's ragtag army marched down the streets of Balaal. The Bruja of Laghouat, in the form of a dragonfly, saw them and thought of all the dead warriors who walked upside down beneath the surface of the land, the soles of their feet touching the soles of the feet of the living rat-men from Sklonište and the bedraggled Bouazizi.

The guns and knives they now carried were barely updated versions of the guns and knives carried by those soldiers from earlier times, when battle had been waged with Chinese fire lances made of paper and bamboo, ribaldis and flintlocks. Now the weapons of war hanging from shoulder straps poked above the line of men like minarets in a cityscape.

They were driven on by songs and chants of "We are the Boo!" and they ignored the spectacular stench, a mix of sweat, gut rot, and moldy feet. At their head was the lumbering ox Bashir, his face shrouded in a fog of cigar smoke. He limped because he had a quarter-inch piece of shrapnel lodged in his thigh, courtesy of the Battle of Matanza Square, but he was indomitable, or so he told himself.

The new regime had dismantled Matanza's system of spies and the Tonto Macoute, but there were few secrets in Balaal, and sure enough, up above, the pilot of the balloon called Freedum soared and saw them. Street hawkers hawked and gawked at them. Ex-spies espied them. Idlers eyed them. And word spread rapidly: Bashir was on the move.

On they ploughed through the heat of the day. With each passing minute the marchers grew weary, lips cracked, skin scorched, legs heavy as trees, because there was no drinking water and the city was parched. But worse than the heat, during the drought Balaal had once again begun to change shape. A road that had led to the palace melted away. Steep streets rose and rose and never descended. Avenues turned into labyrinths from which there was no exit. An area of woodland on the outskirts of the city expanded despite the absence of rain and swallowed up a neighborhood. It pushed its roots deep below the surface of the earth and began drawing on an underground lake that had been there for forty million years.

Where once roads had led to other roads, now they ended abruptly, terminating in mounds of impassable rock or vegetation so thick no light shone through.

Balaal's metamorphosis disoriented Bashir. He went left instead of right. Up instead of down. He crossed a bridge and turned around and recrossed it. He marched by accident into a doughnut factory. He assailed a rundown stable. He inadvertently invaded an ice rink. The street signs were no use. Matanza Square was now called Liberators Plaza. Matanza Boulevard was Camel Walk. Matanza Park was Madrugada Meadow.

Several times Bashir stopped to ask directions.

"Where's the palace?" he said to a street hawker.

"That way. As the crow flies."

But the crow wasn't flying and that way led nowhere. The city was crooked as a camel's teeth.

With the troops flagging, a soldier suggested they send a reconnaissance party to find the way. Bashir agreed. Three of his fastest, smartest rat-men ventured ahead while the others waited in a shady grove. But the three men got lost. They took six wrong turns, climbed two wrong hills, crossed three wrong dried-up rivers, hitched a ride going the wrong way, and soon found themselves in a different city entirely, where no one spoke their language. They were discovered dressed as monks wandering a highway several years later, still looking for the palace.

Worse, the shady grove where Bashir was waiting with his army turned out to be bewitched. Within the hour his soldiers were asleep and transmogrified. Some grew monkey's tails. Some grew fins. Some turned lizard-like with scaly skin. Some grew wing stubs. Some grew fur. Some barked in their sleep and some would purr. Bashir himself turned into a whale with a blow-hole where his eye patch should have been.

As the spell wore off, the men resumed their former shapes and one by one awoke to the smell of the poppies and chamomile which had induced this strange sleep. They recounted outlandish dreams as they staggered to their feet and tried to remember what they were doing in this shady grove.

Only the painted saint, propped up against a tree, witnessed everything and nodded to himself.

"No good will come of this," he said to the tree.

✳

Kin, meanwhile, was ensconced in an anteroom off the palace, the playroom where Matanza's dogs had once cavorted. He heard Bashir's army before he was told about it. Sounds came to him now in the form of snatches of instrumental music. Hoots and thunderclaps, wails and booms. The army was marbles rolling on a snare drum. Bashir himself was the incessant honking of a bass clarinet, the most untrustworthy of instruments, the sound of the universe guffawing.

The betrayal was no surprise to Kin. Bashir reeked of ambition. The painted saint had warned Kin long ago, "Beware the one-eyed basher. He wants the crown." Fundogu too had warned him. *What is a king of rats? A rat himself. A fool leading fools. And which king doesn't want a bigger kingdom?*

Kin felt a pang of fear. He, The Professor, Iquique, and Jesa spent their days trying to send resources to Balaal's poor. Mountain communities were forced to venture into the city for succor. Bears and lions were seen rummaging in city trash cans. With such blight wrought, what use did Balaal have for another conflict? But Kin felt it in his bones: another battle to wage, more blood to spill.

And he had no army. The soldiers from the Matanza regime, having survived the revolution, had deserted and melted away into their communities or found work at the ports or building roads and bridges. Kin would have to beg the Kakurega and the miners, los barbudos and the travelers to come again and fight.

✳

Bashir turned around and stared at his men. They were drooping like wet leaves. Some sweated waterfalls. They barely had the strength to lift their feet off the ground let alone conquer a city.

"Damn it," he said to one of the Bouazizi beside him. "We can't attack today. Look at these idiots."

Bashir stared at the sky. A few birds flitted. The sun was going down.

"We have to find a place for the night. We'll attack tomorrow."

A collective sigh went up as the news trickled down. Men leaned on walls. Sat in the shade. Wiped their brows. At Bashir's command, a small group went ahead to find a place to sleep.

They came across a dilapidated factory with a large open floor, but it had been colonized by feral rabbits with the jaws of dogs. Next, they found a public park with trees for shade and dried up fountains. But this reminded them of the shady grove where they'd been bewitched, and one of them felt the presence of a bruja, so they moved on.

Next, they reached an old theatre and broke in through a side door. There was a stage and aisles in which the soldiers could stretch out. There were working toilets, exits and entrances, high ceilings which meant the air circulated. It was perfect. The only thing standing in their way was a janitor.

"Who are you?" asked the janitor. He was a negro in his seventies, leaning on a mop.

The three rat-men considered their options.

"I said, who are you?" the janitor repeated. "You can't be in here."

"We're using this place tonight," said one of the rat-men.

"Nobody told *me*," said the janitor. "What are y'all, a vaudeville troupe? Classical? Shakespeare?"

"Yeah," said the rat-man.

"Which?"

There was a pause. The janitor dipped his mop into a bucket and made a large circle in the dusty floor, then began mumbling to himself. "Ain't nobody tell me nothin'," he said. "Nobody say they a vaudeville troupe comin'. Nobody say we openin' tonight. Nothin'. They'll want me clean out them changin' room. Nobody tell me nothin'."

Gradually, the circle of water on the floor disappeared. And so did the janitor. He'd been dead for sixty years, but he still cleaned the theatre and went to the shows, standing at the back applauding loudly.

One of the rat-men was spooked by the janitor's disappearance, but the other two shrugged. They'd seen too many dead men and brujas to be worried about a specter with a mop.

"This place will do," they said, and laid down their weapons.

*

Bashir's army wandered into the theatre and those that weren't immediately flat on their backs and asleep began exploring the premises. They discovered a cache of stage makeup and wardrobes full of costumes. Soon the faces of the Bouazizi were painted like clowns or geisha girls, caked in grease paint, lips curved into bows of cadmium red. They dressed in nineteenth-century bustles or full evening dress with stick-on bow ties and shiny shoes. One became a monk and another a cowboy. Two wore tutus and ballerinas' pumps. From the prop cupboard they pulled out hoses, rubber batons, replica revolvers, a plastic skull, Damascene swords, a dial-up telephone, and lanterns with handles and fake candle wicks. They lolled on the stage furniture, rearranged sofas, armchairs, coffee tables, cabinets. Someone was banging away on an organ, someone else thumping a drum.

Worse, the Bouazizi discovered a stash of liquor in a glass case. A collection of novelties. Ghanaian vodka, Indonesian crème de menthe, Slovakian aguardiente. The festivities began. Bashir came in, saw the pageant, and rolled his eye.

Then there was an omen. The King of the Rats reached into his breast pocket for a cigar and to his surprise discovered nothing but the soft flesh of his chest under his faux-military tunic. He was out of cigars. He limped through the city in search of a tobacconist.

*

By morning, Bashir was ready. His cigar stock was replenished and he'd slept a full night in the theater's aisle. He ordered the men to take off their makeup and costumes and retrieve their weapons. They put on their boots, ditching the ballet shoes, high heels, Roman sandals, and tap dance brogues.

Bashir pushed open the entrance, his men behind him. They were met with a blast of sunlight and city noise. Guagua buses sped by, churning up black smoke. A truck snarled.

The previous day Bashir had consulted a map to plot his route to the palace and now he began again the triumphal march. Glorious days lay ahead, he said to himself, and visualized a banquet in the palace, a speech made from a balcony, a parade on Bashir Square.

✳

Kin tried to raise an army. The Kakurega weren't playing ball. They'd already helped rid Balaal of one dictator and lost four men in the process. Now the idiot with the eye patch was throwing his hat in the ring. They'd only returned home a few months ago, and the drought meant they had work to do, digging new wells to source underground streams or harvesting figs and tomatoes. When they weren't doing that, they were in prayer.

Gatillo too said no. He was back in the mountains. They woke him up in the moonlit makeshift schoolyard where he slept on a banana leaf mat. He was in rags, had abjured all possessions and renounced violence. He didn't even hunt rabbits any more, just ate whatever the land gave him.

"Soy el profesor," he said. "No puedo quitar los estudiantes. Ésto es todo. Everything we fought for."

He embraced The Professor and waved a book in his face. "Remember this? This is the weapon now. Son tus palabras, profe."

They couldn't find Cienfuegos and his brothers. The seven giants had gone deep into mining country, the wilds of Balaal. There they expropriated the mines, one by one. Many of the foremen had no idea the revolution had taken place. They were still whipping the miners and stealing their gold. Once Cienfuegos and his brothers brought news of the revolution, the foremen ran. Some begged. Some prayed. Some were beaten with the tools of their trade. Some took off to the wilderness, their houses burning behind them.

Suvaco and the travelers were in no state to help. They had lost two men during the revolution and now in the accursed heat their tiger had grown sick. The giant beast had turned rheumy and melancholic. Its eyes drooped and its face was freckled with flies. Besides the tiger, the travelers were trying to feed their children. At the fairground, food was scarce and the people had no energy for another war.

"Bashir, huh?" said Suvaco.

"Bashir," said Kin.

"I knew he was trouble. Never trust a one-eyed man."

The fighters in The Fishing Village with No Name also said no. They'd seen their homes ransacked time and again, defied the Matanzas at the courthouse-that-wasn't-a-courthouse, and risked their lives at the Battle of Matanza Square. They'd transported cannons and an ancient turtle there and back, borrowed carts and horses from neighboring farmers. Now they just wanted to catch fish to sell in the market and live out their days in peace to the sound of the ocean.

Kin had Balaal's lone radio station make a call for soldiers to fight Bashir. He used the Freedum balloon to drop fliers urging Balaalians to join him. But Balaal was asleep. The heat had driven the people into Lethe, a sea of mourning and forgetting. Those not out drilling or dowsing for water sat comatose in the sweltering shade dreaming of rain. Like the travelers, the fishermen, the Kakurega, and Gatillo, they had no stomach for another fight.

In the end, the only warriors who came were Sombrero and Jesa and a few Bujigangans recently returned from their tours of Balaal building windmills and solar panels. Among them were engineers and inventors, but their dragon had been disassembled and the fake tanks were out of commission.

Sombrero came in from a pueblo where he'd been teaching farmers to read and write. He carried a rifle and was still wearing his hat.

"¿Necesitas mi ayuda, compa?" he said to Kin. "Como siempre."

"So this is it," said Jesa. She dismounted the camel. "A nun, a teenager, two teachers, and some tinkers. Do we have a Plan B?"

"We're working on it," said Kin.

"What would Fundogu do?" said Jesa.

"Levitate and philosophize."

Even as he said it, Kin remembered there was a secret weapon lying somewhere out of reach. A levitator of a different kind, with guns and a bomb chute. Where was that Fokker when it was needed?

✳

Across a field of pampas grass now turned yellow. Through a brass gate tinted with verdigris. Over a crumbling drystone wall hand-packed and spotted with lichen. Past neck-high weeds which still clambered in the drought. There. There in the long grasses. A Fokker A.III M16 Hybrid, built in Schwerin, Germany in 1916 by a Dutchman. Wood and steel. Red and black paint job. Iron crosses on the wings.

"There she is," said Kin.

The tip-off from a former Matanza soldier was correct. The plane was sprouting weeds in a field. But when they tried the engine, it was dead. They called in an engineer from Bujiganga. She twiddled nobs and oiled gear sticks. Nothing. They called in a retired mechanics professor from Sondaj. He took measurements, poked and prodded with a chisel. Nothing. They called in a shaman from the hills. He blew mapacho smoke over the controls and said an incantation. Nothing.

"This plane won't fly," said Kin. "It's rusted to hell, and we're out of time."

They returned to the city center.

✳

When Bashir and his men arrived at the grounds of the palace, they were parched. They lay down in the shade of a tree-lined avenue but didn't sleep because they were terrified of being bewitched again and growing animal parts in their slumber.

Once he'd caught his breath, Bashir said, "Get up. We attack now. We're minutes from victory. There are no guards. Just as before, we walk in through the front door and take over. Are we ready?"

He looked at his army. A fiasco of sudor and grime, red-eyed, swatting at flies. But Bashir clenched his fists and stuck out his chest and gradually his soldiers rose to their feet.

They came to the high gate of the palace. Bashir pushed it open. They walked in. Nobody and nothing. Not a solitary guard. They walked under the portico and came to the main door, which now had a wooden plaque saying Museum—Under Construction. The door was locked.

"Museum, ha!" said Bashir. "They're hiding inside."

He kicked at the door, which came open with an explosion of dust and splinters. They walked in.

The first thing Bashir saw was an oil portrait on the wall, a Matanza dictator, with a hole in the canvas: an eye gouged out, Bashir's own handiwork. The building was bathed in a strange silence. Where was everybody? The child ruler? The nun? The woman with the streak in her hair? The revolutionary in his stupid keffiyeh with his straggly beard? Bashir braced himself to fight but the place was empty. All he could see were one-eyed portraits on the walls and glass-topped tables with little plaques. The museum. Objects of all kinds: maps, dogs' leads, a shield. It was a chaos of clutter, a scene from a Bujigangan junk yard.

One wall was assigned for the recent revolution, adorned with black and white photos of The Battle of Matanza Square, some from the ground up, others from high buildings looking down on the scene. One was from behind the fire-breathing dragon flanked by those fire-eaters.

There were artefacts too. Shovel Belonging to the Rebel Miner Cienfuegos of Bocadelin. Sword Used by the Kakurega. Vintage Grundig 505 Record Player Used to Confuse Matanza Army. Stuffed Parrot Called Madrugada Which Belonged to Rebel Leader Suvaco (Replica).

"We can reminisce later," said Bashir. "Where are they? The boy and those women."

In vain they looked. They combed the upper floors. They scouted the kitchen. They turned the bedrooms upside down, hauling thick quilts off poster beds and rummaging in man-sized wardrobes. There was nobody there and no noise save a constant prattling of antique clocks on the wall and the men's footsteps crashing around the faded luxury.

Bashir stood at the top of the staircase and announced, "I, Bashir, hereby proclaim myself leader of Balaal."

No one applauded. The rat-men were too busy rifling through the kitchen, and the Bouazizi had found a stash of whisky.

"I said, I, Bashir, hereby proclaim myself leader of Balaal!"

Not a whit.

He tried the words of a former Matanza.

"I, Bashir, hereby proclaim myself His Mighty Highness, Conqueror of Balaal and the Surrounding Towns and Lord of all the Beasts of the Earth and the Fishes in the Sea."

The Fanatics of Bouazizi huddled around the booze, backs to Bashir.

"We need to invade the radio station," he said, "and find a goddamned megaphone."

He was about to sit down when the phone rang. It was an old-fashioned hand-dial, ivory colored, with a receiver the shape of a dog's bone. The Bouazizi didn't know what it was, but Bashir was a man of the world and he picked it up immediately.

"It's me," he said. "His Mighty Highness, Conqueror of Balaal and the Surrounding Towns and Lord of all the Beasts of the Earth and the Fishes in the Sea."

"Bashir, this is Kin."

"Where are you?"

"Meet me in one hour, where the four roads converge. Just you and me."

Kin hung up. Bashir thought to himself, the Conqueror of Balaal and the Surrounding Towns and Lord of all the Beasts of the Earth and the Fishes in the Sea doesn't take orders from children. But he decided to go anyway and to take his army with him. What use was a title if no one knew you had it? And what fool would walk into an obvious ambush without an army even if its soldiers were currently draining the dregs of Balaal's finest hooch?

＊

There was only one landmark in Balaal that everybody knew. The fishermen knew Socorro Point, because that's where they were baptized; the soldiers knew Liberators Plaza, formerly Matanza Square, because it was the center of the city, where the giant statue had fallen, and where a dragon had roared; rebels knew Mount Naranco because that's where they ran and hid every time a Matanza wanted their head. But everyone knew The Place Where the Four Roads Converge. It was now little more than a grassy hummock with a rock in the middle, but it was the spot where Balaal had been founded.

It was point zero, where a traveler had lain his head, so far from home, so broken by wars and bloodshed. He was lost, his horse long abandoned to the vultures. Dry gore coated the man's feet up to his ankles. There, that traveler looked to all four corners, smelled water in the earth, heard the distant thunder of ocean waves, and saw the silhouette of a mountain range blurred by sunrays. He fell asleep to the sound of bird squawk and frog croak and dreamed of the great city of Balaal.

Years later he buried his bloodstained shoes at that very point and the mud turned red. After the town was founded, they built four roads off that central hub: one to the river, now dried up in the drought, one to the sea, one to the hills, and one to the wastelands, where, reputedly, the devil played dice with his underlings. They say a city founded in blood always remains in blood.

Now it was midday. The sun burned down from directly above.

＊

"Bashir will kill you," said Jesa.

"Only a fool would face that madman alone," said Iquique.

"Do you even remember the revolution?" said The Professor. "He brought dynamite and knives. He had landmines. He'll use them if he needs to."

Kin looked calmly at them and felt the coral necklace against his chest.

"If you go alone," continued The Professor, "how can we protect you?"

"You're not protecting *me*," said Kin. "I'm protecting *you*. And the city."

Kin stood up. He was no longer a boy. He towered over them all. He had filled out and grown strong while no one was looking. Those days spent hauling nets, eating Jesa's food instead of scraps from the street, the days recuperating in the mountains at the papery hands of the old woman who fed him, meant he had become a warrior instead of a fisherman. Even those days cooped up in a prison cell sustained by nothing but water and bread had failed to wear him down. As a boy, he'd broken into warehouses and stowed away on trawlers. Now, as a man, he was strong enough to work all night for months on end and to take on the King of the Rats face to face, may the best man win.

"I'll be armed," he said. "I'll be ready. Come along if you want, but stay in the shadows."

And the shadows was where Bashir now waited. From there, he could see through a pair of binoculars The Place Where the Four Roads Converge. The city had expanded to the east, so the meeting point was on the outskirts of Balaal, and, despite its history, the area was run down. There were derelict stores, a warehouse, a littered park. Only a massive boulder at the center of the roundabout told the tale. On it were inscribed the words: "De hac urbe condita est sanguis hominem." From a man's blood this city was founded.

Bashir stood under a tree. His army was convened behind him in a faux Roman phalanx, facing outward, weapons drawn. They were down to twenty-eight men and half of those were drunk.

At the appointed hour, Kin arrived. He was wearing army fatigues and scuffed boots.

"Stay here," Bashir said to his soldiers.

He let the binoculars hang down from the leather strap around his neck, felt the gun in his holster, and walked into the light toward the boulder at The Place Where the Four Roads Converge. Kin walked from the opposite direction and they met in the middle, the earth under their feet cracked and still tainted with the red of that first warrior's bloody shoes.

Kin greeted Bashir: "I hear you want to lead Balaal."

Bashir squinted at Kin and appraised him. No weapon, but the boy was now as tall as him.

"You're illegitimate," he said. "No one elected you and you didn't win the revolution alone. Why are you our leader?"

Kin said nothing.

Bashir went on, "Do you have Matanza blood? Is it your birthright to lead us? You have no more right to the throne than I do."

"I have no throne," said Kin. "I'm not a king."

"But everyone says you're our leader," said Bashir.

Kin kept his eyes on Bashir's hands. The King of the Rats looked fat and slow and he had a piece of shrapnel in his leg, but Kin had seen him in battle.

"We offered you a part of the city," said Kin, "for yourself and your men. Remember? It has a water supply and roads. There are trees and fertile land. If it ever rains again, you can run it as you want, as long as you obey the law. We already offered you this, remember? But the next we heard, you were marching to the palace with your army."

"You haven't answered my question," said Bashir. "Why are you our leader?"

"Because Fundogu decreed it. He said it was the prophecy."

Bashir let out a hollow laugh. "You're illegitimate," he said. "And you're a child. Did you rescue your people when their town was bombed? Did you comfort them when their families were murdered? What have you ever led?"

"I led the revolution which overthrew Matanza. You know this because you were by my side. I planned it with Jesa and Iquique. I dreamed it when I was in a cave and then in a prison cell after the first failed attempt."

"The revolution is done," said Bashir. "It's finished. Move out of my way and I'll spare your life. Go back to the fishing village where you belong. You're a fisherman. You can grow old with all the other octopus-eaters. Go home."

"No," said Kin. "I am the ocean. I am the four winds. I am the stars that guide the living. I am the memory of the dead."

A silence passed between them. A remembrance of blood and war. The fire of the dragon's breath in Matanza Square. The toppled bronze horse and rider.

Bashir had a gun in his holster and a knife in his belt. But while he hesitated, the sun retreated behind a cloud and then a drop of rain—the first in ten months—landed on his forehead. Bashir fell to the ground with a thud. His limbs didn't twitch and he uttered no soliloquy. His heart didn't slow to a halt and his life didn't flash before his eyes. He was dead as a stone, killed by a raindrop.

The Fanatics of Bouazizi stared from the shadows. They broke off from their phalanx formation and approached slowly in ones and twos. Like Kin, they were dumbfounded. They looked for the gunshot wound, the geyser of blood. They looked for a poison dart or a rock fired by a slingshot. But they saw nothing because there was nothing to see except a trickle of water on Bashir's forehead, his own personal Nazaré which had washed him off the face of the earth.

In the shadows on the other side of The Place Where the Four Roads Converge, Jesa, Iquique, Sombrero, and The Professor watched in confusion. Bashir was on the ground but they'd heard no gun blast and had seen no attack.

A few of the Bouazizi began wailing. Some dropped their weapons. The remaining rat-men ran back to the shadows and disappeared.

The raindrop that killed Bashir was followed by a steady drizzle which turned into a torrent. All eyes in Balaal were raised to the heavens. In Bujiganga the people rattled pots and pans. In the fishing village they sang to the sky god. In Qo'zg'olon, the miners ditched pickaxes and danced a samba. In the Valley of the Lepers, they strung up tarpaulin between trees to catch the water. In Andantino Dolente, feral cats yowled. Every sound in Balaal was now drowned out by the beautiful hiss of the rain.

CHAPTER 30

The rat-men and the Boo begin to

forget—la bruja—burial—days of

peace and prosperity—Jesa returns

MANY YEARS LATER, A FAMED PUPPET SHOW WOULD DEPICT BASHIR'S REVOLT AS A COMEDY, his army a troop of drunk lollygaggers, vaudevillian villains, lounging indolent on the yellow grass, sunbathing or napping before the imminent attack. They'd get up and trip over cobblestones. A seagull would crap on their heads. They'd shoot themselves in the foot while trying to load their guns. It was the insurgency as slapstick, with the figure of Bashir as the hero-clown blundering in broad daylight toward the palace and succumbing to a raindrop, God's fallen tear.

Only Kin of the Waves understood that Bashir had given his life to bring water to Balaal. Nothing else could have killed him, indomitable as he was. His death was the price of the rain that ended the drought.

✳

Not one of the rat-men or the Bouazizi thought to remove their fallen leader. Even as they turned their backs, their memories began the cleansing brought on by the deluge and by his demise. Who was the one-eyed basher? Why had they followed him in the first place? What was that fetor that stuck to him in death? Could not even the rain annihilate the smell of Macanudo cigars?

They departed to make new homes somewhere in the city. They went in clusters, taking different routes, for there were four roads that converged at the point where Bashir's body lay. Some headed for the sea, others the river, others the hills, and others the wasteland, where the crows cawed long and loud and the devil played dice.

And as the rain came down, the body got drenched. The deluge clung to Bashir's moustache in tiny transparent globules. It turned his military fatigues dark. The binoculars still hanging from the leather string around his neck tipped into the mud like a discarded bauble. His eyepatch was soaked. His beret, rain-battered and crumpled with its own weight, slipped off Bashir's head leaving him exposed to the torrent. His blood turned to clay.

The muddy floor where Balaal was founded now became soft as if beckoning the King of the Rats inside. His massive back formed an indent. Gradually he started to sink.

The Professor, Sombrero, Jesa, and Iquique came out of the shadows to share in the jubilation of rain but also to see what had happened to Bashir.

"What now?" shouted The Professor, as he approached Kin and the fallen rebel.

In the old days, the victors would have tied the dead man to a stallion and dragged him through the streets. They would have left him on a hill for the vultures and hyenas. No gravestone, no marking, not even a wooden post. His name like his flesh tossed to the four winds to be forgotten.

"I can't hear a word!" Kin shouted into the rain.

But Kin knew what to do. He bent down and tugged at Bashir's body, which was sinking into the rain-battered soil where the four roads converged. Using all his strength, he rescued the dead man from this impromptu interment and hauled him over his shoulder in a fireman's lift. To be drowned in earth with no ceremony was almost the same as to be left on a hill, a humiliation saved only for the worst, for the most depraved.

"Are you sure he's dead?" shouted Jesa over the downpour. She could see no blood and had heard no shot.

"Feel his pulse," said Iquique.

"He's dead," said Kin, and he staggered toward shelter—the awning of a shop—where he placed the body in a sitting position against the wall.

Out of the deluge now, Jesa said, "Did you kill him?"

"No," replied Kin. "He was killed by a drop of rain."

And Jesa watched the boy and thought: he pushed a whale into the water, he killed The Butcher, and now he's ended a revolt without spilling blood.

"Shaman," she said, "a drop of rain?"

The inundation turned the sky gray. And from the mizzle, a form appeared but only Kin saw it. At first, he thought it was an eagle or a pterodactyl, but finally he recognized it. Fundogu, way up in the air. Through the blast of rain the old man's spirit shouted, "Heed my words! Find Amador's killer. Bury your enemies. Go to the island. Look in the warehouse."

"I'm going to bury him," said Kin.

And then the rain returned to being rain again.

❋

Fundogu's ghost wasn't the only interloper at the scene. Besides the rat-men and the Bouazizi and Kin and his compatriots, someone else was there. In her previous incarnation she'd been a falling leaf, and before that a dragonfly, and before that a breath of air. Once, a crocodile. Many times she'd taken the form of seagulls, serpents, spiders, dogs, and a fly around the head of a corrupt old judge. Now the Bruja of Laghouat transformed herself into a drop of rain and went hurtling into the face of the enemy. Truth be told, she was aiming at his one working eye, but her coordinates were wrong and instead she landed on his forehead. All the force of a thousand years of brujeria condensed in that watery missile and dropped the would-be despot where he stood.

The bruja then took off, saluting the shade of Fundogu as she went up and he came down.

❋

They wanted to throw Bashir into the nearest hole in the ground. They called for an unmarked grave, and The Professor said Bashir would live on in ignominy, a footnote in the history books.

"He was a traitor," said Jesa. "That will be his legacy."

Even as they spoke, a radio presenter announced that Judas was dead. A puppeteer began sewing a black eye patch and a fat cigar. A graffiti artist depicted Bashir barefoot with a dunce's cap and a dog turd hanging out of his mouth. A troubadour composed a song about the one-eyed turncoat.

But the boy remembered that Bashir had served nobly in the revolution. Kin borrowed a farmer's horse. He slung the dead body over the back of the giant Brabançon and headed for a crypt in the mountains. The others protested, asked him where he was going at this moment when the rain had finally begun to fall. He brushed them off.

Up in the mountains beyond Naranco, there was a necropolis. It took a full day of riding to reach it, but by now Kin knew his way around the hills. His mountainside vigil among los barbudos had taught him everything. He could navigate by the stars or by the sounds of the wind. He could build fires in the dark and survive on the flesh of cacti. And when Fundogu had told him where to find the crypt, he'd listened.

He came to the land of the dead just as the rain eased and saw the necropolis: a collection of twelve buildings on a steep hillside. They looked like outhouses with pyramidal roofs. They had been erected in the thirteenth century in the middle of a plague. No nails were used, just stones and slate, for on nails the dead might snag their clothes.

Inside the buildings were piles of bones dozens deep. This is where Bashir's ancestors lay and this is where Kin would bury him. He peered inside one, through the window slat, and saw bones stacked in a wooden boat and knew this was Bashir's family crypt. Bashir's people had believed that to get to heaven you had to cross a river.

Kin untied the corpse, pulled it down from the horse, removed Bashir's clothes and belongings, pushed open the wooden door and laid the body in among the bones. *Bury your enemies*. In the crypt, he saw a jug made of clay and dropped Bashir's last box of soggy cigars inside it. Then he turned, mounted the horse, and rode away. Truth was, after ten months of battling the weather and now facing down Bashir, he needed time in the mountains with nothing but the company of a horse, the singing rocks, and the vast skies. A whole life spent fighting solitude, and now he realized he needed it like he needed air.

✳

The end of the drought and the end of Bashir heralded new days of peace and prosperity in Balaal. The transformation of the palace into a museum was complete. Kin officially moved into the ante-room where Matanza's dogs had once lived, and other anterooms were found for members of the new government. They turned one into a nunnery for Iquique and her accomplices. Lambu became minister for law and order.

The Professor founded Balaal's first university and called in his barbudos to teach there. They were, after all, the most educated people in Balaal, readers, theorists, and philosophers. The Professor also started a newspaper. It was the first in Balaal for a hundred years that didn't publish solely Matanza propaganda.

Jesa, too, moved into the palace. She met with Iquique every day and governed. But after a few months, she visited Kin in his room. She was wearing her black headscarf once again. Her days as a revolutionary hero were finished.

"I miss the ocean," she said.

"Me too," said Kin.

"I can't stay here. In any case, you don't need me anymore."

"That's not true."

"It *is* true," said Jesa. "You're a man. I don't even cook for you. You have enough food. You and the nuns can run Balaal. It was your destiny, so fulfill it. I need to go back to the village."

Kin saw there was no point trying to persuade Jesa to stay. They went outside. The camel was laden down with trunks and bags, cotton sacks, a battered suitcase.

"Is this all?" asked Kin.

"My stuff is still in the house by the sea. But I left some things here, for you. They're on my table."

"What things?"

"Go and look for yourself."

As she mounted the camel, she removed the black headscarf and shook her hair loose. The streak of white hadn't thickened. She was still beautiful, still his surrogate mother.

"Tell me one thing," she said. "Are you a shaman?"

"You asked me that once before."

"And I'm asking again. There must be a reason Fundogu called you Kin of the Waves. Can you control water? The wave that rescued the whale. The drop that killed Bashir. They say you can divine it in the mountains. Are you a shaman?"

He shrugged his shoulders. "Ride safely," he said.

"I will."

"I wasn't talking to you."

The camel snorted. Jesa and Kin smiled and waved goodbye.

CHAPTER 31

The Wonderer—the taming of wild

horses—The Fishing Village with

No Name—Shadrak and the boat—

the warehouse—the burning of

Ochiades's bed—Jesa

THE TRUNK FULL OF HER HUSBAND AMADOR'S BELONGINGS WOULD RETURN WITH JESA TO the fishing village. It was on the camel's back. But some of its contents she left for Kin: the books, postcards, and maps. He took these to his room and pored over them and wondered what was beyond the mountains, over the sea, far from Balaal where Amador had been. And he wondered if he'd ever find out.

But mainly he wondered when he would go back to the Fishing Village with No Name. Every time he tried to go, something came up with the running of Balaal. The nuns—the worker bees—had everything in hand, but now that he was a man they refused to make any decisions without his consent. And he refused to make any decisions without consulting others. This he had learned from the Kakurega. With The Professor, Fundogu, and Jesa gone, he consulted Lambu or Iquique. Sometimes, he consulted books. Matanza had left a library and Kin spent much of his time dipping in and out of history and politics and philosophy. It was a habit he'd picked up during his sojourn in the mountains with los barbudos.

He thought of returning there too, to the rondavels of Naranco where the rebels had hidden out. Did that little settlement still exist? He wanted to see the hands of the old woman who had fed him, to thank her and tell her she'd saved his life. But somehow time never allowed it. The born skedaddler could no longer skedaddle.

He thought of Silmiya, the woman with the flower in her hair and her hands on the steering wheel of the truck. She would be with her brothers farming the land and taking provisions to those who needed them. He thought to himself, she was the truest revolutionary of us all.

✳

One afternoon he heard a commotion in the stables. He went to investigate and found a group of horse trainers in the paddock trying to rein in a magnificent beast. It was sixteen hands high, tawny brown, sleek and strong, its mane streaked with a shock of white, the fiercest stallion in Balaal. No one had managed to tame it. Kin watched the trainers trying to calm the animal, but it reared up and kicked.

As he watched, Kin understood that the beast was afraid of its own shadow.

"Let me try," he said.

The horsemen looked at him. They were squat and brawny. They'd spent their lives handling animals.

"Be careful," said one. "Stay away from his hooves. If he kicks you, you're dead."

In the paddock, among the horsemen, Kin turned the stallion to face the sun. Now its shadow was behind it. He whispered in the horse's ear just as he'd seen Jesa whisper in her camel's ear and slowly climbed onto its back, stroking its flanks and keeping it eye to eye with the sun. The horse was now his.

*

Years passed and then one night he mounted that same horse and directed it toward the ocean.

The journey was shorter than he'd remembered. All those years ago, when he was a child, it seemed like an odyssey, a trek for heroes. Now it was a matter of hours.

He circumnavigated Shamans' Hill, which overlooked the port. Then he passed Socorro Point, where Fundogu had baptized him, and he glanced at the two iron cannons which faced out to sea. Those too: heroes of the revolution, now returned to their daily duty. He recognized the smell of the ocean and heard the waves lashing at the pilings of a wooden dock.

He arrived in the village as the first rays of sun began to pierce the gloom, and he patted his horse and whispered in its ear.

Nothing had changed except himself.

In the distance he saw a pair of Japanese fishing skiffs and the fishermen hauling in their catch. To the east, he saw an Indonesian jukung listing gently, its double outriggers extending like a grasshopper's legs.

He tied the horse to a post.

He took the same route he'd always taken every morning, for years, combing the beach for whatever the sea regurgitated. As he walked, he saw in his mind's eye the impossible mass of the whale and remembered it as an optical illusion, a trick played by the universe on the universe. Above all, he remembered its smell, the incredible goulash of oil, rotting flesh, and sea debris. He remembered the teeming crowds, the mayor and his dogs, Fundogu in his white gallabiya, harlots in fishnet stockings, acrobats, and priests. How they'd pushed at the whale's back and failed to drive it into the sea.

He reached up now and touched the necklace, two strands of red-brown coral he'd never removed.

He took off his shoes and felt his feet plunging into the soft sand. He shifted his line to the edge of the water where the sand was darker and his stride turned into footprints. A few delinquent dogs nosed their way onto the beach, sniffing at the ghost-smells of scuttling crabs.

He needed to borrow Shadrak's boat.

He found the man, like everything in the fishing village, unchanged. The little pot belly, the mess of a cigarette dangling from his lips.

"Hello, Shadrak," said Kin.

The old man was cleaning his boat. Leaning beside the transom, he looked over his shoulder. Then he straightened, did a double take, and spat out the nub of his cigarette.

"Has it been that long?" said Kin.

Shadrak stared at him.

Kin shrugged. "It's me. Kin."

Shadrak kept staring and then he muttered, "Can't believe it. Can't be." And he kept muttering.

"Shadrak! It hasn't been that long. What, eight years? Ten? I need to borrow your boat."

Shadrak stared at him a little more and then, as if awoken out of some reverie, said, "You be baptized. You be a sailor already. But no. I no let you. My boat my livin'. You no take it without me. Where you wanna go?"

"Will you take me?"

"Depend where you wanna go."

"To the island."

"The lighthouse again?"

"Yes."

"I no been there for years. Since I took the priest."

"Fundogu?"

"The same."

Shadrak finished scrubbing and turned and stared some more. "You be standin' there. You go see Jesa. But I warn her first."

"Warn her?"

Neither of them moved.

"Ain't nobody tell you, Mr Kin?"

"Tell me what?"

"Ah, nuttin'. You wanna go now? To the island?"

"Yes. If you can take me. It's an old promise I made to Fundogu the last time I saw him."

"Wait up. I be needin' coffee and gasoline. Then we go."

✳

The boat bumped across the breakers. Kin waved to the fishermen coming the other way: the lean Somalis, the Japanese lit up like waxworks in the morning sun. They waved back but didn't recognize him.

A breeze came in off the ocean. A line of seagulls flew past, emitting their echoed hark.

The boat pulled in at the tiny bay and Shadrak tied it to a short wooden pylon. Kin sniffed the air and climbed the hill that led to the abandoned lighthouse. The building was barely white any more, its paint having peeled off in the intervening years, but the rubble at the foot of it remained. Kin said to himself, "Nothing survives but the rock."

Shadrak waited outside as Kin walked up the steps that led to the entrance. The door was no longer a door, but a concatenation of splinters. He went in and looked up. He saw the inverted bowl of the cupola, its paint flaked and fragmented.

He looked in all the rooms of the lighthouse but saw nothing but the husks of dead insects and the bones of birds. He was puzzled. *Go to the island.* Fundogu's words, a decade ago. But there was nothing to see.

Kin remembered escaping from Hormigonera and The Butcher and his soldiers, but it was long ago, the time of his baptism. What remained?

He left the lighthouse and walked toward the water.

"Do you want to wait for me in the boat?" he said to Shadrak. "I won't be long."

Kin retraced his old steps. He saw the opening to the cave where he'd hidden from The Anteater and The Butcher. It was no longer filled with water, and he walked in gingerly. He remembered the A sharp of the cave, which he heard again, and the acrid smell of Hormigonera. He remembered shivering in the dark. He remembered the caw of a lone seagull from the cave's exterior wall, telling him to escape.

Now he paused to let his eyes adjust to the gloom. The sand was firm under his feet and he stepped in further.

He saw it almost immediately. At the back of the cave, a skeleton. Or more than one. A collection of bones like a wrecked glockenspiel. Spines leading to the domes of skulls. He saw there were several, clambering over one another or clinging on in death. Was it the remnants of a massacre? He moved closer.

It was only when he saw the rusty weapons poking out of the sand that he realized who they were. His would-be killers. Among them, The Butcher. There were rumors they'd disappeared.

They'd never returned to their vehicle, which had been reclaimed and stripped by human scavengers in the village. The word was that Mayor Matanza had planned to ransack the village to look for his brother.

Kin returned to Shadrak's boat.

"Do you have a shovel?" he asked the old fisherman.

"No. No shovel in the boat. You be wantin' bury those men?"

"You knew?"

"Came here with Fundogu. We saw they skeletons. I say best leave them be. The dead are the dead. They no disturb nobody out here."

Kin borrowed Shadrak's metal bucket and with it dug a deep and wide crater in the cave. Then he interred the bones of the five men, covered them up afterward and kicked the sand level. He knew one day soon the water would dredge them up again, but for now they were at rest. In the mass of bones he'd seen that one skeleton had lost its skull, but he had barely paused. For him, the island had become a cursed graveyard, a place to die.

When he returned, covered in sweat, Shadrak was lighting a cigarette and looking out to sea.

"It beautiful here, early mornin'," said the old man.

"Yes," replied Kin. "But let's go. This place is cursed."

Shadrak switched on the engine and they sailed back to The Fishing Village with No Name.

✳

Kin walked the familiar route to the courthouse-that-wasn't-a-courthouse. The sea air calmed his blood and dried his sweat from the day's labor of burying the soldiers.

He passed the line of fishermen's homes. These hadn't changed in the years since he'd last been there: wooden shacks or tall, thin buildings of many bright colors, barely faded. Outside, on the street, early as it was, the fishing folk had begun placing the signs showing their catch.

A few minutes later, he arrived at the warehouse. Its higher echelons could not be seen because the cloud of mourning persisted, shrouding the roof and louvers like a girdle. On the outside it had become even more dilapidated. Graffiti artists had done their work on the walls, depicted scenes from the Popcorn Rebellion and the Battle of Matanza Square and the depredations of the storm and the drought.

Obscuring the edges of the graffiti was a lamina of maresia: sea rot and fungus turning green to black, and the weeds outside the building were higher than ever despite the drought. An underground source of water had fed them—the residue of Balaal's Plague of Weeping during the Matanza trial.

Kin pushed at the huge metal door and heard the creak as it slowly swung open. *Look in the warehouse.* The heat and the smell of rot hit him immediately. The four-poster bed where Ochiades had lain was in a state of decomposition. Its posts were cracked and splintered. Its blanket had turned a shade of brown and acquired a layer of dust and leaves and animal droppings. The old man was nowhere to be seen.

A flood of images returned to Kin. He remembered the first trial, when Lambu had been on the wrong side. He remembered the turtle Abacaxi, the oldest living creature in Balaal. He remembered the second trial, that of Jesa, which had ended in the Popcorn Rebellion. But above all he remembered the aquiline profile and the cold, dead eyes of Ochiades. Kin had been a child, but even then he'd understood what Ochiades meant in the world. Which is why, aged eleven, he'd escaped from his own trial as the fishermen protected him with their filleting knives and fluked anchors.

Now he combed the warehouse. Nothing. The same junk as before: moldy netting and buoys in the corner. The wreck of a skiff and the four-poster bed.

With the help of Shadrak and a couple of other fishermen, Kin dragged the bed to the beach. They chopped up the wood and stacked it high. Shadrak added a squirt of gasoline and they burned the last existing possessions of Ochiades. The smoke rose into the sky in black wisps and the late afternoon breeze took it over the village. A few loping dogs sniffed the smoke and came to inspect the bonfire. They were joined by a small crowd of onlookers—the village's random collection of mendicants.

"You go see Jesa now," said Shadrak. "She be angry if she know you here all day and no see her."

Before visiting Jesa, Kin returned to the warehouse. Why had Fundogu insisted he look inside? There was nothing there except the empty bed and the flotsam from the village. He looked again, this time more closely. He looked up. The hole in the roof had grown wider, letting in the sun. What he couldn't see were the two bats in the rafters. Even if he had seen them, he would have been none the wiser; there were always bats in the rafters. He would never have known that one of these was the Bruja of Laghouat and the other Ochiades himself transformed. Nor did he know that it was the bruja who had come to him as a seagull on the ledge of his prison cell and hatched a plan to rescue him via the Freedom balloon, or that it was the bruja who had killed Bashir, or that this bruja was his mother, who watched over him in her many forms, the bruja who was also an enemy of the Matanza regime, and who, for the price of having a child, could never appear to that child in human form, such were the ways of her coven. Indeed, she had now lost the craving to appear in human form at all, for she preferred the ways of bats.

As Kin turned to leave, a movement caught his eye. Someone or something behind the wreckage of the skiff.

"Hey," he said and walked closer.

He heard a rustling. Suddenly, from behind the rotting beams of the boat a boy crept out. The boy was in rags, not more than ten years old, rubbing sleep from his eyes. A born skedaddler. The boy looked at him and scampered to the door. Kin chased after him, but the boy was too quick. By the time Kin was out of the warehouse, the boy had disappeared. Furtive, skinny-limbed, rag and bones. Kin looked both ways down the street and then stared at the cloud around the upper perimeter of the warehouse, that covering of smog which had been there a decade.

Had he imagined the boy? It didn't matter, because at that moment he thought he understood why Fundogu had sent him there. He remembered his childhood, the nightly shuffle for a space, a corner of a shipping container, a dry patch under a bridge, the weeks on end in bus shelters and on roofs, braving the bats and wild weather, the night winds and whining mosquitoes. *This will be a home for the homeless. We'll move those children here and feed them fish every day.*

He walked away, glancing to and fro, wondering if the boy was somewhere in the shadows watching him.

*

He knocked on Jesa's door, and when she opened it, she fainted. He caught her and carried her inside, laid her on the bed, and found some water. By the time he returned, she was sitting up.

Kin said, "It's me. What's going on? First Shadrak, then you."

Jesa said, "I thought you were a ghost."

Silently she reached into a drawer and pulled out a photo of Amador, her drowned husband. There in the picture was the very image of Kin. The resemblance, which Jesa had noticed in Kin's adolescence, hadn't fully materialized until now, now Kin had become a man. The same brown skin, the same cheekbones and deep-set eyes. The dead fisherman born again.

He sat down.

"It seems I'm everywhere," he said. "I just saw a kid in the warehouse. He looked like me. He escaped before I could talk to him."

"What?"

"Never mind. We have to demolish it and start again, build a homeless shelter."

"But it's a warehouse and a courthouse. It's not equipped. It has no kitchen, and no. . ."

"We can do it," said Kin. "We overthrew Matanza. We killed The Butcher. We escaped from a high security prison in a hot air balloon. We kept Balaal running through the drought. So we can turn a warehouse into a home. Will you run it, bruja?"

"Yes, shaman."

＊

With the burning of Ochiades's bed and the conversion of the warehouse, pieces of Balaal's history disappeared. But there was more. The statues of the Matanza family that dotted Balaal, each with one eye gouged or chipped out by the hand of Bashir, were now torn down *en masse* as the city set about trying to forget its past. It was only in the museum at the former palace, with its artefacts of the revolution and notes on the many crimes of the many Matanzas, that Balaal's history remained alive, but no one visited. The people were too busy living their lives and tending to their future to worry about the past. And, in any case, Balaal's past was told in stories and songs, not museums.

CHAPTER 32

Trapdoor—Matanza and the

regulating of clocks—ghost—Nazaré

KIN OPENED A TRAPDOOR. HE HAD LED BALAAL FOR A DECADE AND LIVED IN A BUILDING OFF the former palace, but there was one place on the grounds he had never been. He descended a line of steps which led to darkness. He paused a moment to let his eyes adjust. There were four candles attached to the stone walls and these were burning, emitting a faint smell of beeswax. In the summers the prison took on the heat of imus, the underground ovens they used in the wildlands. In the winter, icicles froze on the ceiling. Only one prisoner lived in the catacomb.

"He crazy," said Mukashi Banashi, and the old Kakurega warrior-turned-jailer pointed to his own head and did a circling motion with his finger.

Kin nodded and left Banashi at the trapdoor. He had tried the archives, spoken to fishermen in the village, and interrogated former members of the Tonto Macoute, but he still didn't know the truth about Amador's death. He finally figured there was only one way to know for sure, and that was to ask Matanza.

He smelled the old mayor before he saw him. The fetor of rancid skin. Escarabajo had turned into Ochiades without the hook-nose or the sixth finger.

Porfirio Fulgencio Melgarejo Trujillo Matanza was seated on the floor of his cell, cross-legged, in the white nightshirt he'd been wearing ten years before, which was no longer white and was in shreds. Even in the dark, Kin could see the prisoner was no more than a starving conglomeration of bones and sores, a wretch lower than the animals.

Matanza raised his head. He had smelled Kin too. And heard him. From the footsteps and the lack of jingling keys he knew it wasn't the jailer.

"Who are you?" said Matanza. His voice was little more than a croak.

"Kin of the Waves."

Matanza squinted. He was virtually blind. He'd seen no natural light in a decade and survived on scraps he wouldn't have fed his dogs.

Kin said, "Your brother is dead. He drowned in a cave on the island of the lighthouse. Your dogs are dead too. The Kakurega looked after them but they died one by one of old age. You're the last of your tribe."

Matanza's expression didn't change. This strange interloper who smelled of horse and fishguts was speaking in a dead language.

"Who do you say you are?" Matanza asked.

"Kin das Ondas. I rule Balaal."

"No. You're a ghost. Come closer. I recognize you. I had you killed and now you've come back to haunt me. I don't even remember your name. What does it matter? You're dead. We rammed your boat against the rocks. My brother's men made it look like an accident so there wouldn't be a stupid rebellion. You're a dead man."

"And you?" said Kin. "What kind of a man are you?"

"We only killed the troublemakers like you," said Matanza. "I wanted to bring the people together. I wasn't like my father or my brother. I wanted peace. But I could never get it."

"Peace? You wanted wealth and power."

"No, I had those already. It was impossible in Balaal. The place is ungovernable. All those tribes and little villages, like the one you came from. No one respected the laws. My great-great-uncle Ochiades tried to instill order in that court of yours. He was a judge. But those fishermen threw him out onto the street. And before that, you! You! Fomenting trouble all the time! That's why I had you killed. And in Bocadelin, I wanted better for the miners, but they would have destroyed everything with their greed. There was nothing I could do. They would have stolen the wealth of the whole city. Then the borders kept changing. The place was ungovernable. That's the truth, ghost. And I don't even remember your name. You see? All the dead men, they're forgotten eventually. Even you."

Kin stood stock still and listened. He was dumbfounded. The man before him, far from being insane, remembered things that had happened decades earlier. Perhaps, Kin thought, in Matanza's isolation and silence, his mind went in circles, returning to the past just as Kin's had done in that cave in the mountains all those years ago and in that prison cell he'd shared with The Professor.

"I was a collector of clocks," said Matanza. "I spent my days repairing and regulating them. I wanted them to chime at the same time. It was my obsession, but I failed. Just as one would catch up to the other clocks, another would fall out of sync. You can never trust a clock. How did I ever presume I could unite the people of Balaal when I couldn't even get the clocks to chime together?"

Kin turned and left.

"Wait!" said Matanza. "Wait, ghost! I have more to tell you!"

Kin climbed the steps to the trapdoor and walked into the light. The Butcher was buried. And Porfirio Fulgencio Melgarejo Trujillo Matanza too, buried alive in the dark. Kin had learned what happened to Amador, done as Fundogu asked, and now he returned to his quarters. He would tell Jesa when the time was right. And the truth would set her free. But for now, there was work to do. He had to govern the ungovernable city.

✳

That night he dreamed of the great wave. They called it Nazaré. It broke over The Fishing Village with No Name. He saw Jesa's house split into a thousand parts and the fishermen's multicolored quarters washed out to sea. He saw Shadrak's boat flying empty on the wave, shedding its bucket and tools. He saw the bones of The Butcher and the four soldiers picked up by the water and tempest-tossed over the city. He saw Shamans' Hill and Socorro Point battered by the swell and only the two cannons, the steadfast sentinels, standing firm in the onslaught. He saw the camel kicking through the wave like some disfigured horse of the apocalypse and he saw Abacaxi flying over the now defunct warehouse, neck extended, legs akimbo, shell shining in the deluge. For once, he heard not a single note or even a chord, but a cacophony, a riot of all the notes on the scale. He saw Suvaco's parrot alive and squawking on the shoulder of the great Siberian tiger released from its fairground cage. He saw a fire-breathing dragon rear up on the breaker and heard the cry, "We are the Boo!" He saw the painted saint spinning out of the canvas and yelling, "It's just a trick of the light!" He saw the Freedum balloon floating above the churning water and drifting on the wind. He saw himself as an eleven-year-old running helter skelter over the hills, being chased by Nazaré and always outrunning it.

Above it all, way up in the clouds, he saw Fundogu levitating in his white gallabiya, touching his tribal scars with his long, ringed fingers and whispering, "Yes, boy, everything. Everything. Everything begins and ends in the sea."

ACKNOWLEDGMENTS

I wish to thank my family, my colleagues at Western New Mexico University and Stonecoast, Ramsey Kanaan of PM Press, and my agent Marc Koralnik of Liepman AG. Thanks also to early readers of the novel: Steve Oakes, Victor Acquista, David Henry Wilson, Jenny Wilson, and Chris Wilson, and to my editor Lisa Goldstein.

A version of the first chapter of *Nazaré* was published in *A Public Space* no. 29 (2020) under the title "Nazaré."

ABOUT THE AUTHOR

JJ Amaworo Wilson is a German-born Anglo-Nigerian-American novelist, short story writer, and nonfiction writer. Based in the US, he has lived in eleven countries and visited over seventy. He is a prizewinning author of more than twenty books about language and language learning, and his short fiction, essays, and poetry have been published by Penguin, the *New York Journal of Books*, Johns Hopkins University Press, *A Public Space*, and numerous literary magazines in England and the US. His first novel, *Damnificados* (PM Press, 2016), based on the Tower of David in Caracas, won four awards and was an Oprah Top 10 pick. He is the writer-in-residence at Western New Mexico University, Silver City.

ABOUT PM PRESS

PM Press is an independent, radical publisher
of books and media to educate, entertain, and
inspire. Founded in 2007 by a small group of
people with decades of publishing, media, and
organizing experience, PM Press amplifies the
voices of radical authors, artists, and activists.
Our aim is to deliver bold political ideas and vital stories to all walks of life
and arm the dreamers to demand the impossible. We have sold millions
of copies of our books, most often one at a time, face to face. We're old
enough to know what we're doing and young enough to know what's at
stake. Join us to create a better world.

PM Press
PO Box 23912
Oakland, CA 94623
www.pmpress.org

PM Press in Europe
europe@pmpress.org
www.pmpress.org.uk

FRIENDS OF PM PRESS

These are indisputably momentous times—the financial system is melting down globally and the Empire is stumbling. Now more than ever there is a vital need for radical ideas.

In the years since its founding—and on a mere shoestring—PM Press has risen to the formidable challenge of publishing and distributing knowledge and entertainment for the struggles ahead. With over 450 releases to date, we have published an impressive and stimulating array of literature, art, music, politics, and culture. Using every available medium, we've succeeded in connecting those hungry for ideas and information to those putting them into practice.

Friends of PM allows you to directly help impact, amplify, and revitalize the discourse and actions of radical writers, filmmakers, and artists. It provides us with a stable foundation from which we can build upon our early successes and provides a much-needed subsidy for the materials that can't necessarily pay their own way. You can help make that happen—and receive every new title automatically delivered to your door once a month—by joining as a Friend of PM Press. And, we'll throw in a free T-shirt when you sign up.

Here are your options:

- **$30 a month** Get all books and pamphlets plus 50% discount on all webstore purchases

- **$40 a month** Get all PM Press releases (including CDs and DVDs) plus 50% discount on all webstore purchases

- **$100 a month** Superstar—Everything plus PM merchandise, free downloads, and 50% discount on all webstore purchases

For those who can't afford $30 or more a month, we have **Sustainer Rates** at $15, $10 and $5. Sustainers get a free PM Press T-shirt and a 50% discount on all purchases from our website.

Your Visa or Mastercard will be billed once a month, until you tell us to stop. Or until our efforts succeed in bringing the revolution around. Or the financial meltdown of Capital makes plastic redundant. Whichever comes first.

Damnificados

JJ Amaworo Wilson

ISBN: 978-1-62963-117-2
$15.95   288 pages

Damnificados is loosely based on the real-life occupation of a half-completed skyscraper in Caracas, Venezuela, the Tower of David. In this fictional version, six hundred "damnificados"— vagabonds and misfits—take over an abandoned urban tower and set up a community complete with schools, stores, beauty salons, bakeries, and a rag-tag defensive militia. Their always heroic (and often hilarious) struggle for survival and dignity pits them against corrupt police, the brutal military, and the tyrannical "owners."

Taking place in an unnamed country at an unspecified time, the novel has elements of magical realism: avenging wolves, biblical floods, massacres involving multilingual ghosts, arrow showers falling to the tune of Beethoven's Ninth, and a trash truck acting as a Trojan horse. The ghosts and miracles woven into the narrative are part of a richly imagined world in which the laws of nature are constantly stretched and the past is always present.

"Should be read by every politician and rich bastard and then force-fed to them—literally, page by page."
—Jimmy Santiago Baca, author of *A Place to Stand*

"Two-headed beasts, biblical floods, dragonflies to the rescue—magical realism threads through this authentic and compelling struggle of men and women—the damnificados—to make a home for themselves against all odds. Into this modern, urban, politically familiar landscape of the 'have-nots' versus the 'haves,' Amaworo Wilson introduces archetypes of hope and redemption that are also deeply familiar—true love, vision quests, the hero's journey, even the remote possibility of a happy ending. These characters, this place, this dream will stay with you long after you've put this book down."
—Sharman Apt Russell, author of *Hunger*

Fire on the Mountain

Terry Bisson
with an introduction
by Mumia Abu-Jamal

ISBN: 978-1-60486-087-0
$15.95   208 pages

It's 1959 in socialist Virginia. The Deep South is
an independent Black nation called Nova Africa.
The second Mars expedition is about to touch
down on the red planet. And a pregnant scientist
is climbing the Blue Ridge in search of her great-great grandfather, a
teenage slave who fought with John Brown and Harriet Tubman's guerrilla
army.

Long unavailable in the US, published in France as *Nova Africa*, *Fire on the
Mountain* is the story of what might have happened if John Brown's raid
on Harper's Ferry had succeeded—and the Civil War had been started not
by the slave owners but the abolitionists.

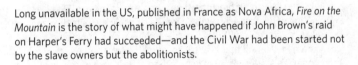

"*History revisioned, turned inside out . . . Bisson's wild and wonderful
imagination has taken some strange turns to arrive at such a destination.*"
—Madison Smartt Bell, Anisfield-Wolf Award winner and author of *Devil's
Dream*

"*You don't forget Bisson's characters, even well after you've finished his books.
His* Fire on the Mountain *does for the Civil War what Philip K. Dick's* The
Man in the High Castle *did for World War Two.*"
—George Alec Effinger, winner of the Hugo and Nebula awards for
Shrödinger's Kitten, and author of the Marîd Audran trilogy.

"*A talent for evoking the joyful, vertiginous experiences of a world at
fundamental turning points.*"
—*Publishers Weekly*

"*Few works have moved me as deeply, as thoroughly, as Terry Bisson's* Fire On
The Mountain *. . . With this single poignant story, Bisson molds a world as
sweet as banana cream pies, and as briny as hot tears.*"
—Mumia Abu-Jamal, prisoner and author of *Live From Death Row*, from
the Introduction.

RUIN

Cara Hoffman

ISBN: 978-1-62963-929-1
$14.95   128 pages

A little girl who disguises herself as an old man, an addict who collects dollhouse furniture, a crime reporter confronted by a talking dog, a painter trying to prove the non-existence of god, and lovers in a penal colony who communicate through technical drawings—these are just a few of the characters who live among the ruins. Cara Hoffman's short fictions are brutal, surreal, hilarious, and transgressive, celebrating the sharp beauty of outsiders and the infinitely creative ways humans muster psychic resistance under oppressive conditions. *RUIN* is both bracingly timely and eerily timeless in its examination of an American state in free-fall: unsparing in its disregard for broken, ineffectual institutions, while shining with compassion for the damaged left in their wake. The ultimate effect of these ten interconnected stories is one of invigoration and a sense of possibilities— hope for a new world extracted from the rubble of the old.

Cara Hoffman is the author of three New York Times Editors' Choice novels; the most recent, *Running*, was named a Best Book of the Year by *Esquire Magazine*. She first received national attention in 2011 with the publication of *So Much Pretty* which sparked a national dialogue on violence and retribution, and was named a Best Novel of the Year by the *New York Times Book Review*. Her second novel, *Be Safe I Love You* was nominated for a Folio Prize, named one of the Five Best Modern War Novels, and awarded a Sundance Global Filmmaking Award. A MacDowell Fellow and an Edward Albee Fellow, she has lectured at Oxford University's Rhodes Global Scholars Symposium and at the Renewing the Anarchist Tradition Conference. Her work has appeared in the *New York Times*, *Paris Review*, *BOMB*, *Bookforum*, *Rolling Stone*, *Daily Beast*, and on NPR. A founding editor of the *Anarchist Review of Books*, and part of the Athens Workshop collective, she lives in Athens, Greece with her partner.

"*RUIN is a collection of ten jewels, each multi-faceted and glittering, to be experienced with awe and joy. Cara Hoffman has seen a secret world right next to our own, just around the corner, and written us a field guide to what she's found. I love this book.*"

—Sara Gran, author of *Infinite Blacktop* and *Claire Dewitt and the City of the Dead*

God's Teeth and Other Phenomena

James Kelman

ISBN: 978-1-62963-939-0
$17.95   384 pages

Jack Proctor, a celebrated older writer and
curmudgeon, goes off to residency where he
is to be an honored part of teaching and giving
public readings, he soon finds the atmosphere
of the literary world has changed since his
last foray into the public sphere. Unknown to most, unable to work on
his own writing, surrounded by a host of odd characters, would-be
writers, antagonists, handlers, and members of the elite House of Art
and Aesthetics, Proctor finds himself driven to distraction (literally in
a very very tiny car). This is a story of a man attempting not to go mad
when forced to stop his own writing in order to coach others to write.
Proctor's tour of rural places, pubs, theaters, fancy parties, where he
is to be headlining as a "Banker-Prize-Winning-Author" reads like a
literary version of *Spinal Tap*. Uproariously funny, brilliantly philosophical,
gorgeously written this is James Kelman at his best.

James Kelman was born in Glasgow, June 1946, and left school in 1961.
He travelled and worked various jobs, and while living in London began
to write. In 1994 he won the Booker Prize for *How Late It Was, How Late*.
His novel *A Disaffection* was shortlisted for the Booker Prize and won the
James Tait Black Memorial Prize for Fiction in 1989. In 1998 Kelman was
awarded the Glenfiddich Spirit of Scotland Award. His 2008 novel *Kieron
Smith, Boy* won the Saltire Society's Book of the Year and the Scottish Arts
Council Book of the Year. He lives in Glasgow with his wife Marie, who has
supported his work since 1969.

"*God's Teeth and other Phenomena is electric. Forget all the rubbish you've
been told about how to write, the requirements of the marketplace and the
much vaunted 'readability' that is supposed to be sacrosanct. This is a book
about how art gets made, its murky, obsessive, unedifying demands and the
endless, sometimes hilarious, humiliations literary life inflicts on even its most
successful names.*"
—Eimear McBride author of *A Girl is a Half-Formed Thing* and *The Lesser
Bohemians*

Judenstaat

Simone Zelitch

ISBN: 978-1-62963-713-6
$20.00   336 pages

It is 1988. Judit Klemmer is a filmmaker who is assembling a fortieth-anniversary official documentary about the birth of Judenstaat, the Jewish homeland surrendered by defeated Germany in 1948. Her work is complicated by Cold War tensions between the competing U.S. and Soviet empires and by internal conflicts among the "black-hat" Orthodox Jews, the far more worldly Bundists, and reactionary Saxon nationalists who are still bent on destroying the new Jewish state.

But Judit's work has far more personal complications. A widow, she has yet to deal with her own heart's terrible loss—the very public assassination of her husband, Hans Klemmer, shot dead while conducting a concert.

Then a shadowy figure slips her a note with new and potentially dangerous information about her famous husband's murder.

"*Judenstaat uses the technique of alternate history to offer biting commentary on modern Israel, on the post–Cold War era in which we live, and on religion and nationhood.*"
—Cory Doctorow, coeditor of Boing Boing and author of *Little Brother*

"*The glory of Simone Zelitch's page-turning alternate history is the uncanny precision with which she has deftly transformed the threads of actual events into the stunning new fabric of her novel.*"
—BookPage

"*Zelitch has had the courage, the wit, and the skill to imagine an alternate history of the Jews of Europe after World War II.*"
—John Crowley, World Fantasy Award–winning author of *Little, Big*

"*With wit and grace, Simone Zelitch draws the collective grief of the generations living in the shadow of the Holocaust. Part mystery, part ghost story, her smart, politically savvy alternative history explores the growth of a nation and the secrets of the major players involved.*"
—Kit Reed, author of *Where*